Dead but Dreaming

Neil Rushton

First published 2020
by Rowanvale Books Ltd
The Gate
Keppoch Street
Roath
Cardiff
CF24 3JW
www.rowanvalebooks.com

A CIP catalogue record for this book is available from the British Library.

Paperback ISBN: 978-1-912655-83-0

This is dedicated to Lord Byron — the only man I ever loved.

Exordium

My little sister; I lost her when she was just a child. One moment we were together, the next she was gone. Her physical memory has become blurred into an arbitrary collection of blue-eyed glances, soft tones, touches and laughter. But underneath the dulled remembrance rests the overwhelming loss; at least a loss that has overwhelmed me. She usually comes to me in dreams, but not always.

***

There was a place at the end of an overgrown garden, down a bank and through some alders to a narrow, dirty brook. I presume it's still there. We used to spend endless summer days in that gloomy refuge. We read, talked, ruminated, napped. Our secret chatter should have made its mark there. But everything else rests only with me, in my memory. Her memory is gone. It has become something other than memory.

She always saw faeries there. When she was a little girl she'd play games with them, but when she was a bigger girl she just talked with them. I was only allowed peripheral glimpses of them amidst the leaves, and their voices were never more than the drone of the brook made fleetingly real during drifts into and out of sleep. But I believed in her belief. She'd always start with the invocation: *We must not look at faerie men; we must not eat their fruits. Who knows upon what soil they fed their hungry, thirsty roots.* And then she would laugh and skip down to her special places within the overhanging trees where she would begin her communions.

She was twelve the last time we went there. It was damp and the brook had a musty smell. She came back from one of her spots amid the trees, pale and tearful. The faeries had sung her a requiem. They promised her she would be able to come back to me as a blackbird for a short while, but only for a short while. After her annihilation she would have to disappear from the world. She cried as we made our way through the garden. There were no words, just tears. I cannot think further about what happened after this. It is not something I have learned to contemplate without despair.

It was a month or so after her death that I finally allowed myself to visit her grave in the churchyard. The thought of her lifeless, decomposing corpse only a few feet away from me became too much, and I retreated to a bench by the church porch. I sobbed and clutched the seat beneath me. Through the tear-mist I saw a female blackbird skip from the branch of a yew tree above me to within a pace of my foot, chirping with vigour. She cocked her head and looked at me with one dark eye.

'I love you,' I whispered.

She preened her wing, cocked her head once more and then darted away to a low branch.

'I love you,' I said again.

I bowed my head and closed my wet eyes. A gust of wind made itself known. It carried within its airy tone the residue of a voice, modulated through the yew tree: *I am dead but dreaming. I am dreaming of you.*

I

4 August 1970

Clickety-clack-clackety-click-tick-tock-speaking-
clock-Puck-pixie-Byron-boy-girl-swirl-noose-grave-
hive-mind-entwined-orchid-twenty-four-clickety-
clack... hypnagogic lurch.

I start awake, loud and stupid. My book thumps to
the carriage floor and I grip the armrest as if I'm about
to fall. The motion of the train brings me back to the
space, and the vague scent of burning oil grounds
me, once again part of consensus reality, although the
remnants of delirium linger. I dart a glance around the
carriage: ten seats as two benches, five facing five, low-
lit, smoky, enclosed, two others with me in enforced
intimacy. The old boy sleeping next to the window is
framed by the dark expanse of countryside passing
by outside, somehow locked together by the kinetic
movement, but the young guy in tweeds opposite is
alert and flashing-eyed, more elemental in the space
into which I awake. He has my book in his hand. He
accords me the same look of bemusement he'd given
when I came into the carriage — the usual once-over,
which I've become so used to from strangers — and
then flips open the book to examine the title page.
The fluttering pages dismantle the last vestiges of my
dreamworld, and the present somehow drifts into the
past.

'I hope you don't mind,' he said, adjusting his
glasses and rolling his thumbs around the book. 'It's the
dimness of the lighting in these carriages — designed
to make folk fall asleep when they're reading.'

'No, that's fine, that's fine.'

He relit his pipe and flicked through the title pages, glancing up and back again. The scent of tobacco trumped the burnt oil from the diesel engine. I fidgeted on the seat.

'*The Stith Thompson Motif-Index of Folk Literature,*' he said, with a question in his voice. 'Volume three, F-H… for reference only. Not to be removed from the library.'

'Yes, I had to get, err… special permission to take it out,' I lied.

'So what's it all about? Not something I've come across before. It all looks very sonorous and scholarly.'

The usual prickle drew itself around my neck. My face ticked. The residue of my half-forgotten dreams lingered, but I checked myself, drew two long breaths and appropriated a smile that did not belong to me.

'Well, it's… um, I'm a folklorist, well, sort of a folklorist. And this is a kind of bible for folklorists. It indexes the motifs from folktales—there are hundreds of them from all over the world. A Finnish chap called Antti Aarne put it together in about 1910 and now it's been reorganised by Thompson. There are six volumes… this is the one with motifs about the… the faeries. I'm coming out to collect… to collect some stories.'

'Ah, the faeries. Interesting.' He drew a long toke and blew it out through his nose, closed the volume and fixed me with a glassy stare. 'My grandmother used to be a firm believer in the *good folk*; not the winged Tinkerbells but, you know, proper faeries, the slightly dangerous types that you'll know all about. She was Irish. As far as she was concerned, they were an everyday occurrence in the countryside around her village at the end of the last century. Seems most people of her generation thought the faeries were to be feared and avoided. She told me lots of stories. I'm sure they'd have included many of your motifs. And here you are travelling into the English countryside to find out what the country folk think about the faeries in 1970. Right?'

'Yes, sort of. I'll be collecting some testimonies.'

'Interviewing rustic sorts, eh? Is this something you've done before?'

'No, not really… well, not ever, actually. I've been based at the university. It's all been a bit theoretical so far to be honest.'

He stared at me from behind the haze of smoke. My tic came on again. My eye flickered.

'And so you'll be based somewhere down here then—a red-brick, no doubt. Not exactly the golden triangle, but pretty decent libraries these days.'

I squirmed now. I contrived a surreptitious glance at my watch; ten minutes until my station. Could I legitimately and politely remove myself and just hang out in the passageway, or was there a social obligation to stay here and engage? I stayed put and tried to control my involuntary facial movements.

'No. I'm actually… I mean it's been arranged for me to stay in a, a… a psychiatric hospital. Not as a patient of course. They've got some quarters for me. My tutor has a contact there. It'll be convenient. Yes, convenient.'

'I'm sure, I'm sure. And I'll bet there might be some distinctive opportunities to find out what some of the occupants think of the faeries.'

'Yes, perhaps.'

He paused, allowing the muffled rattle of the train to create a juncture in the conversation. He was in control of our interaction, and I kind of knew what was coming. It descended into the smoky carriage like the introduction of a bass line in a song. Only nine minutes to go.

'I've had some dealings with psychiatric patients myself. Well, one in particular.'

'Really?'

'Have you heard of Ronald Laing… R. D. Laing?'

'I have. Yes. Um, he treated Syd Barrett, right?'

'So the legend goes, yes. Well, my father knows him, and when I was at Cambridge doing philosophy in '68, he arranged an audience with the good doctor for me and a few compatriots. He took us along to a ward in a psych-hospital in London and introduced us to a patient there. He was a man in his fifties; schizophrenic and wild-eyed but lucid and very articulate. Laing just told us to listen to him without preconceptions about his mental illness or the content of what he said and to then go away and simply think about it. It made quite a mark on me. Do you want to know what he said?'

'Yes,' I lied, again.

'Well, there were five of us, including Laing, gathered uncomfortably around his chair in the corner of the ward. He started talking the moment we arrived. Initially, he was ranting on about Kennedy being assassinated by the CIA, but then he suddenly switched. His entire demeanour changed from agitated nervous tension to a calm Zen-like state in an instant. And do you know what he talked about then?'

'Go on.'

'Solipsism.'

'Solipsism?'

'Do you know what it means?'

'Yes, of course.' Third lie.

'Well, it was the first time I'd heard about it. I'd already had Wittgenstein at Cambridge but somehow I'd missed the whole solipsism hypothesis. I've since found out that it's a bit of a philosophical taboo. But anyway, this chap fixed us with a stare, moving between us. And then he laid it out in no uncertain terms. God knows how he came to the information. I paraphrase of course, but he told us this...'

He adopted a slight northern accent to mimic the patient. I gritted my teeth but listened closely. I had to.

'...Solipsism is the only truth. Our consciousness horizon is all we have, and nobody comes into it and we cannot get into anybody else's. We have nothing but our own horizon, which includes the entire universe from our perspective. We can never be sure that anything that is included within our world truly exists except in our own personal conscious mind. Everything is a subject, just as in a dream. And in a dream you think, at the time of dreaming, that everything is real, but it's not. You've made it all up. All of it. And if you are unable to escape your own mind, your own horizon, in this reality… what makes you think this is any different from a dream? From your perspective, you're all there is. You have no neighbours.'

He stared at me, evidently trying to gauge whether I'd grasped the gravity of the statement. I lost eye contact. I started to feel nauseous.

'And then,' he said, sitting back in the seat and lapsing back into his own Received Pronunciation, 'he spoilt it all somewhat by telling us that from his point of view we were all mere subjects within his mind and that therefore he was God.'

'Ha. Right. Yes. And what did Laing think about this?'

'Oh, he loved it. He'd obviously set up the situation knowing what would happen. He had a skip in his step when we left and said in his sly Scottish brogue: "There you are, the wisdom of a madman. But who can argue that we do indeed have no neighbours? You all need to go away and think long and hard about what he's just told you."'

I had no idea what to say and my stomach still churned away. Fortunately, the guard came stomping down the passageway announcing my station. I jumped up to my feet, rather too quickly, and my head swam for a moment.

'This is me… I'm pleased to have met you and… thanks for the story.'

'Yes, perhaps you might want to think about solipsism when you're studying the faeries. It might bring some new light to the phenomenon.'

'Yes. Yes, indeed. Thank you.'

I retrieved my case from the overhead rack, still

woozy, and slid open the carriage door.

'Your book. You don't want to face those faeries without your motif index.'

I took the book and nodded. I glanced at the old boy still asleep next to the window, and my tweed companion followed my eyes.

'Just a figment of your solipsistic imagination,' he said, winking and taking another draw from his pipe.

'Huh, yes. Goodbye.'

The passageway felt cool and fresh, free from the tobacco ambience of the carriage. I put my book away and dragged the case to the nearest door. The train slowed and drew into the station, but my mind sped up, disturbed by the conversation. It had got under my skin. Suddenly, I could not escape from the thought that I was making all of this up.

I pulled down the window and took a deep breath of the night air, full of unfamiliar scents; the smell of the country. My nausea subsided. The train ground to a halt. I reached outside to open the door and lumped my case onto the platform. No one else got off. The train trundled away and I stood alone beneath the single lamp, still gestating big concepts while having to come to terms with being in the middle of nowhere, embarked on a project that was probably going to be way too much for me to handle. What was I doing here? How would I ever deal with it?

I closed my eyes and for an instant saw my sister's face. How would I ever accept what had happened to her? At that moment, laced with the disturbing residual slant of solipsism, I received the conviction that I was about to find out.

II

As I opened my eyes I realised the station-master was on the platform with me, having dealt with the train and removed his cap: big moustache, brylcreemed hair, still systematically waving his flag to and fro about his person. The usual incredulous appraisal of me was followed by a cough and cursory nod.

'The last train from London this Tuesday. I'm glad you made it. We been expecting you.'

'Have you?'

'Yes. I been engaged in conversation with your lift over there.'

He waved a flag towards the other platform.

'My lift?'

'Yes. I'll be happy to take your case if you so wish. Not in my term o' contract, but you must be tired from your journey.'

I acceded and we made our way over the unlit footbridge. The sound and oily smell of the train had gone and there was a claustrophobic silence about the place, disturbed only by our footfalls.

'Staying at the mental hospital I believe,' he said when halfway over the bridge, his accent causing me a second delay before I worked out what he was saying.

'That's right. I'm pleased they remembered to send the lift.'

'Well, do keep your wits about 'ee when you be there. Lots of damaged souls there, and it can seep out, so to speak. And we do hear things about some going ons there.'

'Do you?'

'Yes. If you ever feel the need during your stay, you can always come down here to chapel. Methodist.

We have a good community, and always ready to help. It's just an offer.'

'That's kind. Thank you. I'll bear it in mind.'

Going ons. My neck prickled, but I smiled again as he handed my case to me at the gate.

'Thanking you.'

'Don't forget—chapel be up on hill just outside town. Always welcome.'

There was no doubt about my lift; just one car in the small tarmac space outside the station house—a low-slung sports car of some type, a long-hair sat on the bonnet with a ciggy in his hand and a grin on his face. I got my third look of bemusement within the last ten minutes, but then he just shook his head and laughed, bobbed forward and took my hand.

'*Dia dhuit*—delighted to meet you. I'm Moore, Thom Moore. I've been dispatched from the looney bin to pick you up. Hop in, and I'll try to fit your case in the boot.'

A few more pleasantries and we were on our way; loud engine, obsidian countryside, an eight-track playing something intense and obscure, and Moore talking incessantly, always with an Irish smile in his voice.

'…So, we're up the hill from the main hospital. It's called the Tertiary Research Unit.'

'TRU.'

'Ha—observant. Yes, the TRU. We are indeed seekers of the truth. It's only been up and running since last year. We cut the ribbon the day yer man landed on the moon. So it's all mod-cons and you'll have the guest suite for as long as you need it. Albé says you've been dispatched down here by Hobby.'

'Hobby? Professor Hobhouse you mean?'

'Ai. Yes, sorry.'

'He's my tutor. Who is Albé?'

'He's the boss man at the unit—head psychiatrist, in charge of all research. He's a cool head. Hobby and him go back a long way, but I've only been here since the beginning of the year. And it's been quite a ride I can tell you. Albé's a… a character, as you'll find out. Brilliant mind though. And I know you're here for other purposes, but I'm sure we can show you what we're all about.'

'And what is it you're about? Professor Hobhouse hasn't really explained. I thought I was actually staying in the main hospital.'

'Well, we keep our independence from the hospital as much as possible. Albé's quite insistent on that. But all our patients come from there; referred to us when there's a chance they might fall into our remit: Hysterical Neurosis, Dissociative Type. ICD-8 300.1.'

'I'm sorry, I don't know what any of that means.'

'People who seem to have multiple personalities, all wrapped up in one mind.'

'Like Jekyll and Hyde?'

'Heh, sort of. It's usually a lot more complex than that though, and there are never just two personalities. Some of 'em have dozens. There's a long history to it, but a lot of misunderstanding, and the luminaries at the hospital don't want to believe in it at all. They just want to label it as schizophrenia and pump them full of Chlorpromazine. But we know better.'

He looked at me, a question in his eyes, or maybe a challenge.

'Believe me, we do know better. But all this can wait. You'll have loads of time to find out our modus operandi once you settle in.'

'I'm sure. I wonder how this fits with solipsism?'

'Solipsism?'

'Yes. I had a slightly odd conversation with a chap on the train about it just now. Do you know what it is?'

'I do indeed,' said Moore, interest clear in his tone. 'But I think that might have to wait as well because we're only about twenty minutes from the ranch and are about to enter into an absolute classic that needs to be listened to loud and with great concentration.'

'Oh?'

'Oh indeed. Do you know Van der Graaf Generator?'

'I'm afraid not.'

'Well, buckle up and brace yourself for eleven and a half minutes of twelve-tone profundity. It's called "After the Flood", and it's absolutely bloody marvellous. Totally outta sight. Released this year.'

He turned up the volume, put his foot down and off we went into the night with the sound of an apocalypse. Despite the background hum of creeping anxiety, I relaxed back into the seat, closed my eyes and listened to the music. It rumbled into place, organs, saxophone and electric guitar with an intense vocal.

'Who's the vocalist?' I asked, still with eyes shut.

'Peter Hammill. Fecking genius. Listen up.'

Drums into the mid-section, some sort of pipes, and repeated lyrics describing the end of days: *And when the water falls again, all is dead and nobody lives.* The saxophone and rhythm section stirred things up to the musical equivalent of a nervous breakdown over several minutes, then wound down to mimic the falling of water levels with an acoustic guitar and bass. But the best was yet to come and, as things ramped up again, Moore couldn't resist joining in, singing along in full gusto to a crescendo that sounded like heads being smashed together.

'*And then he said: every step appears to be, the unavoidable consequence of the preceding one. And in the end there beckons, more and more clearly, total... ANNIHILATION!*'

Both Hammill and Moore sounded like deranged Daleks, screaming the word through a distortion box. I stiffened up in the seat, eyes wide open, and stayed there as the song wound out with a guitar and organ solo, ending in a rumble created by God knows what, which vibrated the speakers, unable to cope with the depth of the bass. My background anxiety had turned into a tangible presence in the air.

'Fecking amazing, eh?'

'That was, indeed, something else.'

Moore was pumped up and driving too fast along the narrow, black road. I gripped the seat, taken back to *that* day and the ensuing cataclysm. My hands shook.

'I'm sorry,' he said, after a few moments, with softened tension and a release of the accelerator. 'You're probably starting to think I'm actually an escaped lunatic from the hospital. It's just that some of this music we've been getting lately is blowing my mind. But don't worry, I'm in full control of the vehicle.' He grinned and winked. 'It's Albé's. He's always let me drive it but says: if I ever damage the E-Type, I'll be a dead-type.'

'Ha, well, yeah. Car accidents are always bad things. I've never been in anything so powerful as this. But the speakers couldn't handle Van der Graaf Generator.'

'Indeed, indeed. You're right there. They need an upgrade.'

We turned through an avenue of trees and onto a driveway with some buildings scattered around.

As we ascended a slope, Moore pulled to a stop and pointed beyond. 'There's the main hospital: Gilbert Scott, 1840s. It can appear quite severe if you're not used to it.'

All I could see was a darkened hulk with a central tower of some sort, vaguely silhouetted against a black-blue sky, with a few winking lights in its upper windows. It was disquieting, like a Grimshaw painting. I turned away and Moore drove on, chattering away. We pulled up in front of a single-storey building and he cranked up the handbrake as if to announce an end and an arrival. We got out and Moore retrieved my case before moving to the entrance. He rattled with some keys but then stopped and looked at me, with an air of the awkward.

'I hope you don't take this the wrong way, but... you have a very distinctive look. Do you mind me asking if you're... if, err —'

But there was no time for anything further, thank God. Another thirty-something long-hair opened the door and threw up his arms in welcome.

'Halloo. Thought you'd never make it. Welcome to the TRU. I'm Scrope, Scrope Davies, and delighted to meet.'

He shook my hand and looked at me sideways — the usual look — then exchanged a glance with Moore I couldn't work out. I was ushered in, through a couple of corridors to a door that needed both of them to grapple with the keys and lock before it was opened and I found myself in my quarters.

'No need for further words tonight,' said Scrope. 'I'm sure you can work everything out for yourself. Someone will come a-knocking about nine o'clock in the morning and we can take things from there. Just make yourself at home. Bathroom's down the corridor to the right.'

'Thanks. And thanks for the lift, I appreciate it.'

I closed the door and turned around to my new life.

III

My shoulders dropped and I relaxed a little. I'd had more interaction with people during the last hour than I'd had in the previous month. The drive had put me on edge and my head was buzzing, but I was all right. I inspected the room: single bed, wardrobe, dresser, sink, chest of drawers, small desk under a big window looking out to I knew not what. There was also a shelf with a couple of dozen books: some Hardy and Brontë novels, volumes of 19th-century poetry, and a few scientific-looking tomes. But on the bedside table was just one book, conspicuous in its placement. I picked it up: *The Three Faces of Eve*. It was over a decade old, something about a woman with Moore's Hysterical Neurosis, or whatever it was called. Maybe this was my primer. I threw it back onto the table and turned to stare into the mirror on the dresser. I could never stand to look at my own face for long, but I gazed hard, knowing why I always elicited bemusement on first meetings. The blue eyes stared back at me. Was I all there was, as my fellow traveller had suggested? Did anything exist outside of this room right now?

I pulled away from the mirror and snapped myself from the thoughts with a shake of the head. I needed to extract myself from these burrowing ideas, so I unpacked, occupying myself with the practical to suppress the metaphysical. But once I was done I was on my back on the bed and again allowing my mind to drift into an esoteric territory.

As usual, it was Sis who appeared in my mind's eye. The whispered words of the wind in the churchyard came back to me: *dead but dreaming*. Where was she? It continued to be inconceivable to me that her consciousness was null and void. She had to exist somewhere in some form. Or perhaps that was just me making up a story to stifle my guilt, to convince myself I could be exonerated because her physical vehicle was just a temporary trifle and her greater, more expansive mind was now free and infinite, but still able to communicate with me.

Next, as per custom, came thoughts of her faeries. Her implacable belief in their existence was what had taken me to the university to study their ensconced position in cultural history. I didn't see how they could possibly be a real phenomenon, but there was something deep and knowing in my sister's interactions with them that I could not dismiss. She never lied. She was the most honest, beautiful, little empathetic being in the history of the world.

I started to cry. I always did when she was with me. And the tears brought tiredness. I was not used to travelling and mixing it up with other people. I'd been holed up in a room reading folklore for the last couple of months. This day had been an intensification of my life, and now it was ending with desperate, coded memories of my sweet unimpeachable Sis and the supernatural entities that would forever be wrapped up with her. I wanted to stay awake. I wanted to think about things. But I couldn't. I stripped, slipped under the blankets, curled up into a foetal position and allowed the globular forms of darkness to overwhelm me and take me to my dreams, where I was the sole arbitrator of reality.

IV

She is with me, of course. We promenade outside a villa in the get-up of 150 years ago. In the air, some skewed version of Van der Graaf Generator plays from an unknown source, and an E-Type Jag whirls around above us. It changes into a diesel train. Neither of us is concerned about this. We laugh and hug each other, hand in hand. Her cheek is pressed against mine, and there is an inexpressible intimacy as we communicate our love with telepathic promptitude.

The scene changes and the atmosphere darkens. I am suddenly afraid of something undefined. We are in the E-Type, but it's not really the Jag; it's my father's car. I glance behind me and there is a band of faeries playing up in the back seat, but I'm not too bothered about them. Their archaic clothes and stick-like appearance concern me, but they are not the centre of attention. My sister is the focus. She sits in the passenger seat, still in the garb of 1816 (I just know it is from 1816) and rocks to and fro, crying.

'What's the matter, sweetie?' I ask, even though it feels like a thought.

'It's coming,' she whispers. 'You should have known it's coming.'

She turns to look at me, and a second of ineffable love passes between us. We may as well be one person. But it is only a second. The next second contains a calamitous, uncontrolled explosion; a maelstrom of crashing glass and metal. For another second I am at the eye of the storm in silence, and hear the softly-spoken words: *And in the end there beckons, more and more clearly, total…* There is another second of silence before the world fills with the distorted scream: *ANNIHILATION!*

***

I lurched awake with the detonation and screamed. My body was clammy, heart thumping away like a stuck clock. I pulled on the sheets as the crashing percussion of the aborted dream dissipated into the near silence of the room. *Tick-tock*. I squinted at the carriage clock on the bedside table. I would have sworn it wasn't there when I went to bed, but it was definitely there now. *Tick-tock*. I harboured an instant dislike for it.

The dream began to fade, but its intrinsic elements remained and the usual hopelessness began to wash over me. It was eight o'clock. My head seemed to weigh a ton. I sank it back into the pillow and resorted back to my days in my university room, where sometimes I didn't get out of bed until five in the afternoon, too horrified at the prospect of facing the world, and most especially people.

One day I had got up mid-afternoon and walked to the hardware store, listless and abstracted. I bought a thick rope, returned to my room and stared for an hour at the cross-beam eight feet from the floor. Then, spurred into a certainty of what I needed to do, I made a haphazard noose out of the rope, climbed on a chair and tied the rope as best I could around the beam. I then lay back on the bed and stared at the waiting noose for another hour. There was a carriage clock there too: *tick-tock*, *tick*-fucking-*tock*.

I pulled away from the image, got up out of bed and quickly dressed. Why were my memories always so disheartening? Why were my dreams always so full of love and horror? I went to the window. This place was green. It was the tired green of a summer on the verge of waning, but still full of the vitality of nature. Outside the window was an apple tree with tentative green fruit starting to bend its branches, and an ash tree curving its limbs over the eaves. Its curvy arms popped into my head the M. R. James story of an ash tree outside an ancient manor house, the tree's hollow interior inhabited by a witch and a gang of giant spiders who would break in through the casements on late summer nights to smother and poison the hapless incumbents. I turned to the bookshelf. Sure enough, there was a volume of M. R. James' ghost stories, book-ending the Hardy volumes.

'Miserable old bastards,' I muttered, before returning my gaze to the expanse of green outside. The trees, grass and the distant valley-side began to dispatch memory and dream in favour of a revised Arcadia.

***

The knock came at nine o'clock as promised. I was still trying to penetrate the details of my dream, but it was dissipating and returning to wherever it belonged. A few deep breaths and I opened the door. It was Scrope, accompanied by some raggle-taggle who gawked at me with unreserved incredulity.

'Sleep well?' asked Scrope, his public-school accent stamping its authority in two words.

'Yes. Some recurring dreams, but yes.'

'Ah, we'll need to apply some Jungian analytics to your dreams — have them all worked out in a jiffy. But meanwhile we need to work quick, as Albé wants to meet you before we go over to the hospital, and we're due there in a quarter of an hour. Are you all good to come now?'

'Sure.'

We walked through the corridors. Scrope was as insistently verbose as Moore; they were like the Irish-English equivalents of each other. Our compatriot loped along, just behind us, grunting occasionally.

'And who are you?' I asked him, between a pause of breath from Scrope.

'Most rude of me, most rude,' said Scrope. 'This is Eddie; Eddie Epsilon.' He reached back and ruffled Epsilon's wild ginger mop of hair. 'General dogsbody, aren't you Epsilon?'

'Fuckin' right, yeah, fuck.'

They were the first words I'd heard from him. I looked at Scrope, quizzical.

'You'll, err, get used to young Epsilon. Just don't try to elicit too many words from him. He's fine for fetching and carrying and such stuff but has a bit of a limited vocabulary. You'll get used to it.' He curled his mouth into a knowing smirk, before locking me into confused eye contact. 'There are simply different types of people in this world, my friend. We all need to fit in, in different ways. But the differences are indestructible.'

I breathed shallow and my tic started to move my face, but before I could think of anything to say, we reached the common room.

'Now, you need to brace yourself a bit for Albé,' said Scrope, reinforcing his words with a hand on my shoulder. 'He can seem a bit overbearing at first. In time you'll get to know why, but for now… don't take anything too… personal. He's cool.'

This was great. I was only an hour away from a dream that smashed in my sister's head, all mixed up with some prog-rock insanity, propagated by a ride in a sports car with about a million horsepower alongside a louche Irishman, marinated by being greeted first thing in the morning by an Old-Etonian and a sweary roughneck. Now I was about to be presented to some eminent big-timer who might not be too concerned with my wavering sensitivities. My shoulders tensed up to maximum, facial tic ticking. Scrope opened the door, and in we went.

The room smelled of tobacco underlined by cannabis. At the far wall, about fifteen feet away, Moore banged on the side of a telly, ciggy in his mouth, cursing under his breath. Watching on was, I presumed, Albé.

'It's busted,' said Moore. 'It was acting up last night. Maybe this is providence. Time to get a colour one. Join the modern age.'

Scrope coughed, and they both turned around. It was not a cold morning but Albé wore a long greatcoat, which swished in dramatic fashion as he turned. He had a well-coiffured set of dark locks, a pale aquiline face, and a curl on his lips I had almost expected. He immediately zoned in on me and moved in our direction. His limp was pronounced. It was incongruous with the rest of his fast-emanating persona, which filled the room like ink in water.

'So here we are,' he said, shaking my hand with a soft touch—no look of bemusement here. 'Hobby's student, come to find out about the faeries. I like your hair—short, blonde, unusual. I'm going to call you Blondie, if you don't mind. What's the line, Moore? From the Eastwood film… "Hey Blondie, it's only seventy-five miles, I think a *man* like you could make it."'

'Something like that,' said Moore, grinning as per last night, giving up on the telly and coming to stand beside Albé.

'But I do detest everything which is not perfectly mutual, and so you are to know me as Albé, whatever Hobby may have called me.'

'Ok, yes, certainly.'

I was being probed by a superior being, and all I could do was rock back and forth. I smiled and tried to suppress the tic.

'Now let's see,' said Albé, eyes narrowed, and somehow coming closer to me without moving. 'The product of a somewhat infected upbringing, amidst a provincial working-class family, who thought that you going to university was a joke. A father whose life revolves around betting on horses, and who thinks that Heath will be a damned good thing for this country… and a mother who hasn't spent a day unanaesthetised with gin and tonic for twenty years.'

I gulped hard. I couldn't help it.

'The only place to escape to was London, once you understood your untenable position at home, and that most of the received wisdom passed on by your father was at best a lie, and at worst a deliberate attempt to stifle you out as a creative person. But you have escaped, haven't you, Blondie? I'm guessing that '67-

'69 were very good years to be in London; flushed out most of that post-War conventionalism that had been forced down your throat, and replaced it with a more open-minded, progressive attitude. With the Floyd thrown in as well—brilliant.'

'I, um... yes... that's...'

Again, I felt him drift towards me somehow, never once losing eye contact. 'But there's a bit more to it than that isn't there... I'm sorry about your sister, and the estrangement from your family.'

I realised my mouth was open. I gulped like a fish. I was also aware of the others watching me, and my blush followed. This time, Albé moved to me properly, dragging his foot slightly as before, and put a hand on my shoulder. There was a low-level buzz as he did so, akin to a fly whipping around the room. But it felt more insidious than that, more inside my head.

'You'll fit in nicely here, Blondie. I think your presence will be mutually beneficial.' He leaned forward and whispered in my ear, 'Don't worry, we'll get on fine if you just don't mind my words. You'll understand all this soon.'

I closed my eyes for a moment and breathed deep. When I opened them, Albé had retreated and was beckoning us through from the common room back into the corridor.

'Come on, Blondie, you can tag along. Have you ever been in a psychiatric hospital before?'

'Nope.'

I was surprised he didn't know the answer before he asked it. A second's thought and I realised he probably did.

'Well, you might have turned up in the nick of time. If Enoch Powell's plan comes to fruition, this place could be an empty shell in the very near future, along with all the other mental institutions. Perhaps not a bad thing, but only if an alternative provision is made. And I somehow doubt that'll be the case. Imagine half a million lunatics turned out into *the community* with nothing but anti-psychotic drugs to keep them in order.

It won't end well. But that's a discussion for another day – come on, we've an appointment to keep.'

We all trooped down from the TRU along a path to the hospital. The morning was sunny but hadn't warmed up yet. The neo-Gothic brick façades of the hospital reared up in a way that made me not want to go inside. It was a beautiful, intimidating building, emanating something I could not get my head around. Albé marched on at the front with a stick, his pronounced limp not constraining his speed. He gesticulated about something with Moore as they struck up ciggies. Actually, no, one whiff of the smoke told me it was weed. I felt like a prude for being shocked.

'Fancy a drag?' said Scrope, offering me the joint. 'We usually fortify ourselves before doing battle in the HQ.'

I accepted, took a few tokes and things calmed down a little.

'And what are we going there for?'

'A possible referral to the TRU. A newly certified patient, female, displaying potential symptoms of dissociative Hysterical Neurosis. But the powers that be in there are not going to want to countenance it. They'll want to keep her and fill her with anti-psychotics, or maybe even try ECT or a leucotomy, God help her. But I think you might be about to witness Albé's powers of persuasion. Probably a bit too much for your first day, especially as this isn't what you're here for. But life is for living, eh?'

'I suppose.'

Epsilon trudged behind us, muttering obscenity-riddled sentences under his breath. Scrope passed back the joint to him, and he puffed away, hungrily. I had questions to ask about all this, but one resonant lesson I'd learned in life was when to keep my mouth shut. I kept my mouth shut.

Albé led us into the main entrance, the joint being stubbed out. A couple of nurses watched us wide-eyed, but Albé was zoned-in on a mission and we turned right, past a sign for *Female Wards*. We went through some corridors, up a flight of steps and arrived at the doors of a ward.

'Murray ward, right?' announced Albé.

'Yep, Murray,' replied Moore.

In we went. The communal ward stretched a hundred yards, partitioned cubicles on one side. It was quiet apart from some general shuffling around inside the partitions and some moaning at the end of the ward where a few nurses bustled in and out of a cubicle. But the doorless cubicles we walked past only allowed momentary glimpses inside, revealing nothing I could make sense of. The smell of disinfectant mixed itself up with the weed, constructing lightheadedness.

'Cubicle twenty-four,' announced Moore.

And there we were at cubicle twenty-four, an officious-looking sister waiting for us outside. She stiffened up as Albé approached her. We all squeezed in, except Epsilon, who hung around at the threshold.

'Twenty-four,' said Albé, switching glances between the patient and the sister. 'A very special number, you know.'

The sister glanced between each of us, agitated, unsettled. I felt sorry for her.

'They say virtue is its own reward… it certainly should be paid well for its trouble.'

She flinched at Albé's words. I was starting to understand I was in a situation that had probably, in many and various forms, been carried out innumerable times, and there was some type of implicit stage-management going on. It made me shrink back in front of Epsilon, who was slouched just outside the cubicle, oblivious to what was happening.

'An appraisal please, sister,' said Albé, looking at the woman in the bed; in her twenties, wrapped up in a white nightdress, dishevelled, staring into the middle distance, meeting no one's eyes.

'Miss Caroline Lamb. She was brought in yesterday by her doctor under a certificate, after a…

after a psychotic incident. Hearing voices, violent, unable to communicate. Dr Dawkins says—'

'Spare me the thoughts of Dr Dawkins, sister. Where is he anyway? We had an appointment here for nine fifteen. We're here, why isn't he here?'

'I'm not sure… I'm sure he'll be here at any moment, I'm—'

'Whatever,' said Albé, moving to the woman's bedside and putting his hand on her arm.

He swayed for a moment and gained eye contact with her. She came out of her catatonic state, smiled and brought her other hand to his. There was a moment of vacuum. It enveloped me. It was broken by the intrusion of new people.

'Dr Dawkins,' the sister exclaimed. 'I'm sorry, I was unable to—'

'No need to worry, my dear. No worries.'

Dr Dawkins, flanked by two male orderlies, placed himself at the end of the bed, obliging me to shuffle along in the constrained cubicle. I glanced to Scrope and Moore—they were grinning at each other. I didn't want to be there, but I was. I stiffened the muscles in my face to control the tic.

'Now I do not have to tell you,' said Dawkins, bristling, his bald head sweating, 'that it is highly irregular for you to be interfering with a new admittance less than twenty-four hours after their arrival. The certificate explicitly states that—'

'Twenty-four,' said Albé, never taking his eyes from the young woman. 'What is your diagnosis, doctor?'

'I was only able to briefly examine the patient when she was brought in yesterday. It appears to be a schizophrenic episode, but she will require further assessment—'

'And large doses of Chlorpromazine no doubt.'

Dawkins turned red and scrunched his jaw. 'As you know, my lord…'

My lord? I looked to Moore and Scrope for an answer to that, but they were both just watching the action with unconcealed enjoyment.

'…we have protocols for anti-psychotic medication for newly certified patients that are tried and tested —'

'She has been having dissociative episodes since she arrived, has she not? There have been at least three distinct personalities manifesting, and the person she is at the moment, Caroline Lamb' — Albé smiled at her and squeezed her hand — 'has attempted to tell you about her blackouts and loss of memory but was ignored.'

'I fail to see how you can possibly ascertain such a conjectural…' Dawkins spluttered, too agitated to articulate his sentences, '…a conjectural diagnosis, based on information from thin air.'

'Well, we do have our sources,' replied Albé, his coolness making him seem like a different species than Dawkins. 'And I think that perhaps I should be allowed to spend some time with our patient here before you sedate her further. I mean, surely we need to listen to the people we incarcerate. They are, after all, *people*, are they not?'

'This is preposterous. I do not see why —'

'What do you think, Caroline? Would you like to talk with me a little while, just so we can get to know one another and hopefully help you out? Because you do need help, don't you?'

Miss Lamb, who had been static, silent and wide-eyed until this point, re-grasped Albé's hands with hers and nodded, mumbling an affirmative.

'I appeal to your good grace, Dr Dawkins. Please just allow me ten minutes with our patient and then I will leave her in your capable hands. I beg your allowance.'

Caroline grasped his hands even tighter. Dawkins glanced at his expressionless orderlies and then waved his hand.

'Fifteen minutes. The first group of patients from this ward will be taking the air at a quarter to ten before their occupational therapy, and I would like you to be gone by then. Most irregular… most irregular.'

Dawkins stomped off with the orderlies, leaving the sister to wring her hands and flick her eyes between us. They rested on me, and sure enough, up went the eyebrows before she pulled her gaze away and back towards Miss Lamb, who sank back into her pillow as the tension dissipated.

Albé turned and nodded to a stool next to the cubicle entrance. Epsilon caught the look, brought it over and Albé sat down on it, never releasing Caroline's hands.

'We're here to help you, Caroline. Everything will be all right. Do you trust me?'

She nodded and bit her lip.

'So just try to relax and tell me what happened yesterday.' He gestured back to the rest of us, standing at the end of the bed. 'These good people are with me. You can trust them as you trust me. So stay calm and let me know what happened.'

Caroline took a minute; recollecting, grimacing, tears reaching her eyes. But after a quick glance around us, she gripped Albé's hands tighter and began to speak, her voice tremulous, high-pitched, but well-enunciated with just a slight regional burr.

'I know you won't believe me; nobody ever does. But I have some others within my head. Others. They just take over sometimes. Not always, but I am not always Caroline, I'm just not. And there is one called Caro. She wouldn't want me to be talking about her, because I'm a good girl, but she's a bad girl. She really is.'

Albé stroked her arm. 'Stay calm, it's all good. Just let me know what she's about.'

'I only know her in the dark place. She doesn't like people. She likes to tell them exactly what she thinks of them. She likes to hit them and shout at them. She's been doing it for so long. She takes over and just does it. I beg her not to, but sometimes she is so much stronger than me. And she pushes me back into the dark place, where I have to stay while she does what she wants. And I can sometimes see and hear her doing all her stuff, but because I'm in the dark place I can't do anything about it. It's like I'm in a dream when I'm in the dark place. Yes, like a dream, when you know something is happening outside but not quite sure what it is. She put me there yesterday and started her violent ways in a shop. I didn't know what she was doing but have been told. She likes to scratch and slap and shout at people... she's so horrible. I hate having to share things with her.'

She breathed heavily and tears rolled down her face. She began to mutter disjoined words before Albé stopped her with a look.

'I understand, Caroline,' he said, soft-toned. 'I do understand. I know you're telling us the truth. Are there others inside your head? You said there were.'

'Yes. But they're not too bad. They like me. One is even a beautiful little girl called Innocent who comforts me often when we are both in the dark place together. I only know them there, not out here in the real world. As I said, the dark place is like a dream. They know I'm number one. But Caro won't have that. She's jealous. She wants to be number one. And she wants to hurt everyone. She wants to take over. She says humans are a scourge upon the earth, and that she wants them destroyed. She says she wants *annihilation*.'

I looked sideways at Moore. He didn't look at me, but I guessed we were both rehearsing the mutual song in our head—Peter Hammill screaming the word.

'All right. I understand all of this,' said Albé, leaning closer to her. 'You know I do, don't you?'

'Yes. Yes. How? You can join me and them, can't you? In the dark place. How do you do this?'

'Don't worry about that now. Just be assured that I, and my friends here, are on your side. We know what's going on and we are going to help you. You'll need to spend a day here so that you can rest, and then you will move over to another place, a special place, where you'll get the help you need. Then everything will be dealt with. We'll talk with Caro and the others and come to some agreement. Do you trust me?'

'I do. Are you a god?'

Scrope and Moore let out involuntary snorts. Albé just smiled.

'No, none of us are. We all suffer as humans. But remember this, Caroline... concentrate.... Adversity is the path to truth. You have been through adversity, but we will help you find the truth. Keep love in your heart.'

Albé extracted himself from her grasp and marshalled us to leave.

'Sister—no Chlorpromazine. I know you've got the final say on this. If we find it in her blood when she comes over to the TRU, I'm going to be mightily fucked off.'

'Please, your language.'

'Apologies... I shall be extremely displeasured. But she will be coming to the TRU, either tomorrow or Friday. So please bear that in mind. Have you got that?'

The sister nodded. I could feel her muscle tension from five feet away, and something passed between her and Albé; subtle, insubstantial. Albé went back to kiss Caroline on the brow and then off we went, back through the corridor, where now several curious faces appeared in cubicle doorways and a couple of nurses made way for us with suspicious glances. I tried not to meet any of their eyes.

As we trailed back up the path to the TRU, I fell back a little, retreating from the conversation. What had I let myself in for here? I'd spent the last few months in almost total isolation, and now here I was in a literal and metaphorical madhouse, surrounded by competing egos I had no idea how to deal with. The interactions this morning had only taken three-quarters of an hour, but already all I could think about was getting back to my bed to curl up beneath the sheets.

V

I was curled up beneath the sheets. There was no sleep, but I needed the comfort and seclusion that only a bed could provide. It was gone noon, and I was once again going over the morning's events. I couldn't make sense of them—too much nuanced behaviour. I'd lost the ability to interpret these things. I'd been too long without social interaction.

I conjured up Caroline Lamb's face and found there some resonance with Sis. Were there similarities, or was it just me sympathising with someone who had lost control, causing me to project the patterns of someone I had known intimately onto someone I knew barely at all? And, although I made assiduous efforts to suppress it, my conversation on the train kept intruding its way into every thought and memory, sowing the seeds of doubt into the experience. Was Miss Lamb still lying in her bed at that moment, or was she nothing more than a subjective moment conjured up by my Universal mind, non-existent except in what I called my memory?

I wished I hadn't had that conversation. The solipsistic idea had burrowed into me and insisted on providing a possible interpretation for every move I made. It felt unhealthy; like an addiction gaining traction.

I get up, annoyed at my retreat to bed. I am going to ask for the carriage clock to be removed. I cannot stand its incessant tick-tocking counting out the minutes of the days. I turn to look at it. There is no carriage clock. I stare at the bedside table, a prickle running around my neck and down my back. I look around the room. *Clickety-clack, clackety-click.* I shake my head, squeeze my eyes shut then reopen them. For a fraction of a second, I am back in my university room. *Tick-tock*. I am in bed again.

I woke up shaking from the momentary images. The carriage clock was on the bedside table. It told me it was almost one o'clock. I slithered out of bed, pulled on jeans and a baggy jumper and made myself sit at the desk. I needed to calm down. I also needed extraction from the delirium setting itself up in me. Perhaps I was coming down with something; the result of my immune system not being able to cope with the stress and anxiety of the last twenty-four hours. Twenty-four. Why had Albé been so insistent on it being a special number? I was twenty-four. The solipsistic parasite wheedled its way into me once more. Were all words and actions meant as clues?

I rubbed my eyes, opened my notebook, and spoke aloud. 'What am I here for? What do I need to do? Get yourself together and do it.'

A few seconds passed. A ray of sunlight made itself known through the window and fell on the open notebook. I took it as a sign and read my scribbled notes. They were the product of my last nine months, a bumpy transition from degree to research assistant for Professor Hobhouse. I had made every effort to fall into place and understand what it was he wanted of me, but the truth of it was I wasn't very good at it. He was putting together some magnum opus on the faerie folklore of the British Isles, and just because I'd shown interest in the subject and written some ropey dissertation on the faeries in literature and popular culture (much of it plagiarised shamelessly from the works of Katherine Briggs and Evans-Wentz), he copped onto me as someone who could do the research he didn't want to or didn't have time for. What I had never told him was that my real interest in the faeries was because my sister used to play with them.

I flicked through the pages. They made for sorry reading, a litany of half-baked connections between the Aarne-Thompson Motif Index and folkloric anecdotes about the faeries from wherever I could find them in the historical record. I sat back in the chair and stared out the window. This was what I'd been doing for most of the last nine months — staring out of windows, always visualising my sister and secretly hoping her union with whatever amorphous entities she had found would somehow dribble into my mind and allow me some greater understanding. It never happened. And the further she drifted into memory, the less sense I had of what she could possibly have been contacting. In my bleaker moments, I just concluded she'd been strung along by her overactive imagination. Those bleak moments always coincided with the assurance that I wanted to end my own life. But when I came back up above the suicidal waterline, I *knew* she had known something I didn't. I closed my eyes and pictured her. As always, the tears came then.

I cried for a couple of minutes, let it subside, took some deep breaths and returned to the notebook. In the back pages there were some names and addresses of contacts I was supposed to visit while down here, to collect testimonials. Professor Hobhouse was convinced there was a generation of countryfolk about to die out who held the last vestiges of faerie belief. Their testimonies were essential. That's what he thought. I thought it would be impossible to overcome my social awkwardness and actually visit people who believed in the faeries. I'd never done it, I didn't know how to do it, I'd had no training, but here I was.

I flitted to Evans-Wentz, an American at the beginning of the century who, with great charm and charisma, travelled around the Celtic fringes extracting anecdotes and beliefs about the faeries from the rural population. He was clever. He was likeable and engaging. I wasn't and, sixty years down the road, things were going to be different.

I snapped shut the notebook. The gloom was coming. It always did when I realised I could not cope. My vision blurred through some new tears as I stared out the window. The greenery swirled and congealed into an unholy mess. My train conversation reasserted itself. If I were truly the only solipsistic consciousness in existence, then the universe was in deep trouble. If this were the totality of existence, then surely non-existence would be better.

There was a knock at the door. My chest contracted. But I got up and answered it anyway.

VI

Albé stood at the threshold. He came in at my nod and shuffled over to the window without a word. He picked up the Aarne-Thompson Index and flicked through it for a moment without looking at it.

'I hope you didn't find this morning too distasteful,' he said, meeting my eyes. 'But I thought you should see the main hospital as soon as possible. We are but an adjunct to it here at the unit.'

'No. No, it was an experience. I don't think I'll want to spend too much time in there though. It's not really what I'm here for.'

Albé stared at me. My face ticked.

'Quite. But I think that you may benefit from knowing a little more of what we get up to here at the unit. It may inform your project in ways you don't realise. Hobby was au fait with us taking you under our wing when we discussed you coming down here. And you won't be able to escape the ambience of the place… it is all-pervading.'

'Right.'

'Moore tells me that he explained dissociative Hysterical Neurosis to you.'

'Sort of.'

'And young Caroline Lamb should have given you a taste for what might be going on with these people. But you will need to see it first-hand for a proper understanding. All I can tell you now is that it is a very real phenomenon. The likes of Dr Dawkins just don't want it to be true. They are materialists, reductionists, and their concept of reality is severely constrained by their thinking that consciousness is an epiphenomenon of the brain. In their worldview, the idea of more than one mind operating inside an individual is an impossibility. It is simply a brain malfunction. But they're wrong.'

'Right.'

He stared at me deeper. The words weren't quite sinking in. All I could think about was my twitchy face giving away my nerves. He did his trick of moving closer to me without moving a muscle.

'We'll show you why they're wrong soon. But you might like to read up on what dissociation is. I know you have a lot to do with your project and all, but there are a few easy-reading books here' — he pointed to the bookshelf — 'that will give you the outline. This is also pretty good.' He picked up *The Three Faces of Eve* and dropped it back on the bedside table. 'You could also think of the analogy of actors.'

'Actors?'

'Mmm. Disassociation is achieved by actors all the time, good actors anyway. The difference between them and our specimens is that they have control over the switches between personalities.' He paused to gain my full attention. 'A few years ago I was on a film set, watching Richard Burton in action.'

'Really?' I blurted.

'Yes. I watched him closely. Set filming consists mostly of hanging around and waiting. He was pretty louche and amiable to everyone when he was sitting around chatting, smoking and drinking tea between takes. Then he'd limber up a little when called for a scene, but just moments before the clapper-board clapped, he switched in an instant. His entire demeanour shifted. Every muscle in his face and body changed. And with it, his mind moved. There was suddenly someone else inhabiting his body. He was capable of totally overriding his own considerable personality and replacing it with another. The crew had all become used to it, probably never noticed what was happening anyway. But I did. I'd watch the scene closely; watch his every action in the minutest detail. There was no correlation between the man who'd just been laughing over a joke with the make-up girl, and the character he then allowed to become manifest. And when the cut came, the change back was just as instantaneous. He'd exhale the character out of himself, pick out a crew member, or anyone hanging around, and smile or wink at them. It was his way of letting us know that he was in complete control and that he could do this anytime he liked.'

'Richard Burton,' I said, like an imbecile.

Albé gave me his curled-lip smile and made as if to leave. He turned at the door and once again lowered his gaze, forcing me to lose eye contact.

'But the analogy only goes so far. Our patients are not actors. The condition has been forced upon them, for a variety of reasons. They need help, and we've found a way of providing it. If you can spin out the anticipation of your project for another day, I can give you an idea of what's going on. And as I say, I do strongly believe that getting a handle on the vagaries of the human mind in one of its most fragmented forms may give you some insights into your supernatural entities.'

'Do you?'

Albé took a couple of steps back into the room. 'Your being here is not a complete accident, Blondie. I'll have you know that I'm extremely interested in the metaphysical and all the creatures that may abide there. This will be made manifest, but not just yet. In the meantime, I'm keen for you to meet our TRU patients before you advance further with your studies. So I'd like you to put tomorrow aside and Moore, Scrope and I will open your eyes to it. Is that acceptable?'

'Yes, of course… I don't think a day will delay me much. So yes… yes. Of course.'

'Cool,' he said, looking me up and down as if it were the first time he'd seen me.

I needed to break the moment. The first thing that came into my mind was: 'And how many patients do you have here at the TRU?'

'Currently two. Caroline Lamb will make three, and we may have to take a recalcitrant from the hospital tomorrow, taking us to full capacity.'

'A recalcitrant?'

'Eugh. I'll explain later. But now I need to get on. I'll leave Moore or Scrope to organise the logistics for tomorrow. But I'm really glad you're here. Every place could do with a bit more folklore. I'm a big fan of it. And I do understand where you are coming from. I know it's been difficult for you. I know.' He came to me and placed a hand on my shoulder. 'The great art of life is sensation, to feel that we exist, even in pain... But now to business. I need to get on. Treat everything as you would a home. Moore and I have residence in an annex just up the path, but Scrope has a room here and is always on site. There's usually a nurse here too... and Fletcher. Mmm, Fletcher.' He went to the door. 'Fletcher!' He shouted. 'Fletcher!'

Twenty seconds later a forty-something man came rumbling up, and Albé drew him into the threshold.

'Here's Fletcher—my personal assistant. In the good old days, he'd have been a valet, but in these bad old days, he's called an assistant and deals with all the things I don't have time for. If you need anything, he'll be at your disposal: post office runs, organising taxis, fixing light bulbs, anything like that. You just need to ask. Fletcher, this is Blondie.'

A polite 'how-do' was followed by the usual searching look of incredulity. But I shook hands, and in a few moments they were gone and the door was closed. I pressed my back to it. Albé was right: I could spin out the anticipation for another day. And this still left me with an afternoon to kill. I had no idea where I'd take my meals, or where everyone usually spent their evenings, or whether I would be expected to socialise. But that could wait. With an unusual focus, I decided I needed to get shod and take a walk around the hospital grounds. I wasn't sure why, but Albé had left me energised. I needed to take advantage of it before it wore off.

VII

It was warm. I started to regret wearing my jumper but just carried on. There was a big spired chapel, buried somewhat within the other hospital buildings but a discernible focal point. I aimed for it and came across a small patch of grass and a bench outside. Leaning against the chapel wall were half a dozen small iron markers, rods with rounded heads, each with a moulded number. I picked one up—twenty-four, of course. Were these grave markers? I ran my fingers over it and then sat down on the bench. I drew back to the day spent crying in the church porch with Sis's grave only a few yards away. The spell of death crept up on me. I thought about that rope tied to the cross-beam. Why had I not followed through with my design? Probably because I was a coward, too afraid of the pain. But a few more moments' reflection and I realised there was a deeper fear. Suicide would mean further punishment. I was not sure how the punishment would be delivered, but I was quite sure that my life was not my own to end. And having been responsible for the ending of another life, I felt doubly sure that if I strung myself up, there would be retribution. But from who? What was my consciousness without my body and brain? Would death not just bring non-existence? And if so, why would it matter how I died? Non-existence could not administer further punishment.

The silence was disturbed by a rustling behind my bench, in some lavender bushes. I looked around and saw a blackbird fishing around underneath the bush, intent on grubbing up some morsel of food, apparently oblivious to the big mammal sitting on the bench only two yards away.

'Hello,' I said, looking into her black eyes. 'I'd like to believe you're Sis. But I can't believe in anything anymore. Give me a sign.'

The blackbird ceased her beakings and looked at me. Two seconds later she winged up to the bench and stood on the arm, only a foot from me. My instinctive urge was to reach out and stroke her, but I knew I couldn't. I was excited, enlivened. Something was attempting to show me things were not how they might seem. She jumped on to my lap. I stiffened, delighted at her trust, but afraid to scare her with movement. She cocked her head at me. My heart thumped.

'Am I forgiven?' I whispered.

She seemed to oscillate, a very un-birdlike movement. I thought she was about to speak to me.

'Ah, good afternoon.'

The little world was broken. The blackbird flew away, depositing some excrement on the bench next to me, and I turned my face up to the breaker of the bubble. From the side of the chapel, Dr Dawkins emerged. I looked up to the branch where the blackbird had alighted. I wanted to follow her there. But I couldn't—I had to interact with Dr Dawkins. He had a nurse towing along behind him as he stood himself in front of me, fingers fiddling with his watch-chain.

'I believe you're a guest at the unit. I saw you this morning, am I right?'

'Yes. Yes, I was invited along.'

'Well, I am sorry if it gave you a poor impression of our institution. We only have the best interests of our patients at heart here, and procedures and protocols must be adhered to lest the standards of care are not maintained.'

I nodded and smiled, hoping he'd leave it there and go away. He didn't.

'But the Tertiary Research Unit has a lot of funding and exerts much influence, even though its patients are few and the research parameters are very narrow.

At the hospital we have hundreds of patients with a myriad of conditions, who, I can assure you, are receiving the very best care and assistance, with the very latest medicinal thinking.'

'I'm sure. I was only tagging along. I'm not really here to engage in the activities of what goes on here. I'm just a guest. I'm a… err, I'm a folklorist.'

I was making the usual hash of explaining myself, but Dawkins seemed pleased at my disengagement from any partisan affiliation.

'Yes, I have heard about you. A very worthwhile study, that of folklore. A part of what this country is built upon. I hope you will find some stories in these parts. But… please do look after yourself while you are at the unit. I do not apologise for retaining scepticism about what they are attempting to do there. I am a materialist. I believe that our patients need to be treated via their brains. It is their brains that need to be dealt with and cured, not some occult mumbo-jumbo involving consciousness and minds that are separate from the physical brain.'

I squirmed in my seat. I wanted him to go away. I looked at the nurse for the first time. She stared at me — the usual look, but with some vitriol thrown in. She disapproved of my existence, I was quite sure of that.

'But I'm glad you've found our chapel,' continued Dawkins, perhaps picking up on my uncomfortable bearing. 'It provides a haven of peace.'

'Yes. What are the iron markers?'

'Ah, they are awaiting return to the hospital cemetery; it's about a mile away, on the road into town. Each marker designates a buried patient, obviously, but the last burial was seven years ago as the cemetery is now closed — most of these markers are from decades ago, some going back to the foundation of the hospital in the last century. We bring some of the uprooted ones here sometimes — certain of the more stable patients enjoy drawing them or taking rubbings.'

'But they're just numbers. Do you know who they are?'

'Oh yes. Each number is recorded to the patient in our archive. They were real people. They lived and died here.'

The nurse coughed, prompting Dawkins to whatever business they were on. He took the cue and bustled into a leaving demeanour.

'I hope your stay is productive,' he continued, 'and that if we may be of service to you at the hospital then please do not hesitate to come to us. And please… do be careful of your compatriots. I say this in an advisory fashion. Good day to you.'

Off they went. I gave myself a few moments to readjust from the interaction then got up and went back to iron marker number twenty-four.

'Who were you, my friend? What's your story?'

I stroked the marker again and looked up to the tree. The blackbird was nowhere to be seen. There was just the splash of sunlight finding its way through the canopy and glistening on the iron markers below. They were signals of death. I needed to extract myself from them, so I trooped up away from the chapel, through some vegetable gardens, onto a footpath and out of the hospital grounds into a lane that led uphill through to enclosed fields. I found a corner of hedgerows, sat down and attempted to work out how I was going to deal with the situation in which I found myself.

The sun was on my face. I squinted into the distance beyond the hospital: hills levelling out onto a broad flat expanse, made hazy and gossamer-like. I closed my eyes and straight away felt the drift, the events of the last day becoming invested with the mild delirium of oncoming sleep. Dawkins and Albé became mixed up with the grave markers and the blackbird, and the hum of the E-Type ran alongside the clickety-clack of the train, while Fletcher somehow bustled around my quarters, piling up books, asking if I wanted light bulbs changing and when I'd like supper.

***

Now I am by the brook. The sun is harsh. Why is it so hot? The light is whiter than it should be, making it impossible to look at the reflection in the running water. I shield my eyes from it. On the other side is Sis. She wears a white dress I've never seen her in before and plays with two foot-high faeries with little hats that mimic the fly agaric mushroom. I squint hard at them and see that they seem to be made of wood, all gnarled and morphing into different forms moment by moment. She tells them to stop misbehaving with a wag of her finger and then looks into my eyes. Her black hair billows in a way that upsets me, but I don't want her to know this, so I smile and wave.

'You're going to find out what I know,' she says, her words reverberating inside my head rather than in the air. 'They are going to show you what it's all about. I think you've come to the right place… Do you know how much I love you?'

'As much as I love you.'

The faeries start dancing around again, happy at our declaration of love. Each has an iron grave marker in their hands, and they wave them around with abandon as they sing: *We must not look at faerie men; we must not eat their fruits. Who knows upon what soil they fed their hungry, thirsty roots.* Sis shushes them, and then I am standing at the bank of the brook. I am about to jump over, but she holds up both hands to halt me. The faeries copy her gesture.

'You cannot come to this side. I am here and you are there. In many years you'll be here too. I'll still be here then. I so want to hold you. I want your warmth.' She becomes stern. 'But don't you dare come over the water before you have to. I shall be cross with you if you do. And anyway, you're about to fall in love. That will be worth staying over there for.'

'Can I ever love someone more than you?'

But she is gone now. The faeries slink into the undergrowth and the heat of the sun causes a whoosh;

the upward travel of something imperious… I am transcending…

***

A moment of hypnagogia with sing-song words: *Row, row, row your boat, gently down the stream. Merrily, merrily, merrily, merrily, life is but a dreeeeeam.*

I came round, clammy, clothes sticking to me. I wanted to get back to the dream, but I knew I couldn't. Her face and voice had been so super-real. I teared up but pulled myself to my feet. A few cows mooched around on the other side of the hedgerow. I stood on tiptoe to look at them. They stared back with bovine, bland curiosity.

'Is this a dream?' I asked them. 'Will I ever be able to tell?'

They chewed their cuds. I went back to the TRU, the resonance of the dream buzzing inside me. It infected my every thought.

VIII

At about seven o'clock Fletcher came knocking at my door, Epsilon trailing behind him with a tray of food, cutlery and a bottle of cider.

'I hope you don't mind,' he said, never quite meeting my eyes. 'But I was asked to bring you some supper. We usually serve up in the common room but thought you might like room service on your first night.'

'That's so kind. Thank you.'

'It's just some pasta, spiced sausage and sauce. We get it cooked up in the hospital kitchen. Miss Rood there makes sure we always have something amenable for the unit. She and I have an agreement.'

He coloured a little, but I couldn't decipher the meaning.

'Spiced sausage pasta. That's quite exotic.'

'Well, m'lord and I spent some time in Italy — Ravenna and Venice — developed a bit of a taste for it. Even young Epsilon here has got used to it... eh, Eddie?'

'Fuckin' right, yeah. Fuckin' lovely grub.'

Fletcher rolled his eyes and told Epsilon to put the tray on the desk. They turned to leave, but I sensed I needed to take the brief opportunity to get some information.

'Have you been Albé's assistant for long?'

'Ai, we go back a long way,' he said, finally meeting my eyes. 'He's a good sort really. He has his ways, but then don't we all?'

'Indeed. And where are you from?'

'Nottinghamshire, born and bred.'

'And Albé?'

'Ha, all over. But his seat is in Notts.'

'His seat?'

Fletcher started to shuffle, and I realised I needed to cease the questions. A few more pleasantries, then he and Epsilon left. I sat down to my meal, swigging back some cider, which had the ambience of something potent.

'Fuckin' lovely grub,' I mumbled, smiling at my image of the hapless Epsilon. The food was delicious and the cider was strong.

An hour later I was in bed with pretensions to start reading *The Three Faces of Eve*, but the blackout came quickly, and I was soon back into the alternative dream reality.

***

I remembered no dreams when I awoke. The carriage clock said half past seven, and the mourning sun was forcing its way through the flimsy curtains. I eased myself awake, locked into the tick-tock of the clock. All else was silent.

I got up, brushed my teeth and washed my face in the basin, then crept along the corridor to the bathroom with my towel and soap. I allowed myself to soak in the tub for half an hour, attempting to find some neutral space without the usual cascade of mind-chatter. I was almost successful, but once back in my room, I began heating up again with the thought of what might happen during the day. Spinning out the anticipation of starting my project was one thing but delaying it to find out about insane people was another. It was too late though.

I sat on the bed waiting for the nine o'clock knock and tried to control the spasming muscles in my face and neck. How long before someone realised I was not firing on all cylinders? Christ, if things took a few wrong turns, they might suggest, with subtle intent, I needed to be given a certificate and committed into the hospital.

The knock at the door came.

'Walk in.'

It was Moore, ciggy in mouth and smile on his lips as usual. He offered me one. I declined.

'Ready to come and see our part of the madhouse?'

'I think so. I'm a bit nervous, to tell the truth. Have you got five minutes to tell me about what will be happening?'

'Yeah, of course.'

He came in and we both sat down on the bed. I knew I was squirming, but I tried to allow his nonchalance to wash over me. At least my ticking face seemed to have abated.

'We managed to get Caroline Lamb over here last night,' he said, making himself comfortable with a pillow behind his head. 'As you've already seen her in the hospital, we thought it might be a gentle start for you to see us in action with her first off. Y'know — a sense of familiarity.'

'I guess. Did you clock onto her saying *annihilation* when we were there?'

'You bet. Scrope would call it synchronicity. All that Jung and the Collective Unconscious stuff. Scrope's the psychologist — worships Jung. He's been in the Observation Room for the last half hour with Caroline, warming things up so to speak.'

'The Observation Room?'

'Yes. It's all a bit *Star Trek* — you'll probably be surprised. I know I was when I came here. But it's so useful. You'll see.'

'Ok... ok. And what about you, Thom? What do you do?'

'I'm a chemist. A poet too, in the style of Anacreon, but that doesn't make me any money, so I do chemistry instead. We have a tiny lab here.'

'Oh, I'd got the impression Albé disapproves of drugs for the patients.'

'Only certain types of drugs,' he said, an inscrutable look coming over him behind the smoke. 'There is a place for some chemical intrusions. You'll get this in time. But the TRU operates a very different ethos from the hospital. As I say — you'll need some time to understand what we're about.'

Moore's obfuscation triggered my face tic. The carriage clock behind me seemed to become incessant and loud: tick-fucking-tock. But I'd worked out my questions; necessary primers before I dived into something I didn't understand.

'All right. And I know we need to get going and all, but could you just give me some idea about what to expect. If Miss Lamb has Hysterical Neurosis —'

'Dissociative Type.'

'Yes, that. What will she be doing? Will she be ranting and raving?'

'Who knows? We've had over twenty patients through here since last year. They all have their own idiosyncratic behaviour patterns, caused by a variety of traumas. But it's become quite clear to me that they have all had multiple persons within them. I mean, *real* different minds within the individual. We've worked out techniques to extract these personalities and to treat them. I wouldn't say we've cured them all, but we've definitely helped them all. It's difficult to explain. You really need to see it for yourself — some time to see what we're all about.'

'And will I see it today?'

'Yes.'

Moore made motions to suggest we needed to get going. But as he stood up, he allowed a moment's pause.

'And the faeries? Why are you so interested in the faeries?

'Well… it's a long story. You'll need some time to understand what *I'm* all about.'

He grinned and gave me a concessionary nod. He left another pause, as if deciding whether he should say more.

'You'll find that we know a little more about the faeries here than you might think. It's no accident that Hobby and Albé have manipulated you to be here. And there's a girl here that you'll need to meet soon.

She's the co-ordinate that will connect you and us. She's important in so many ways. She's quite special. I think you'll get on with her like a house on fire.'

'Right. A girl. Does she work here?'

'She's a patient at the hospital.'

'A patient?'

'Yes. Her name is Fernanda. She's very cool. But once again, my friend, this is going to have to wait. We need to get along to the Observation Room. We have some observing to do.'

IX

We went down some steps at the far end of the unit and stopped in front of a door.

'So this is the monitoring chamber part of the Observation Room,' said Moore.

He knocked the door and in we went. The room was narrow, low-lit, but had a massive window on the left-hand side, which gave a view into a bright room. Albé was sat down in front of some kind of electronic panel with buttons and lights, like a mini recording studio. Moore and I took up seats next to him. He spoke without taking his eyes away from the window.

'Ok,' he said, 'no time for explanations, Blondie. This is a one-way mirror; a reciprocal mirror. They can't see us but we can see them. We're soundproofed as well, but their room is miked up.'

He twisted a dial and the volume of voices from the other room increased. I breathed deep and squinted into the room, my eyes adjusting to the light. No more than ten feet away, Scrope was in an armchair. Caroline Lamb was on a small sofa, sitting up straight with her hands on her lap. She wore a close-fitting, plain white dress. She looked manicured and well turned out compared to her distressed condition yesterday. Her eyes seemed huge. She looked so young.

'Is she still Caroline?' asked Moore.

'One minor change so far,' replied Albé. 'But we're just getting to the crux of it.'

'Recording?'

'Of course.'

I gulped hard and hoped Albé and Moore couldn't hear my breathing. The blood pumped in my ears. Scrope leaned forward, folding his hands together.

SCROPE: …and so when did this start happening? Take your time. Remember, I'm on your side.

CAROLINE: I don't really know. I was maybe twelve or thirteen. I don't know exactly though. I'm sorry, doctor. Please don't hate me for it. I'm a good girl, I really am.

SCROPE: I know. There is no hate here, Caroline, only understanding. Can you remember the first time?

CAROLINE: Yes, like I said before… he came to my room. Like he used to, as I told you. But this time was different. Not for him but for me. He touched me down there… you know. Oh, I hate to think of it. No, I cannot speak of it again. Please don't make me.

SCROPE: I won't make you do anything you don't want to, Caroline. I don't need to hear about what he did. But you say something happened this time. What was that?

CAROLINE: She took over. She put me in the dark place and took over. She took control.

SCROPE: Could you see her from the dark place? Hear her?

CAROLINE: Sort of. It's hard for me to explain. It's a little like dreaming. I've told you that already. You know when you dream and are just waking up — you sort of know what the real world is like but not quite. You're never sure where you really are.

SCROPE: Yes, I understand. Do you know what she did?

CAROLINE: She hurt him. Oh, how she hurt him. He screamed. Mummy came down. Please don't make me speak more. Please.

SCROPE: It's ok. You're safe here. No one can hurt you anymore.

CAROLINE: Oh, but you've done it now. I can feel it. There is a shiver in me. I don't want to go to the dark place. She's not nice. I'm nice. I'm good, I know I am. But she's not…

Albé leaned forward, adjusting a dial.

'Here we go,' he said.

Moore glanced at me, biting his lip. No Irish smile now.

Caroline eased back into the sofa for about a minute. Her face creased up and she spread open her legs, fingers tapping the cushion. She was smiling, maybe sneering. She looked suddenly different.

SCROPE: Are you all right?

CARO: Oh, I'm fine. What do you care?

SCROPE: Well, I'm here to help you. We've been talking about how I can help, have we not?

CARO: You can take your help and shove it up your ass.

SCROPE: Who are you?

CARO: You know who I am. She's told you. I'm the reason she's here today, cos without me she wouldn't have gotten away from that fucking monster.

SCROPE: Do you want to tell me about that?

CARO: Yeah—I'll tell you about it. I was born to protect her. She's useless. She's compliant. She tells you she's a good girl. Well, maybe, but she doesn't know how the world works. She just lets things happen to her. But I don't. You mess with me and I'll fuck you over, I can tell you.

SCROPE: How were you born?

CARO: Ah, so clever. You think you're a real smart cookie, don't you? Another public schoolboy observing people like me. Well, I'll tell you how I was born. One day that monster came to do what he had gotten used to doing with Caroline, and there was a snapping of something. Like a massive elastic band snapping. One moment she was her, laying down and letting it all happen, as usual, the next I was there, scratching that bastard's face off. I bit his dick. Is that what you want to hear? I can tell you, he fucking howled at that. Blood everywhere. He deserved it.

SCROPE: Where did you come from?

CARO: Mmm. You know all this. The dark place. It's where we live when she's calling the shots.

SCROPE: We?

CARO: You're manipulating me. You know how this works. Why are you trying to get it out of me?

SCROPE: I don't think I do know how it works. I don't know what the dark place is, and I don't know who else is there.

CARO: I think you're lying about that. I can tell these things. Your friend Albé has been there. I don't know how. The dark place is like a dream. I don't know how he managed to get there, but he did. He has no right to be there.

SCROPE: Can you tell me more about the dark place?

CARO: No.

SCROPE: Ok. Why did you take over in the shop? There was a violent incident there, I've been told.

CARO: You've been told. You're such a deceptive bullshitter. But yeah, for the record, she was taking some grief from some dude for no reason in particular. This seeps through to where we have to live most of the time; the dark place. I rose to the top, kicked his bollocks and slapped him in the face. Sorted him out. If I could be in charge all the time, there'd be no problems.

SCROPE: But it's because of that incident that you're here now.

CARO: Eurgh… I feel sick. You've made me sick. I am. Just. So. Angry…

She collapsed back into the sofa. Scrope barely made a move. Albé and Moore were on tenterhooks. I couldn't believe what I was seeing. It was like some dramatic performance being played out in a theatre.

I looked closer at Caroline—she was a beauty. But when she changed, transformed, whatever it was called, she seemed to become so much older, hatefulness distorting every feature. As she sank back into the sofa, her demeanour slumped. Her mouth became skewed. And when she spoke again, her voice was that of a little girl.

INNOCENT: You should not have done that. Why are you doing it? You brought out Caro. Caro is a baddy.

SCROPE: Who are you?

INNOCENT: My name is Innocent.
SCROPE: Where have you come from?
INNOCENT: Pffft. You know.
SCROPE: Who else is there now?
INNOCENT: A few others. They hug Caroline. They love her. Caro does not. You know this. Please send Caro away.
SCROPE: We have no power to do this.
INNOCENT: We?

She looked directly at the window as she spoke. I balked at her gaze. I was quite sure she could see us, sitting there in judgement. She took her sulky gaze back to Scrope.

INNOCENT: I don't like you. I'm going back now. Caroline talks about Albé. We've seen him in the dark place. He is an angel there. But he's not one of us. We don't understand how he gets there. Please ask him to get rid of Caro. Caroline is the big girl. She'll tell you.

She wriggled on the sofa, clasping her hands together and shaking her head. There were a couple of minutes of silence and stillness. She felt her breasts over as if ensuring they were there.

SCROPE: Caroline?
CAROLINE: Yes.
SCROPE: Are you all right?
CAROLINE: I don't like this world. I don't like the things that happen to me. Are you going to help me? Because I don't like this. Sometimes I want to just stay in the dark place. But when I'm there, I don't really know what's happening out here.
SCROPE: We will help you. But you need to trust us. Do you trust us?
CAROLINE: I trust Albé. I want him to come back to the dark place. He's an angel. No one from outside has been there before. I like him to come there. But now I am tired… so tired.

SCROPE: Well, he'll be there for you. I promise. Would you like to go back to your room now?
CAROLINE: Very much. I would like to sleep. I am so very tired. Please tell me everything will be all right. I'm a good girl. I really am. Please don't blame me.
SCROPE: We don't blame you for anything, Caroline. We will help you. Now come with me, and we'll get you settled back in your room.

There was a collective release of tension in the monitoring chamber. Albé fiddled with a few switches and then swung round on his chair. He spoke to Moore.

'There are at least half a dozen personalities there. Caro is the main sub-operator and will need to be the focus of our treatment. Usual story though: sexually abusive father, introduction of a character who can deal with him, and ostracisation when it happens. Then when she escapes the abusive familial relationship the alternative personality refuses to relinquish her element of control and starts to cause problems. Accurate?'

'Yep. But the little girl... Innocent? She was interesting. She sounded about six or seven, but her vocabulary and enunciation were quite advanced. We'll need to keep her separated from the rest of them.'

'Agreed.'

They both looked at me. They must have realised I was not part of their world. I didn't know what was going on, but the implicit assumptions were starting to turn over my mind.

'That's probably enough for you, Blondie,' said Albé, curving his lip. 'In at the deep end, I guess. But better you saw this sooner rather than later. If you don't mind, I'll come to your quarters at five this afternoon... just to go over some things. Would that be acceptable?'

'I'll be there.'

'Splendid.'

I left. Yes, I left.

X

'Here you go,' said Albé, entering my room with his usual limping swish. He deposited a red plastic box on the desk and opened it up. 'An Olivetti electric typewriter for you. Travelling version. Our friend Richard Burton has one, so I hear.'

'For me?'

'On loan, while you're here. I presume you'll be needing to type up notes and suchlike, so you may as well have the latest technology to smooth the passage.'

'I don't know what to say; that's so kind.'

'Well, it's the least we can do.'

He sat himself down in the chair and motioned for me to sit on the bed. I did.

'I've been starting to think this morning's episode may have been a bit much for you, so soon after your arrival. I do realise you're not here to engage with our research or patients. But I think the longer you're here, the more you'll realise that your study of supernatural entities and our investigations into how the human mind works are more closely correlated than you might think. Did you understand what was going on with, Caroline?'

'Imperfectly.'

Albé did his curled-lip thing. 'I like your language, Blondie. You don't give too much away, do you? Did you believe what you saw?'

'I think so. Though it was kind of unreal. It was a bit theatrical.'

'That's probably because it's so rarely seen. We've become used to it over the last year at the unit, but it's not a well-known disorder, and even when it manifests under psychiatrically controlled conditions, it will usually be diagnosed as schizophrenia. This is why we have such a battle with the Dr Dawkins types. But I think your moments in the monitoring chamber this morning should have demonstrated to you that one physical person can have many minds. To speak plainly, a person such as Caroline has several minds operating through the conduit of her brain. These aren't just variations on her personality showing themselves during a neurotic episode. They are individual minds, unique consciousnesses operating within one body.'

'But where do they exist when they aren't... you know...'

'Primary? Well, you heard the different characters talk about *the dark place*. That's a common way for them to talk about it. It's a distinct location — a metaphysical location, where consciousness can exist without material form. As Caroline says — a bit like a dream. Each consciousness remains aware but is suppressed. Then at certain moments, and for a variety of reasons, they can take primacy in the host. They never have any interaction with each other out here in the *real* world — only one personality manifests at any one time — but it's quite clear there is communication between them in the dark place... although this differs between patients. And though there is only a limited recognition from repressed personalities about what is being done by the primary personality in the physical body, it does seem there can be some awareness. As young Caroline eloquently expressed: like experiencing the edge of wakefulness from a dream.'

'Yes. I think I get it... sort of. Do you think we all have these multiple minds? It's just that most of us repress them?'

'Mmm. Perceptive. Possibly. The lack of any repression in these individuals is, I'm afraid to say, usually the result of some form of abuse in childhood, which forces the psychological reaction. But as you say, perhaps the multiple minds are latent in all of us. We don't know. And as all institutional bodies in need of funding grants say: "More research is needed."'

I laughed.

'You should laugh more, Blondie—it is cheap medicine.'

The unreasonable sensation that Albé was burrowing into my mind made me shift on the bed, as though that might stop him being able to do so.

'Because without laughter, love and hope, our traumas will get the better of us won't they? Before we know it, we'll just give up and string ourselves up from a beam, just to escape it all.'

I gritted my teeth and hoped he was guessing, because if he weren't, the only possibility was that he had access to my memory. Memory. An association brought itself up from my memory; my tweed travelling companion on the train and our conversation about solips—

'Solipsism. You did mention that before, didn't you? I guess multiple minds inside one person would disprove solipsism once and for all, wouldn't it? But then an adherent of solipsism might argue that even all the multiple personalities were actually just another group of subjects interacting within the primary consciousness. If I were the solipsistic God, then even if I appeared to have a number of minds taking over now and then, I could still simply see them as aberrations within my one, universal consciousness. I would still be all that really existed.'

My face started to tick. I was having a conversation with someone several intellectual divisions above me, and I was pretty sure I didn't have the social skills to fit into where I was expected to be.

'But perhaps this is all too unnecessarily esoteric. All that parsimonious philosophy, eh? Perhaps the basic concept you need to take away, before you start finding out about your supernatural faeries, is that the mind is not the brain. Aldous Huxley called the brain a reducing valve for Mind at Large. I think we should probably take notice of clever people like Huxley, even if the Dr Dawkins of the world try to tell us otherwise.'

'Yes.'

'You can look into the brain as deeply as you like, but you won't find the mind there. Scientists with a materialistic outlook will try, but they'll fail. I've heard there's a lot of excitement about a prototype brain scanner—computed tomography it's being termed—developed by an engineer called Hounsfield. It can supposedly scan the brain in slices. Very useful, I'm sure, but even if Hounsfield's bit of kit is improved to the extent that it can map every neuron in the brain, a materialist scientist will still have nothing to say about the mind, about consciousness. You can measure physical reactions to external stimuli in the brain, and even invoke feelings and memories by stimulating certain parts of the brain. But the feelings and memories themselves will remain unexaminable. No scientist will ever see or measure a feeling or a memory by looking for it in the brain. And yet feelings and memories are all we have—they constitute the totality of consciousness. A particularly dogmatic scientist, of which there are many, would get around this by saying that consciousness is just an epiphenomenon of brain function. The three-pound lump of flesh trapped in your skull simply produces... this.'

Albé held his hands up and looked around him to demonstrate *this*. He then did his trick of shifting closer to me without actually moving in any discernible way.

'That's why they so dislike the concept of Mind. They will do anything to take it out of the equation in order to reinforce their worldview. They cannot admit that consciousness is non-physical, metaphysical... because their worldview is predicated on everything being physical. Their science is dependent on matter, and how that matter interacts within the universal laws of physics. But consciousness operates outside of those laws. Our minds have very little to do with the laws of physics—they are only constrained to interact with this physical reality during their time as causal prisoners of the brain and body.'

I squirmed on the bed. 'Can you give me an analogy? To help me… understand.'

He beckoned me to move to the desk, drew out a sheet of paper from the pocket in the Olivetti and rolled it into the typewriter.

'Type LOVE.'

I complied.

'What you have just done conforms to the laws of physics in a totally predictable way. A typewriter is a physical object constructed of matter, that will respond to you, a physical person also made of matter, typing LOVE, in the same way, every time. It will punch out the four appropriate metal arms, and output in ink on that piece of paper the word LOVE in an undeniably causal fashion. It's a machine operating within this physical reality under the rigid laws of cause and effect.' He waited for me to meet his eyes. 'But the machine doesn't know what LOVE means; how it feels; what it's like to have a memory of LOVE. Only we know that. Only our non-physical minds. The typewriter is the brain. You, the operator, are the Mind.'

'I think I see. I think I do.'

Albé stepped back and regarded me for a few seconds. 'Think about the love you had for your sister. Where did it, and does it, exist? It can't be pinned down to anything except your non-physical thoughts. We cannot get behind consciousness.'

I bent in the chair, the wisp of Sis materialising behind my closed eyelids. I didn't want to cry in front of Albé, so I got up and turned my back on him for a moment. I stared at the carriage clock. *Tick-tock*.

'I'm sorry,' he said, with a lowered voice, 'I don't mean to intrude on this. I know what a sister's love means. She used to interact with faeries, did she not?'

'She did,' I said, controlling my breathing as best I could and turning. 'I guess I must have said something to Professor Hobhouse about it.'

'Yes. Maybe. Did you ever see them when you were with her?'

'Not as such. You know, peripheral things. Maybes and mights.'

'But you know she saw them and talked with them.'

'Oh yes. She was always scrupulously honest.'

'Do you think she was delusional?'

'I don't know… there was something intense and real about the way she talked about them. And in every other respect, she was so level-headed. She used to say: "They're real, even if you don't believe in them. You've just got too big and grown up to believe in them."'

I started to crack and tried to dampen my heaving chest. The buzz came into my head again, this time as a weird undercurrent to my train of thought that almost had the quality of a human voice. I finally met Albé's eyes and could not escape the intuition he was putting it there.

'Well, I might suggest that your sister simply had access to a realm of consciousness from which most people have become disconnected. I think perhaps our patients here in the unit, and many of those in the hospital, are in the same position, only they have lost the ability to control any interaction with that ulterior consciousness. And the way it represents itself can just overwhelm them. It then makes them insane.'

I nodded, too afraid to speak in case I burst into tears.

'But there's one in the hospital who has full control over her insanity. Has Moore mentioned Fernanda yet?'

'Yes.'

'Well, we'll arrange for you to meet her in the next few days. She knows all about the faeries, and I feel you might see some of your sister in her.' He paused, a pregnant pause. 'She's very important to us at the unit.'

'Really?'

'Yes, as you'll see.'

'What's her story?' I asked, still trying to keep the tear-choke from my voice.

'Well, she's the only South American in the hospital… Actually, she's probably the only non-English person in the hospital.'

'So why is she here?'

'Chile. They're about to elect a Marxist called Allende. Her father saw which way the wind was blowing a couple of years ago, didn't like it and cleared out the family over here. He's some sort of diplomat—ties to some Tory big-nobs apparently. But Fernanda had already been here for a few years at college for some reason. Once the father got here, he found out she'd been having some *problems*, extracted her from said school and used his influence to get her admitted here.'

'So what are her problems?'

'Delusional psychosis, according to Dr Dawkins at mission control. But we've found out different. She's quite special. You'll like her.'

Albé moved as if to leave. The buzzing ceased.

'What have you planned for the next few days?' he asked, before reaching the door. 'Hobby's given you some contacts?'

'Yes. I've been in touch with the chap who runs the local folklore society. I need to phone him and get some more contacts from him. You know, people with stories about the faeries, past and present.'

'Oh, I'm sure you'll find lots of those. I know Hobby wants to get it all out of them before they pop their clogs. Who is the folklore chap?'

'Mr Goodfellow.'

'Ha. Excellent. Do you think that's his real name?'

'I suppose so. We've exchanged a few letters and he does sound a bit… err, eccentric.'

'I bet.' Albé opened the door but glanced back at me. The light from the corridor made his eyes appear to flicker. 'We'll need to come back to your sister… for your own sake.'

He left me swaying next to the desk as the first tear escaped. I turned and looked at the piece of paper hanging out the top of the typewriter. LOVE… indeed.

XI

I decided I needed a few days more to acclimatise before I jumped into interviewing real people. I managed to convince myself this was a sensible option, all things considered, but knew I was just fooling myself and that, in fact, I was afraid of beginning the project. I also knew if I didn't force my way out of my room I might start to atrophy and end up cowering in there for as long as I could get away with it. I'd spent months in my university room, only venturing out to walk in the park at dawn or dusk when nobody was around to collect provisions from the shop. I'd grown afraid of people.

But despite the unorthodox nature of my new environment, and the even more unorthodox companions I found myself with, there was a kernel of ease beginning to give me some confidence. I'd been treated with kindness ever since I'd turned up at the station. Albé scared me because I felt inferior to him, and for his apparent ability to know what I was thinking, but I was receiving attention and a modicum of respect, which, apart from Professor Hobhouse's loose faith in my abilities, I had been starved of for so long. Maybe I wasn't utterly useless after all.

But any sub-stratum of positivity never lasted long. I sunk onto the bed and stared at the ceiling. One thing I was good at was staring at ceilings. The Artex pattern swirled and within that strange land of memory-visuals, I reworked my last confrontation with my parents. It was after Sis's funeral. The mandatory gathering at the family home was in full swing with barely recognised relatives, awkward neighbours and well-meaning friends. The moment transferred from past to present; the scene overlaid in mysterious realism on the swirling plaster ceiling of my current being.

I am talking to two male cousins whose names I cannot remember. They are both a bit intoxicated and becoming sentimental. My father comes over to us. We hadn't spoken since the autopsy. My mother, thoroughly gin-and-toniced, dutifully follows in his wake. He is a small man but has a way of making himself seem bigger. He eyes me up and down, disapproval dripping from every pore.

'I think you should leave now,' he says. 'I've held me tongue too long. You've got half an hour to pack yer bags and clear off.'

'Really? Um, ok.'

One of the cousins pipes up that this might not be the right time for this, but my father is having none of it.

'She's dead because of you. We all know it. You may as well have knifed her in the heart. I want it to be known that from this point on you are not part of this family. And as for yer *lifestyle* choice... you have brought total shame on me and yer mother. You are a disgrace. And now speaking with yer posh voice. I wish you'd never been born to us, you piece of fucking shit, you —'

He goes for me, but the cousins manhandle him away, as he continues to shout obscenities. My mother, drunken anxiety all over her face, sidles up to me and touches my arm.

'You should go, dear. We'll sort this out later but go now. Please.'

I pack and leave; bleeding, bereft. I've not seen nor heard from any of them since.

***

I walked around the hospital grounds. The sun burned away some of the remembrances, but the harsh words from past days lingered, tipping into my thoughts when I wasn't concentrating on some aspect of what was before me. I passed the nurses' hostel. Four nurses came out, laughing and spinning talk. When they passed me they became quiet and looked at me while pretending not to. It wasn't what I needed. What was it I needed? Perhaps I needed action. I checked for notebook and shillings in my pocket and made my way past the lodge-house, down to the road and on to the phone box, which stood incongruous at a junction a hundred yards away.

'Mr Goodfellow?'

'I be him.'

'We've exchanged some correspondence. You kindly suggested I come and see you about my folklore project... about some local people who might be able to talk to me.'

'Ah, I do indeed remember. London sort.'

'Err, yes.'

'Wanting to know all about our faeries, I do believe.'

'Um, yes, that's right, I was —'

'Then you've come to the right place. You can come down to the Shervage Arms on Saturday and we can go over things.'

'The Shervage Arms?'

'Ai. As in the Shervage Vyrm.'

'I'm sorry?'

'Shervage Vyrm... the gurt vyrm of Shervage Wood.'

'Sorry, I'm not sure what you mean. Is this a pub?'

'That it be. You be at the big mental hospital, do you not?'

'Ah, yes.'

'They'll know where it is. Not too far from you. I'll be there for about zeben, in the public bar. We can talk before skittles at nine. Just ask for me at the bar.'

'At seven?'

'Yep, at zeben.'

Christ.

I walked back past the lodge into the hospital grounds, now more unsure than ever I should be there. How was I going to deal with these people?

I'd never been in the countryside in my life, and rural sorts were just characters in my folklore, usually distanced in time by a period of several generations. I doubted the country types of 1970 were going to be anything like the literary renderings of my motifs and anecdotes from the nineteenth century. I stopped and rolled a ciggy, trying to think of ways I could cope with what I was about to be thrown into. Perhaps I could have a chat with Moore or Scrope. Maybe one of them would come with me on Saturday to dilute my dread of walking into a country pub and interacting with someone who I had already convinced myself was as mad as a mongoose.

As if by immediate osmosis, I saw Moore, about a hundred yards away, heading down the path from the unit. I instinctively ducked behind a tree trunk. I peered out from beside the trunk. He strolled along with his usual casual gait, but turned towards the nurses' hostel, whistling as if to create an air of nonchalance. A few furtive glances around and he slipped into a side door without a sound.

I leant on the trunk and finished the ciggy.

'You dirty dog, Moore,' I whispered.

I smiled. Moore had broken my spell of anxiety, and I was grateful to him for it. But it was time to get back to my room before I was forced to engage with anyone else. I needed some solitude.

XII

'Take that grimace off your face Fletcher; it's no more than four miles. The walk'll do us good,' announced Albé over his shoulder.

We trooped up the country lane, Albé leading on, waving his walking stick and making comments about various flora in the ditches, Scrope and Moore laughing and joking about something or other, and Fletcher huffing and puffing behind me. They'd appropriated my Saturday evening meeting with the ostensible promise of helping me out, but with the evident reality of having a boozy night out at the Shervage Arms. I walked on, the early-evening August scents of the country creating an ambient haze, only partially infiltrated by Fletcher's grumbling.

As we reached a crossroad at the crest of a rise, an old open-backed truck spluttered along the adjacent lane. It stopped and an old boy, as decrepit as his vehicle, leaned out the window.

'Where you lot traipsing off to then?' he asked, eyeing us all up. His gaze finally rested on me. As always, up went the eyebrows.

'The Shervage Arms, my good man,' said Albé. 'And there's a very large drink in it for you if you'd care to give us a lift.'

The driver's face creased into a grin. 'Get theeselves in the back with dog then, and we'll be there dreckley.'

The suddenly rejuvenated Fletcher was first in, relief and satisfaction riding over him in equal measures. We followed him and hauled ourselves into the back of the truck, finding space between the detritus and nameless small machinery. I spent the rattling journey stroking the collie dog, putting up with his bad breath and half-listening to the never-ending banter between Scrope and Moore. Fletcher spread himself out with an aura of contentment, and Albé just watched the passing rurality. A joint was passed around, and in the ten minutes it took us to get to the pub, I found myself reeling a bit from its weedy strength.

The Shervage Arms was a rambling affair; soft yellow stone made even softer by the dulling light. Inside, the smoky ambience was complemented by the low dialect chatter as the locals carried on their timeless ruminations amidst their familiar watering hole. I'd half expected them to all stop mid-track and stare us down, but our arrival seemed to go unnoticed and we somehow melded into the condensed environment as if we belonged there. Moore was clearly quite at home. He leaned over the bar and beckoned the barmaid with a knowing smile.

'Six ciders please, darling. Ice in the ciders.'

'Coming right up, my lover.'

'I bet,' winked Moore, his eyes flashing with anticipation.

We sat down. Fletcher gulped down his pint in an instant and was back at the bar buying our driver another drink with money from Albé's pocket. I sipped at mine, still heady from the joint, and wondering how I would recognise Goodfellow. At the far end of the bar, a couple of crusty locals plucked away on banjos, to general indifference. Suddenly their tempo changed, and one of them started to mumble some indecipherable lyrics, all wrapped up in a folksong cadence. I felt the change; the passing of something. One of the players seemed to look at me from across the room. His words became distinct, sung in a folky resonance:

'And in the end there beckons, more and more clearly, total annihilatiooooon.'

I triggered a look at Moore, but he was just rolling a ciggy. He hadn't noticed. Was the weed having an abnormal effect on me? The buzz was in my head again. I looked at Albé—he was squinting at me. The tic took its hold on my face as usual, but I breathed deep and brought my attention back to the banjo players. They were now singing about a maid walking out amidst the dew in the merry month of May or something; innocuous, subsumed folkiness. I sipped my cider, chewed the ice, and tried to gravitate to Scrope's ongoing monologue about the importance of public houses to local communities. But the buzz continued and I decided I needed to get up and take some air outside. Too late though — Fletcher returned from the bar with news that Mr Goodfellow was in the snug and keen to talk to me.

'Do you want me to come with you?' asked Albé.

'I wouldn't mind. I'm feeling a bit, err… odd.'

'Well, I won't hang around. I'll just set you up. Got your notebook?'

'Yep.'

'Come on then.'

Goodfellow was a small man, sixty-ish, tweed jacket, brown tie, pipe in mouth. He greeted me with suspicion, and Albé with even greater suspicion.

'Don't mind me,' said Albé, 'I've just come along in mutual support. We understand you're the local aficionado on matters of folklore.'

'Well,' said Goodfellow, pipe still in mouth and meeting Albé's eyes rather than mine, 'I've been the president of the local folklore society for five years and lived here all me days, so I know what I'm about. Can't say I have confidence in Youngster here gleaning too much from people. But I know how it is; London types coming down here with all sorts of ideas.' He eased back into his chair a little and stared at me over his glasses. 'But having said that, a good-looking young thing like you may well be able to illicit some stories from the old folk. And there are stories aplenty about the faeries. People are sometimes reluctant to talk about them though. Nobody likes to seem foolish, and so if I'm to bide you some names and addresses, I need to know you'll be showing all due respect.'

'Oh, I can assure you of that, Mr Goodfellow. I'm simply here to collect —'

'Because there've been some salacious newspaper pieces in recent years, with know-it-all journalists making fun of some of the genuine folk beliefs of the older people here. If I let you know some of these people, I don't want no comeback on me nor the society if you're going to portray them as backward, or as silly countryfolk.'

'I can confirm to you, Mr Goodfellow,' said Albé, imposing his innate superiority, 'that my colleague here comes with the highest credentials from one of the foremost folklorists in the country. Professor Hobhouse has much deference and regard for belief systems of this type and in no way would ever disparage any anecdotal evidence. He's a social-scientist who I happen to know thinks of entities such as the faeries as representations of a metaphysical reality, which may become observable to certain people when particular circumstances are met. My colleague has a moral and scientific duty to adhere to this outlook and will ensure that the utmost delicacy and respect is shown to anyone divulging information.'

Goodfellow tensed and puffed quick on his pipe. 'Well... well, that's good to hear. Yes, I don't doubt it.' He held his hand to his right ear and flicked his eyes as if attempting to work something out.

Albé continued. 'Now if you don't mind, I think I should probably leave you two together to talk business. As you know, we're at the hospital, so quite central to all the surrounding environs — easy to reach everywhere. Delighted to have made your acquaintance, Mr Goodfellow.'

Once Albé was gone, Goodfellow continued, hesitant, looking around as if in recognition of someone listening in on his words. But he relaxed after a few minutes and began talking about the locality with evident affection for the landscape and its embedded folklore. A little longer, and after

Fletcher had appeared with a pint of cider for him, he sank back into the chair, re-lit his pipe and (after some convolution regarding the difference between faeries and pixies) told me a story about his father being 'pixie-led' by a band of entities while walking home through a field one evening in his youth.

'...but as his mother had always advised, he took off his jacket, turned it inside out and threw it to the ground. The next moment them faeries vanished, his disorientation was over, he found the gate and dashed home, without his jacket, but at least with his wits.'

'And what did he say they look like? The faeries?'

'Like you and I, my young friend,' he said, smiling for the first time. 'Like you and I, but just somehow different. They have their ways, but they are real. Please do remember, when you go a-collecting your testimonies, that we are not just making up stories for fireside telling. The younger folk think it's all baloney, but there are still people, in the quieter, slower parts who know the faeries are still here, and that they need to be reverenced.'

We chatted some more about the locality and some of the characters I could expect to meet. I jotted down some names and addresses of contacts and made to leave.

'Your colleague?'

'Albé?'

'He has something about him.'

'Indeed.'

Back in the main bar, Moore was still chatting up the barmaid, Scrope and Fletcher were engaged in a game of cards with some locals, and Albé was nowhere to be seen. I took the opportunity to slip outside for some air. I sat down on a bench. The road was silent.

'Here you go.'

I started. Albé appeared from the shadows and handed me a joint.

'Thanks.'

'Get what you needed?'

'I think so. But getting the addresses is one thing. Visiting these people is another. I'm a bit, err... inexperienced when it comes to collecting folklore. It's a delicate task and I'm not totally sure I'm up to it.'

The buzzing in my head started. It was like an electrical charge. Was it the weed, or was it Albé? Maybe both.

'Well, see how you go. And if you're having problems, then we'll see what we can do to help. There are ways and means of getting inside peoples' minds. We have it down to a fine art at the TRU.'

'Yes, I guess you have to.'

'You see, for us, one of the most important things to understand, and get to the bottom of, is where our patients' disassociated consciousnesses are going to when they are not operating the physical person. What is that space?'

'The dark place?'

'That's what they call it, some of them anyway. But these characters are not just bunkering down in some neurones of the brain. They are existing in a numinous, metaphysical reality. I know you don't see it yet, but I have a feeling the people you're about to meet, who have seen and interacted with faerie entities, are going to the same space, by whatever means they do it. They probably don't understand where they really are. But it's not the physical world, and so who knows what sort of beings exist there?'

'So you think the faeries might be real?'

'Blondie...'

He took the joint from me, and as he did so, I felt a curvature of thought that was not mine run through me: a momentary lucid insight, which conjured up some sylph-like creatures swarming over a tree.

'Blondie... you are coming into something by being here. We're going to help you understand, but you must keep your mind open. You will need to let me in sometimes.'

The buzz intensified, becoming somehow like the sound of running water.

'I think, I think… I'm a bit stoned, Albé.'

'And one of the first things we're going to have to get sorted out is that beautiful little sister of yours.'

'Oh?'

'Because there's a big blockage there, isn't there? A big mountain of grief and guilt that you don't seem to be able to move beyond. This will need to be removed.'

'Will it?'

'You know it will. We can't have you staring through a circle of rope again, can we?'

The pub door opened and slammed against the wall, breaking Albé's conjured moment of noose and imminent extinction. A flushed Moore tumbled out. He gave us a brief quizzical look, then eyed up the joint in Albé's hand. It was handed to him. The buzzing ceased.

'The good news,' said Moore, taking a big toke, 'is that Fletcher's arranged a ride back tonight from one of the local sorts who's heading that way. You'll have to wait till after skittles though. Usually done and dusted by midnight apparently.'

'And the bad news?' asked Albé, re-appropriating the joint.

'Well, I won't be joining yous. The charming Miss Elizabeth Dyke behind the bar has invited me up to her room after the bell sounds, for some philosophical dialogue, which I have been persuaded into on account of her evident intellectual repartee.'

'I'm sure.'

We finished off the joint and headed back in. At the threshold, Albé pulled me back by the arm.

'Don't forget what we've talked about. There are things that need to be done…. Sorrow is knowledge; those that know the most must mourn the deepest. The tree of knowledge is not the tree of life.'

Great.

XIII

I am in a bubble. I levitate within it. It appears to contain the entire universe. But then there is another bubble. It floats towards me from a distance, and I realise there must be something existing outside my bubble. Albé is in the other bubble, or is it someone else? Whoever it is communicates with me, the voice buzzing with static interference.

'She walks in beauty like the night, of cloudless climes and starry skies…'

The static drowns out further words. I now notice the space between the bubbles. From a stratospheric viewpoint, I see the Shervage Arms in the middle of patchwork fields. It then becomes the hospital, and there is the sound of a bell tolling as if in warning. The faeries are in this space; luminous, looking human but not moving like humans.

'We live here. We live here,' they shout. *'You must not look at faerie men.'*

I catch a scent. I somehow know it is an orchid. At the same moment, the other bubble conjoins with mine and we become one. There is a rush upwards, and the spoken words are sublime and loud. They are inside my head rather than coming from without:

'The smiles that win, the tints that glow, but tell of days in goodness spent. A mind at peace with all below, a heart whose love is innocent.'

Bang. Bang. Bang.

***

Bang. Bang. Bang. I wake up… no, I woke up. The knock on the door sounded again. I looked at the carriage clock, but my newly awakened vision was blurred. There was just the tick-tock insinuating that time still existed. I got up, heart thumping, and opened the door. As I did so, the pulse of a big hangover headache hit me and I swayed, looking at the figure before me without recognition.

'Blimey, Blondie. Nice legs. I hadn't realised.'

'Moore?'

'The very same. Are you all right?'

'Yeah. I thought you were staying at the pub. Why are you here?'

'I did. It's one in the afternoon. Have one too many ciders last night, eh?'

'I think I may have. Oh God.'

'Good craic it was. Do you remember the skittles?'

'It's starting to come back to me.'

'Well, if you can regain your equilibrium by about three, we'll go over to the vegetable gardens to meet Fernanda. She'll be there today.'

'Ok, see you at three.'

Moore eyed me up one more time and trotted off with a smirk on his face. I shut the door, fell back on the bed, fought off the nausea and started to piece together the parts of a five-pint night at the Shervage Arms. I hadn't drunk five pints of anything over the course of the previous six months, and so packing in five scrumpies in one night, alongside all the weed, had been a pretty stupid idea. But I had two hours to break the hangover, bathe and get ready to meet the increasingly mysterious Fernanda. Aspirin, a jug of water, some buttered toast and a bath would do the trick.

***

The trick had only been half accomplished. My head still throbbed and a shakiness ran through me as Moore escorted me through the damp grounds; evidently, there had been rain while I slept away the morning. We walked past the laundry building and oil tanks, then under the grey neo-gothic elevations of the chapel, dripping rainwater from their eaves high above.

'I don't want to tell you too much about Fernanda,' Moore said, lighting up a spindly joint. 'Don't want to bias your opinion, so to speak. But you do need to know that we've benefited from her... her abilities, at the TRU.'

'Abilities?'

'She has what the old folk back in Ireland might call the second sight; clairvoyance, or whatever you want to call it. And it doesn't really matter whether anyone believes it or not, because we have proof of it.'

'Do you?'

'She's brought the metaphysical into the physical, like an alchemist. And she's trusted us with her gift... but you'll have to wait to find out about that. I'll be interested what you think of her. She can be quite odd. I guess it's a combination of being a Chilean in an English mental hospital and having the ability to enter an otherworld. That would make anyone odd, wouldn't it?'

'Indeed.'

'But she's special, and we very much want you to get on with her. I think she'll appreciate someone who will talk to her about the faeries.'

'Is that the real reason why Albé agreed for me to stay here?' I asked, regretting the caustic tone.

'Well, you'd have to ask him. But I think you'll soon understand why our work with the TRU patients is somewhat dependent on our Chilean inmate. But this can wait. You need to meet her first. Got your notebook?'

'Yes.'

We passed the west end of the chapel, with the vegetable gardens in front of us. Moore stopped to re-light the joint, took a drag and handed it to me.

'Anyway, there she is, over there in the red top, doing some weeding, or whatever it is you do in a vegetable patch.'

A couple of tokes on the joint calmed me a bit. I gave it back to Moore and went to find out just how odd she might be.

There were a few inmates engaged in something or other at one end of the gardens. A nurse sat on a bench, reading a book and keeping a dilatory eye on them. But Fernanda was apart, working alone in a patch that seemed profuse with greenery. The sun came out. A cloud-breaking ray fell over the gardens, picking out colours that hadn't seemed to be there a moment before. Fernanda's hooded red top pulled her out of the background; made her seem physically separated from it.

I walked over to her, hiding anxiety with a smile. She was crouching to place some nuts onto a tree stump next to the vegetable patch, but saw me, stood up and stretched out her hands as though she expected me to take them in my own.

'*Hola.*'

'Hello. Fernanda?'

'You are just in time for the ravens. They are being called now.'

Her accent was slight but distinct. She looked through me somehow. But her eyes were smiling. She'd already taken some control.

'They only trust me, but I think they will trust you too.'

She walked to the end of one of the garden paths and I followed. She closed her eyes and swayed while another ray of sun found her face, and I was able to take in her features. I could feel my pulse in my fingers. When she opened her eyes, they seemed black, iris and pupil, and I couldn't tell what she was looking at.

'*Dos cuervos,*' she announced, 'coming to us now.'

Sure enough, from the tree-line to the North, two ravens appeared and silently flew down onto a fence at the far end of the gardens. They tarried there, conspiring and ensuring their coast was clear before gliding down together to the tree stump, where they put their beaks to work on the nuts. They hopped about, taking some more nuts before retreating back to the fence.

'Now observe,' she whispered. 'They will silently call their comrades.'

We stood in silence for about a minute, Fernanda staring into the middle distance, while I shuffled around hoping this wasn't going to go on too long. Then six more ravens appeared above the tree line, making their way towards us. They flew down in ragged tandem, alighted on the fence with the other two, then, two by two, drifted down to the ground and hopped over to the nuts on the tree stump. We were only ten feet from them, but they carried on as if we weren't there.

When they'd finished and moved back to the fence, Fernanda crouched down. One of the ravens broke ranks and landed closer to us. It bobbed its head a few times in our direction, then flew off, taking the others with it back into the sky.

Fernanda stood up and said, 'I know you want to know about the faeries. Albé has told me about you. *Las hadas...* they are the nature spirits, the elementals, as well as the tricky ones you know about. They are everywhere.'

'Do you see them now?'

She laughed, then smiled. I blushed.

'The ravens see them. All animals do. The faeries fix themselves onto the minds of the ravens and then give them instant speech with others of their kind. The faeries summoned the ravens by riding on their minds... their thoughts. "Hey, my friends! Come get the nuts at the tree stump."'

I chuckled. 'But do you see them?'

She stared at me for the first time but said nothing. Instead, she took my hand and led me around the vegetable patch to some spinach leaves. She got me to crouch down next to her and pointed at the biggest leaf in the patch.

'Stare at this green leaf,' she said. 'Just stare at it for some moments.'

I complied. The leaf was crumpled a little at its top, making a ball-like shape. At first I just gazed at it, seeing nothing but its spinachy form. But I relaxed my shoulders, attempted to zone out Fernanda's presence beside me and squinted hard. The longer I looked at it, the more I started to see patterns in the natural chaos of its shape: first a green rose flower, then a scrunched up piece of green paper, which seemed to momentarily expand and contract before forming into a small childlike face. It appeared to wink at me. I started, blinked, looked again, and it was gone. There was just a snail-nibbled spinach leaf.

'You see,' she said. 'They are here, but you just do not want to see them. *Las hadas* are part of the minds of the plants… the earth, the rocks, everything.'

I turned to her; she was close. I could see she meant it. But the usual rational stream of thought pulsed through my mind, first explaining the optical illusion of the crumpled spinach leaf, then aligning itself with the reasonable view she must be delusional and making this up from within a damaged and beguiled mind. But even as the stream of rationality assured me this must be so, I knew it wasn't. And there was an adjacent thought. I resisted its shallowness, but the prattling voice in the back of my mind was telling me she was too beautiful to be mad.

'You are a modern Western person, my friend,' she said, touching my arm. 'You have grown up in a world of science and material things. It is quite simple, really. You've disconnected from Spirit. Once you disconnect, you stop seeing what is really there. If you were *una niñita* I would be able to show you. But you have grown up and disconnected. There is Spirit everywhere, but you no longer recognise it.'

I fiddled with the notebook in my hands, coming to terms with my abrupt perception of inferiority to someone deemed insane. And, as she looked through me, I was pretty sure she knew this.

'I need to be alone now,' she announced, standing up and running her hands through her black hair. 'But come again tomorrow, without notebook. I will talk to you about the faeries. I think you might be one who will listen.'

Without another word, she packed her trowel into her little gardening bag, smiled and started off back to the hospital. She turned at the edge of the vegetable gardens and waved.

'*Mañana*,' she called.

I watched her disappear behind the chapel, red top contouring her from the grey stone. It started to rain again.

'*Mañana*,' I whispered, looking first at my unopened notebook, and then back at the plain old spinach leaf, now quivering under the raindrops. A raven passed overhead, cawing as if laughing at me. *Mañana* indeed.

XIV

It rained the whole of the next day. I knew this curtailed any meeting with Fernanda, so I stayed in my room and attempted to plan out some kind of itinerary for the week ahead. But my inner vision kept sliding back to her. It slipped into fantasy, and I began to dwell on what I might say to her when we did get to meet, and how much I'd like to just touch her. But her domination of my thoughts started to disturb me, and I made a conscious effort to put them to one side. However, when I did manage to do so, she was replaced by laced memories of Sis.

I closed my eyes and pictured her pale face. Our age difference had put a gap between us that allowed me to act like a parent to her, especially as mother had always been in absentia via alcohol and father was so distant and cold. It allowed us to hold each other and be touchy. We took and gave affection from each other. Whenever she found out I had a girlfriend, there would be much jealous pouting at first, but then always an acceptance. She somehow understood what I needed, unlike my parents. But girlfriend or not, she always wanted me with her; to listen, to wonder, to hug, and to love her. And I always gave love to her, without condition. Until I brought about the final curtain-call of course. That put a fucking stop to everything.

Just before seven I put a line under my introspection, braced myself and went along to the common room for supper. As I turned the corner to the door, Miss Rood—as I supposed from Fletcher's description—and Epsilon had got there just before me, both carrying two big trays of covered food, emanating spices and gravy. She was scolding him about something but tempered it down when she saw me. She looked me up and down, with the usual look, and then glanced at Epsilon as if he might offer some explanation, which he did.

'Fuckin' good 'un, yeah.'

Miss Rood huffed, gave me a nod of acknowledgement and eased herself into the room. I followed Epsilon in. They were all there, gathered around the new colour television set, with the addition of two women, who I took to be nurses without any definite confirmation of the fact.

'Food, Rood, Epsilon and Blondie,' announced Albé. 'Excellent. Come and join us.'

Fletcher rushed to help Miss Rood with the tray and Moore caught my eye and patted the empty space on the old leather sofa next to him. I sat down, feeling a bit prim.

'*Star Trek* about to start,' said Scrope, looking at me and rubbing his hands with delight. 'Every Monday night is *Star Trek* night here… and now for the first time in glorious technicolour as well. This one's called "The Immunity Syndrome", according to the *Radio Times.*'

Epsilon gawked at the new colour television as if it were a descended angel, and Fletcher had to prompt him to lay out the food on the low table in front of us. Two minutes of settling down ensued as we filled our plates, and everyone shifted their positions before the collective concentration returned to the television where the Enterprise crew were preparing for an R&R break from duties.

'Look at Kirk eyeing up the bird in the mini-skirt,' announced Moore. 'We all know what he's got on his mind for when they reach Star Base 6.'

The nurses giggled, Scrope nodded approval and Albé smirked. The screenplay continued and, of course, things soon took a turn for the worse as Spock sensed the destruction of a Vulcan starship and the Enterprise was redirected to investigate. The prologue ended with the usual melodramatic close-ups and the main title theme struck up. Moore and Scrope broke into a singalong with it.

I'd never seen a colour television before, but as the plot developed, I was as interested in everyone's reaction as in the gaudy vision of an interstellar future, magically projected in primary colours onto the screen. I glanced around the room and attempted to pretend I was still watching the telly. Scrope and Moore grinned like enrapt schoolboys, nodding away at every nuanced trope, the two nurses were wide-eyed at the cosmic spectacle, Fletcher and Rood had lost interest and were whispering into each other's ears, and Epsilon (still standing) continued to goggle at the television with his mouth open in an air of total incomprehension. I pulled a sideways look to Albé. He was watching the screen intently, brushing his fingers over his chin. His eyes met mine and I twitched back to the telly.

The Enterprise was approaching some mysterious dark space, which suddenly engulfed the starship with a high-pitched buzz. Albé and Moore exchanged a look. I wanted to read it but couldn't. A few minutes more and Albé seemed to somehow impose a note of expectation on the room through a change in his posture, a tension that demanded everyone concentrated on the unfolding drama. Even Fletcher and Rood felt the magnetic pull, ceased their whispered conversation, and turned their attention to the television.

'Here we go,' said Albé, as if he knew what was coming. 'Listen to this.'

Kirk and Spock engaged in a prickly conversation about what caused the buzz:

'That sound was the turbulence caused by the penetration of a boundary layer, Captain.'

'What boundary layer?'

'Unknown.'

'A boundary layer between what and what?'

'Between where we were and where we are.'

Albé curled up his lip and chuckled. 'The unknown is penetrating the known. This is going to be edifying.'

I stiffened up as the drama continued. The dark space turned out to be an enormous single-cell entity, which swallowed up any energy it came across. Spock volunteered for a suicide mission in the shuttle craft, fired into the entity to unravel its secret and help the Enterprise escape its grasp.

'Suicide for the greater good,' said Albé. 'A logical decision, eh Blondie?'

I squirmed. But the episode ended with the inevitable denouement of Spock escaping and the entity being destroyed through the application of scientific logic. The last scene once again had Kirk eyeing up a mini-skirted minion, much to Moore's delight, before the end-title music broke the spell. There was a general singalong and then, as the titles faded, a brief discussion about how *Star Trek* was without a doubt the best boundary-pushing sci-fi in popular culture, created by people who had evidently taken LSD.

But the collective moment was over and soon there was a natural dispersal from the room, as if watching *Star Trek* had been the central element of the evening. I found myself between Albé and Moore, the latter lighting up a joint, listening to them discussing the next day's workload, as Fletcher, Miss Rood and Epsilon cleared up. I soon felt I was intruding, but when I got up to leave, they seemed to remember my existence, broke their conversation and decided to come with me.

'You've seen Fernanda?' asked Albé.

'I did. She's quite… otherworldly.'

'Indeed she is.'

'I was supposed to meet her again today, but the rain stopped that.'

'Well, you've plenty of time. She's not going anywhere, even though she's probably saner than anyone in the hospital… including the staff.'

I followed Albé and Moore through the doors and into the corridor leading to the secure rooms. There was a peculiar floral scent. I wanted to relate it to my dream and deem it orchid, but I had no reason to think this beyond a vague sense.

'Now if we're lucky,' said Albé, slowing his limping pace a little before the narrow first room window, 'Gloop will be asleep and we won't have the dubious honour of having to witness one of his displays.'

'Gloop?' I asked as we stopped before the window.

'Mr Gloop: our recalcitrant. True identity not currently known. An exhibitionist with a penchant for masturbation in public places.'

'Oh. So why is he here?'

Moore took over the narrative with evident glee. 'He kept escaping out of the male ward during his sedative inter-glacials, through the kitchens to the female wards so that he could put on some shows for the inmates. Yesterday he was caught by a nurse giving a spunky wake-up call to one of the new patients, which as you can imagine, caused some hysteria. So here he is, under lock and key with us as there's no secure space for him in the hospital at the moment.'

Albé beckoned us forward. 'Come on, quickly past his window and we should... oh shit, too late.'

Gloop's shiny bald head and even shinier and balder face appeared behind the glass. 'My lord, my lord! You must come in and see me. Please, I beg you!' he hollered.

Albé sighed and Moore grinned. Albé unlocked the door and in we went.

'Now then, Gloop, I don't want any of your— '

But again, it was too late. Gloop already had his smock and Y-fronts around his ankles and his rapidly erecting penis in his hand.

'I have been expecting you, my lord, and what a show I have for you... and more visitors... even better.'

He stared at me for a couple of seconds, nodding and wide-eyed. But he quickly recovered his composure and proceeded to grip his shaft for a thorough going over. I had never seen a man with his penis in his hand and instinctively turned my head away. I glanced at Moore (smirking, lighting up a ciggy) and then Albé (implacable, lighting up a ciggy) before steeling myself to look back at Gloop who now grinned insanely, gurgled, grunted and worked over his gland. After no more than thirty seconds, he was at the point of no return.

'Hooyeah... hooyeah... yeahaaaaah.'

His fleshy face contorted into a spasmed gurn as he fountained out his load, which splashed onto the linoleum at our feet. I drew back in case there was another pulse, but he was already into his post-ejaculation wind-down, squeezing out the last few drops from his wilting member and adopting a slouch of satisfaction. A brief moment of silence ensued.

'I'm delighted to make your acquaintance, Mr Gloop.'

Moore spluttered on his ciggy and laughed out loud.

'Indeed,' said Albé, blowing out a noseful of smoke. 'And your aim was admirable, Gloop. A perfect trajectory, right onto the lino... nice and easy to clean up. Good job we put you in this room; the others have carpet.'

The spent Gloop put on an inane grin and chuckled, no longer able to meet our eyes. Albé nodded to Moore, who proceeded to scrabble in his jacket pockets.

'But I think we've all had enough of seeing you bashing your bishop for one day, so pull up your pants and smock. Mr Moore here is going to give you something to help you sleep it off, and we'll see you in the morning.'

Moore gave him the injection and helped the unresisting Gloop over to the bed.

Outside in the corridor, Albé looked at me — he must have seen my reddened face — and raised an eyebrow. 'Sorry about that, but you can see why he's a bit of a nuisance on the ward.'

'Quite. What are you going to do with him?'

'Well, I don't know what you think, Moore, but I think our willy-wanking exhibitionist friend might well benefit from a few sessions of... supplemental therapy.'

'I think you might be right,' Moore replied, lighting up another ciggy, 'and quickly too, otherwise he'll have to clear off back to the main wards; we can't have him jacking off and dumping his load here every time someone goes into his room.'

'Sorry about the injection, Blondie,' said Albé, looking at me sidelong. 'You know we don't like to use sedatives, but under certain circumstances, it's a short-term solution. We'll get him into the Observation Room at the first opportunity and see if we can find out what's going on. We can usually get to the bottom of these things.'

XV

A few days have passed. I am walking the three miles to the residence of Mr and Mrs Pigot, who are first on my list of interviewees. They have agreed for me to collect some of their anecdotes. But something is wrong. I smoked a weird floral joint given to me by Moore this morning, and now the midday sun isn't how it should be. It appears to be moving in the sky. It is unnatural and unhealthy. There is a storm in my head. Sis, Fernanda, Caroline Lamb, Albé, the spinach leaf, Gloop—they are all punching away at my thoughts with feverish delirium.

I feel sick and sit down on a bank by the side of the lane. The birdsong echoes. I look up at the tree line and am sure I can see the sound, but I don't understand what the vision means. The song becomes the whooshing of a wind. It then turns into the buzzing I have heard before, but I am unable to place where I've experienced it.

A horse-drawn cart rumbles along the lane and comes to a standstill in front of me. The man at the helm says something, but I can't understand the words. I feel as if I'm about to vomit. Before I can, I shift without moving; closer to the man. I have the overwhelming instinct that I am an enormous thread of cotton attempting to pass through a tiny needle eye. The eye is passed through somehow, and for a moment I am panting, the taste of mulched hay in my mouth and an intense pain in my shoulders. My shoulders feel enormous.

Forward. The road, the load, the road, the load. Forward.

I sink into something big and small at the same time. But then I am snapped upwards as the buzzing intensifies. The taste of cider is in my mouth, and for an instant, I look at myself doubled over by the side of the lane.

'What are 'ee?' I speak the words and hear them in two different places. But my mind is filled with memories that are not mine, utterly confused and mixed with what I had been previously thinking about only seconds before.

Wife annoyed. Harvest. Gammy leg ache. Cider press needs collecting. Flossy seems lame and disturbed. Hope. Where is the hope? Who is this person? She seems to be me now. Fear is in me now.

Darkness. I grope around in the darkness. The buzzing continues. I try to open my eyes but can't. I grip my temples. The world returns and I see the cart disappear into the distance. There are a group of diminutive characters on the back of the cart laughing and pointing at me. Their chuckling morphs into the buzz, and I look away, trying to stop it.

But by looking away I am brought outside Southwell Bungalow, home of Mr and Mrs Pigot. I knock on the door. He answers. There is the usual incredulous once-over, followed by indecipherable words. I am invited in, and in the small living room on a spongy, uncomfortable sofa I manage to regain some control over what I'm doing. The buzzing is in the background, but I'm on top of things. At least I think I am. They seem taken with me.

We drink tea, pleasantries are exchanged and stories are told. I don't know how I'm doing it, but I am invoking their testimony about the faeries. Mrs Pigot does most of the talking. I hear her words and see the scenes she calls up as if they are my own memories. The clarity of her tale is absolute and rolls out as if on a cinema screen, or a colour television. All sensory perceptions are energised and engaged. I can smell the manured fields and hear the wood-pigeons as she weaves her story:

''Twas after Great War, when Mr Pigot and I were a-courting. My father never went to the Front as he was too old and infirm. It always held with him… had much guilt about it after knowing so many poor young souls lost their lives there. It made him disturbed, no doubt about it. But he was always a loving man and a great storyteller. I think that gave him solace. Always telling tales of the faeries, was 'ee. He used to tell me as a small infant that there were more things in Heaven and Earth than are dreamt of in our philosophies. I don't know where he got such highfalutin words and ideas, but he always told us that there was a magical world separated from this one by a hair's breadth and that the faeries were part of that world.

"But anyways, shortly after the war, there was this incident. It's the one that has stayed with me all these years—half a century—mainly because it happened when I was in womanhood and I have it in my mind as a real occurrence rather than just another story from olden days.'

I luxuriate in the memory, playing out to me as a moment in the present.

'My father worked the low fields and cut the peat when time of year was right. Our house fire was always made up of peat. I used to love the sweet smell of it. Anyways, he had this friend—Uncle John we used to call him, although he was no blood relative. He was younger than father and a bit simple. There was talk of him going into the hospital where you are biding, but that never happened and he was able to earn a crust working out in the peat fields. He never went to the war due to his backwardness. Well, one day he went missing, which was most unlike him. Search parties were sent out but there was no sight nor sound of him for a week and a day. He'd been given up as dead or kidnapped by some ne'er-do-wells. But after the eight days, he was found by my father and some labourers less than a mile from here amidst some scrub woodland. And do you know what he was doing when they found him?'

I do know, but I motion her to continue.

'He was dancing around in a circle, oblivious to all else around him. Well, Father pulls him up, half relieved and half annoyed, due to the trouble that's been caused. But on seeing the poor state of the fellow… what's the word…'

'Emaciated.'

'Yes, indeed. He was emastiwasted. All skin and bones and making even less sense than he usually did. So he was brought back to our then home, and I remember the night as if it were yesterday.'

The scene is in front of me, startling and super-real. The parlour is filled with the overbearing scent of peat as Uncle John is dragged onto a wicker chair next to the fireplace and forced to down a big glass of brandy. The servant girl is sent away for some food as Father and the men bustle about in a state of excitement.

The food is eaten and Uncle John starts rocking in the chair and shaking as he realises what is happening. There are a few moments of stillness; a readiness in the air. He looks around at us, nervous and unable to meet anyone's eyes. He stares into the middle distance and, after some coaxing from Father, begins to speak.

'I took shortcut. Back from work. You knows the one. Well, I sits meself down for a rest—feeling blue as I often do; not knowing what is up or down. I had half a mind that I didn't care what happened to me that day, so on seeing one of those toadstools with red and white tops, I just munched it down, thinking not whether it would poison me as sure as the devil. Oh, it did take on me. The world became so strange. And no sooner than I was leaning back on tree stump with the wooziness, they start trooping through the glade and singing so merrily and dancing. They forms into a circle, what 'ee might call a Gallitrap. Such small folk they were and with looks that frightened me halfway to heaven. I was rooted to the spot. But then a beauty broke off and came to me. Oh, Mr Pigot, I never seen such beauty. She looked me in the eye like no woman ever has and I felt like she could be my wife. Her eyes were big and black and her smile was like nothing I seen in this world. She told me I was a special one and that special ones were always invited to dance. She pulled me up and before I knew where I was, I was dancing with the merry crew in the circle, round and round. Funny thing is, as soon as I was in the circle, I heard the music coming from I knew not where. Pipes and whistles and some drums... such a wonderful air... I could not resist the dance. They were so full of merriment. It be like a dream, but it was not a dream. And she held my hand all the while and asked whether I'd like to come to the land where she and her fellows lived. She told me it was always summer there and that the rivers flowed with the sweetest nectar. I wanted to go, so I did. But after what seemed only a few minutes dancing to their reel, there was a yank on me... I was pulled up and all the music and dancing vanished in a second. Then I was with you, with your hand on me shoulder. Oh, this world seems so dark and dreary next to theirs.'

Uncle John returns to a glazed stare. But after a few seconds, he pulls up his eyes and looks directly at me. He laughs an insane laugh and needs to be calmed by those closest to him. He is pulled up from the chair and taken away by two of the men, but he does not take his eyes off me. After this, there is a fading. All my senses fade.

***

Back in my room, I stared at the ceiling. Dark and dreary indeed.

XVI

I needed to find Moore and discover what was in that joint. I had awoken thinking my trip to the Pigot's bungalow was a delirious dream, but five minutes contemplation convinced me otherwise. Had he spiked it with LSD? My one previous experience with acid told me otherwise. This had been radically different.

I flicked through my notebook. There were just a series of sketches: faeries in a ring with Uncle John, a horse and cart and a distorted faerie queen brandishing a tambourine with a sinister smile wiped over her face. I never made sketches. I couldn't draw. These were good drawings: beautifully rendered and detailed in their composition. My face ticked. The carriage clock tick-tocked.

There was a scratching at my door. Was I still in the altered state? What would possibly be scratching at my door? I stared at it. The scratching continued. My heart seemed to fall in line with the tick-tock of the clock and then sped up. I stepped to the door, bleary-eyed and with feet of lead. The scratching continued and I opened the door.

A big black and white Newfoundland dog burst through the gap and circled around the room in great excitement with a doggy smile. My shoulders sank with relief and I crouched down.

'Hello there.'

S/he piled into me, knocking me over, and began to lick my face, whimpering with excitement. I gained a sitting position and allowed the joy to wash over me as I rubbed the dog's muzzle.

'Boatswain! Boatswain!"

Fletcher appeared at the threshold, out of breath. He took in the scene.

'I'm sorry about this. He's a bit of a rascal. Never wants to be where he's supposed to be.'

'It's fine, really,' I said, as Boatswain continued to slaver over me. 'He's a beauty. Why haven't I seen him before?'

Fletcher came into the room with an apology on his face and put Boatswain under collar and leash.

'He's m'lord's. Just returned from a stay with his sister. He's usually here all the time, causing mischief… *aren't you?*'

Boatswain turned his attention to Fletcher, thwacking my face with his wagging tail. Fletcher pulled him up and gave me the once over. I realised I was sitting on the floor in a t-shirt that only just covered my arse.

'Is *m'lord's* sister here then?' I asked, pulling the shirt down and watching Fletcher's reaction closely.

He blushed and I regretted the facetiousness.

'Yes, she came last night. Augusta. You'll meet her tonight, no doubt.'

Fletcher made his excuses and pulled the still-excited Boatswain from the room, who woofed as he went. A few moments of mindless canine enthusiasm had dispatched the tremors inside my head and I was able to dress and sit at the desk with a smile on my face. I looked over the sketches again. They now held a less sinister aspect; Boatswain's soft fur and trust had percolated into me.

I squinted at the faerie queen and recognised there Sis. The eyes, the chin, the wayward hair; I had drawn my sister once removed from reality. I turned over the page and started to make notes of what I could remember from my incoherent visit to the Pigot's bungalow. It may have been an unhinged episode, but the lucidity of Uncle John's story lived in me as more than a memory, and for the first time since I'd been at the hospital, my enthusiasm for the project outweighed the anxious rhetoric of my inner voice. I was so enthused that the jottings soon became the first typed page on my Olivetti typewriter: *Mr and Mrs*

Pigot and Uncle John's Faerie Dance with Time Lapse, c. 1920.

***

By the evening, my zeal had dampened. I'd got the whole testimony from Mrs Pigot into coherent note form, but the clarity had dulled and I was obsessing about the fragmented, surreal nature of what had happened. As in a dream, the passage of time had been non-linear and non-local. I could not recollect how I had got from the lane where I met the cart to the bungalow, and I had no idea how I'd returned to the TRU. But then memory was non-linear too. The in-between times become squeezed out to leave only the relevant incidents. This had been different though— radically different. I put on my baggy jumper and went out to find Moore and an explanation.

I stopped in front of the common room door and peered through the window. Albé was inside, locked in an embrace with a woman, running his hands through her blonde curls. My instinct was to retract, but I hung on a moment longer as they kissed, long and deep. With heat in my face, I turned away, thinking I might stay in my room that night after all. But my intentions were headed off by Scrope, who appeared from the direction of the Observation Room with Boatswain at his heels.

'How-now?' He smiled. 'Bit of a reunion going on in there, I am guessing.'

'Is that Albé's sister?'

'Half-sister. A close spousal relationship they have.'

'I should say. Have you seen Moore?'

'He's repaired to the Shervage Arms, to reacquaint himself with the philosophical thinking of Miss Dyke no doubt.'

'Right. I really do need to speak to him as soon as possible.'

'Well, I think you'll have to wait until tomorrow. But for now, come on in and meet Augusta. You'll like her. Everybody does.'

Scrope knocked and made sure he left a few seconds before we entered. Boatswain made straight for Albé, who had disengaged from Augusta, and much fuss was made of him.

'You're the very best dog in the land,' said Albé, acknowledging us with a side-glance. 'Goose, this is Blondie, our resident folklorist and expert on all things to do with the faeries.'

Augusta sprinted a questioning glance at Scrope then slid over to hug me. She grasped me longer than was necessary before pulling back to inspect me.

'My children love the faeries,' she said. 'Always playing faerie games in the garden at home. I'm sure your faeries are much more serious though.'

She had a sing-song voice. She decided to hug me again. I liked it. She sidled back to Albé and put her arm around his waist.

'Moore tells me you were out and about collecting testimony yesterday,' he said, pouring out some wine into glasses for us all. 'Any good tales?'

'Yes. It was all a little fraught though. Moore gave me something to smoke before I went and it had a… a strange effect.'

Albé looked at Scrope. 'Mmm. But did it help?'

'Yes and no. Can you tell me… do they still use horse and carts around here?'

'They do indeed. In out of the way places it can be more like 1870 than 1970 sometimes.'

I wanted to ask some more questions, but Boatswain became excited about something, started barking and broke the moment. The dialogue moved elsewhere; Scrope talking about a patient, Albé suggesting Boatswain could be used as a therapeutic tool in the TRU and Augusta reminiscing on childhood days. As usual, I was socially awkward, not able to contribute much. Augusta noticed and started to pull me into the conversation; her kind eyes relaxed me a tad. But I knew the question was coming sooner or later. Fortunately, I'd sunk a glass of wine before it did.

'And what about your family?' she asked. 'Where are they from?'

'From a London suburb. I don't really see them anymore though.'

I controlled my tic and looked from Albé to Augusta. The buzz returned. I was quite sure Albé knew my history as well as I did, but at that moment it was Augusta's empathy that seemed to sweep over me. Which one of them was reading my mind now? Augusta's eyes beseeched an explanation.

'There was an accident you see. My sister died. My parents blamed me. And that was that. Yes, that was that. My sister died… and I'm to blame.'

The tears welled up. Augusta came to me on the sofa and held me, stroking my hair and putting her cheek next to mine.

'Albé will show you otherwise,' she whispered, her mouth touching my ear and her hair falling over my shoulder. 'He'll show you otherwise. And your beautiful sister. I can tell you, she may be dead, but she is dreaming. She is dreaming of you.'

XVII

The next day I was in search of Moore again. I found him going into the monitoring chamber of the Observation Room.

'Thom. I need a word about the other day.'

He knew what I was talking about and adopted his guilty-amused look.

'Sure, sure. But it'll have to wait, Blondie. Albé and Scrope are about to start a session and I need to get to the control deck. Come on, you can join me.'

In we went. The monitoring chamber still had an overbearing feel to it, enhanced by the recording instruments making some whirring noises, rising up and down in pitch. Moore fiddled with some switches and we sat down. Albé and Scrope were sitting in the Observation Room behind the window chatting away in earnest, their voices audible once Moore turned on the volume:

'...*so we have at least three personalities underneath the primary, Jacob,*' said Scrope, reading his notes. '*As usual he has limited knowledge of them and has frequent memory losses. He's been groping kiddies and has been in police custody before being brought to the hospital under a certificate. But he has no recollection of what he's been up to. He's been talking about dreams and how he thinks them to be real. In the dreams he believes that men are rubbing themselves over him. That's his description. And...*'

'*And?*'

'*And we've got some information of sexual abuse in his childhood. The usual disparate records though. But when I did the session with him three days ago, he was definitely switching. There are some personalities that sound like older men. I would suggest they might be his abusers made manifest as distinct personalities for whatever reason. But they only surfaced for a few seconds at a time. I could never get anything out of them.'*

'Yes. I heard the recording.'

'But there's a woman in there too. We missed her on the recording last time… didn't we, Moore?'

Scrope turned to the mirror and Moore shrank back a little. He opened up the mic.

'A technical glitch, gents. Don't worry, we're all set today.'

'She's some type of protector — a typical archetypal Great Mother figure. She seems quite powerful. I think he's lucky to have her. He's talked about her as someone he always dreams about and protects him in the dreams. I think if you can bring her up to the surface, it will be useful… are you dosed up?'

'I am.'

Albé held his hands up with forefingers touching thumbs as if to prove it.

Moore silenced the volume.

'This is gonna be a bit extreme, Blondie. Are you ok to be here? Based on the last session, this guy's all over the place. This is why Albé's in there.'

'Dosed up?'

'Just go with it, my friend. I promise this will all become clear to you in time.'

'He can get inside these patients' minds, can't he?'

Moore squinted at me, uncomfortable. 'He can.'

The moment was disturbed by the door opening. Augusta sidled in, slid the spare chair over next to mine and gripped my arm.

'Don't worry,' she said. 'I'm used to this. It always upsets me, but I've been here many times. I saw you being tempted in here by Moore and so thought I should come and give you a prop.'

Moore winked at us, altered some dials and then our collective attention shifted to the other side of the mirror as a nurse and an orderly ushered in a slight, dark-haired man, maybe thirty, pale, holding his hands together and grimacing. He was placed on the sofa. The nurse and orderly left. The patient stared at the ground, hands still together. I took a deep breath and started to wish I were elsewhere.

SCROPE: Jacob? Jacob?

JACOB: Aye. Why am I here again?

SCROPE: Well, you've been having some problems, haven't you? We want to get to the bottom of things and help you out... make you better... get you back into the world.

JACOB: Don't want to go back out. The world is too dangerous. I'm a nervous type, doctor.

SCROPE: We'll just ask some questions and see where we go. My colleague here is called Albé. You met him briefly when you arrived here.

JACOB: Aye.

ALBÉ: Hello, Jacob. I'm going to touch you on the arm. Don't be afraid. I just need to get a bit closer to you.

JACOB: I don't really like people touching me. You can, but I'm nervous. I've been told I have been doing horrible things, but I cannot remember them. I have these blackouts, see.

ALBÉ: What are the blackouts like, Jacob?

JACOB: They are like falling asleep. And when they happen I dream, just like when I am asleep. But it's different than dreams. The same people are always there. It's a dark place but they are people. I don't like them, except one. She's like my mother. My real mother is dead, but this person is like my mother. She's kind. But the others are bad. They are bad men.

SCROPE: Do you know these men, Jacob?

JACOB: Ermm... maybe. I cannot tell sometimes. I don't know. But I do not like them. I think they might take me over sometimes, but I don't know how or why. I've been told that sometimes I become a bad man. But I'm not... I'm not.

ALBÉ: Ok, just relax. We don't think you're bad. Just relax and look into my eyes.

Albé touched his arm. There was a minute of silence after which Jacob straightened up from his slouch and looked around with renewed eyes and an enhanced posture.

'*Aye, Jeremiah,*' he announced in a thick Yorkshire accent, unlike his own.

ALBÉ: Jacob?

OBADIAH: Eh? Ah, I'm here. I'm Obadiah. Who are you?

ALBÉ: I'm a lord of the realm. And I'm here to find out something about you. Where have you come from?

OBADIAH: Ah, I think you know. Jeremiah and I have felt you rustling around in the dark place. You don't belong there. I don't care how lordly you are, this be our province. You may have an impressive box of tricks, but you can't come in there and start ordering us around.

ALBÉ: Where's Jacob?

OBADIAH: In dark place.

SCROPE: Are you aware of him?

OBADIAH: And who are you? Some sort of sidekick to m'lord?

SCROPE: Are you aware of him?

OBADIAH: Aye. But he's just a memory now. It's me here. Last I remember was being in police station. Why am I here?

ALBÉ: You were arrested after some indiscretions with small boys. You've been certified and brought here. This is a psychiatric hospital.

OBADIAH: Uegh. I remember. Yes. I guess this is like some Soviet gulag. You take people who don't adhere to system and lock 'em up for re-education.

ALBÉ: Do you consider fiddling with young children acceptable behaviour?

OBADIAH: Mmm. I can tell by your lordly title, accent and language that you be a clever one. And moving around in the dark place… that's quite impressive, I have to admit. But I'm having none of this. I, and Jeremiah, have a fondness for children. We like to touch them and feel their young bodies. We always make them comfortable before doing it. We are sexually attracted to youngsters. Just because our society says it is wrong does not mean it is wrong. Your ancestors, m'lord; they were marrying eleven year olds and nobody batted an eyelid. Our predilection for children is society's crime, not ours.

ALBÉ: But you don't give them a choice, do you? They're children. They can't consent like adults. You're a predator. You're not here for re-education, you're here so we can deal with you and protect innocents from your inability to control your sexual desires.

OBADIAH: You don't know what it's like. You don't understand the desire.

ALBÉ: Is this what you did to Jacob?

OBADIAH: I barely know who Jacob is. He's a dream... a memory. Why do you talk about him?

ALBÉ: You're using his body. You and Jeremiah used him in the past for your own sexual needs and now you are inhabiting his consciousness and his body. It's damaging him. We are here to help Jacob. And I'm afraid that means me putting you back in the dark place with Jeremiah and then coming in there and expelling you both to a location beyond it, where you won't be able to come back. Do you understand?

OBADIAH: You bastard. Who do you think you are? I have rights. I have a mind. If you kill me, it's murder.

ALBÉ: Obadiah... I'm not going to murder you. I'm just going to dispatch you. Jacob is more important and more worthy than you and Jeremiah. You two will ruin his life. If you continue to take him over and do your thing, he's going to be in prison for the rest of his days. Your consciousness is going to have to be extinguished. The body will remain, but it'll be Jacob's. You're gone. Your existence is over. So now I'm going to send you back to the dark place, and then I'm coming in there to send you over the edge.

OBADIAH: You can't.

ALBÉ: Oh I can. But the good news is that there's a collective consciousness. It's an otherworld. You'll be subsumed into it and everything will be forgiven. You won't be you; that's probably a good thing. But your consciousness, as it now is, is about to be eradicated.

OBADIAH: No. Please don't. Please. I can explain.
ALBÉ: Too late. The die has been cast.

Jacob, or whoever he was, stiffened back onto the sofa, inert. Albé and Scrope just sat there, but Albé was staring at Jacob. Five minutes passed without any words or movement, broken by Albé relaxing back into his seat and smiling. Jacob followed his shift and spread out on the sofa, a smile on his face for the first time. He felt over his chest, then ran a hand over his crotch. When he spoke, it was a husky, disorientated, but distinctly female voice.

THE MOTHER: How did you do that?
ALBÉ: You're the Mother?
THE MOTHER: I guess. What have you done with them?
ALBÉ: They've been dealt with.
THE MOTHER: How?
ALBÉ: They've been dispatched. They were quite weak personalities. We have worked out methods here for consigning them elsewhere.
THE MOTHER: Is that so? I didn't know people like you existed. But I was born to protect Jacob from them. Do I now need to die? I don't want to die. My life has been spent protecting another when we are in the dark place… I deserve something more than death, do you not think?
ALBÉ: I do. You may stay. Jacob may need you in the future. You are good. But you'll need to live in the dark place. It's not so bad, is it?
THE MOTHER: No… no. It is not so bad. It is like a dream. As long as Jacob is Jacob… and *they* have gone. That's all I really care about. He has suffered so much. They were real people once, then they became part of him. If you tell the truth and they have been removed, then I'll stay in the dark place. I will exist there, as long as Jacob exists. If he needs me again, I'll be there for him.
SCROPE: Have you seen what happens out here… in this world? To Jacob, I mean.

THE MOTHER: Does the dreamer know what happens to the sleeper? The dark place is a dreamworld. Jacob suffered there until I could protect him. But I am not *here* often. This world seems peculiar to me — too light. My presence here is not required.

ALBÉ: Ok. We respect you. You can stay as long as you like this time, but we will need Jacob back when the time is right.

THE MOTHER: Yes. I feel myself fading now. I think I want to sleep and dream. But just one more question.

ALBÉ: Yes?

THE MOTHER: Where does your power come from?

ALBÉ: Orchid-24.

THE MOTHER: Oh.

Jacob shifted again, as if under pressure from an unseen force from above. After a few minutes he attempted to speak but all that came out were sobs. Scrope joined him on the sofa, putting an arm around him.

'*Do you understand what has happened, Jacob?*'

Jacob made some incoherent sounds and continued to weep. Albé got up, nodded towards us and left the room. Augusta gripped my arm tighter than before and made sure her breasts touched me.

'I want to walk out with you, Blondie,' she whispered. 'I think you've had enough of the crinkum-crankum of this Observation Room for today. You need someone to talk to, don't you?'

'Um, yes. I think I'd like that.'

'It's a nice day. Let's go for a walk.'

XVIII

We walked out into the grounds. Augusta took my arm and we moved on in silence for a few minutes. She glanced at me occasionally but said nothing. We climbed the stile at the top edge of the hospital perimeter and began walking along the lane, made into a holloway by the overhanging trees.

'I know you saw me kissing Albé,' she said, breaking our subsumed silence. 'You probably think it a bit odd. But think how close you were to your sister.'

'I never kissed her like that,' I said, blushing up.

'I'm sure. But Albé and I have a special relationship. I hope you can understand. We are half-siblings, but there is a bond between us—the bloodline makes us close... makes us almost one.'

'Right.'

'But I don't want to talk about that. I want to talk about you.'

'What do you want to know?'

She widened her eyes and curled her lip—so like Albé. We left the lane and came to a small grove with a fallen tree trunk marking the boundary. It felt like a private space with the summer greenery casting a warm shadow. She coaxed me to sit down with our backs resting on the trunk. I still felt stiff and uncomfortable, exacerbated by the session with Jacob, but she pulled me to her and coerced me to fall in tandem with her body. She kissed me, briefly and lightly, on the lips. It just seemed the natural thing for her to do. It calmed me.

'So let's talk about you. You don't have many people to talk to, do you? How did your sister die?'

I drew back for a few moments. But what was the point of retreat? I told her how she died and then I cried. I hadn't cried in front of another person for many years. But then I hadn't known an empathetic person like this. She held me in silence for a while. After the natural saturation of emotions had subsided, we pulled apart.

'I'm here because of my sister really,' I said, recognising the dullness in my voice. 'She interacted with supernatural beings. I never understood it but I appreciated it. I guess everything I've done since her death has been an effort to understand what she had been a part of. She saw faeries. She talked with them. For her, there was no doubt they were real. I'm just trying to unravel it all. To be honest, the whole folklore thing has become a bit tedious. I'm more interested in what the faeries might be right now. Do they exist? And if they do, where do they come from? If I can get some kind of answer to that, then maybe I'll get closer to Sis. She often dominates my thoughts.'

The buzzing started up. My shoulders tightened and I squinted at Augusta, the sunlight through the canopy making her face seem to shift in an unquiet way as it fell on her.

'You haven't been told about Orchid-24 yet have you?' she asked, her words somehow amplified as if her mouth were next to my ear.

'No. I heard it mentioned in that session in the Observation Room. But I don't know what it is.'

'Well, they need to know you can handle the truth of it before you're… initiated.'

'And what is the truth?'

'That's not for me to say. But it's rather magical.'

'Is it?'

She drew closer to me, her vivid turquoise eyes becoming all I could see.

'This life is a type of dream. That's where your solipsism comes in. It's no accident you were confronted with the hypothesis when you were on your way here on the train. What you are experiencing at the TRU might well suggest it is the true explanation for your existence. It's as reasonable an interpretation as anything else, isn't it? When you transcend from it, it'll all fade away like a dream, and you will realise that you are all there is.'

'Mmm. How do you know about my conversation on the train, Augusta?'

She smiled an Albé-smile, sidled back up to me and kissed me again, her tongue probing around my mouth for a brief few seconds. She turned me on, but I pulled away. She put her hands around my head.

'We're all here to help you, Blondie. But you're going to have to open up your mind if you are to benefit. I'll only be here for a short while. I'll be gone from your life in a few days, and you might never see me again. But you will remember this walk and me. Maybe you've just conjured me up at this time because you needed someone to listen to you… to be close to you. Isn't that what you've always wanted? A female to love you and caress you… to help you overcome all those old-fashioned dogmas of your parents. Your *annihilation* is a personal one. You have to embrace it if you are ever to move on from your sister-love to a new life. The old life requires a level of *annihilation*.'

I closed my teary eyes, but Augusta's presence penetrated my blood-red darkness. The buzz and she were somehow the same things. Peter Hammill's screamed word rattled through me.

'How do you know all this, Augusta?'

'All minds are one. We just need some help to get to the one.'

'Do we?'

'You know it, but you've yet to be shown it. Your sister, the faeries, all of your hang-ups. This is the right place for you. And Fernanda's the right girl for you. I think we need to get back so that I can have some words with Albé. They need to stop teasing you. But before we do, let's nap a while. Let this moment sink into you.'

We held each other. Sleep was suddenly irresistible. My head slouched onto her shoulder and I was gone.

She infiltrated my dreams; smiling, sun-kissed, surrounded by chattering faeries with Albé looking on. Sis crouched behind him, perhaps levitating and touching her comrades. When Fernanda appeared among the little folk, laughing and flashing-eyed, I snapped awake to find Augusta standing and staring at me.

'Time to head back,' she said, pulling me up. 'Our time here is done.'

***

Back at the TRU, there were raised voices in the main corridor. Moore and Dr Dawkins were waving their fingers at each other, embroiled in a disagreement. Dawkins was red-faced, and two orderlies shuffled around behind him while Moore bristled, his anger heightening the Irish accent and lacing his words with some Gaelic. They didn't notice us slip through the main door and continued.

'…and I must protest at you calling him Mr Gloop,' shouted Dr Dawkins. 'It is an absolute disgrace and demonstrates a degree of unprofessional incivility, which I am not prepared to countenance.'

'*Truflais*,' scoffed Moore. 'You have no idea what his name is, and so we've given him an appropriate one. And besides, you were unable to contain him in Mission Control, so we've been doing you a favour, have we not?'

'The agreement was that he was to be given secure accommodation until one of our own secure rooms became available. There was no accordance that he be taken into your Observation Room for interrogation.'

'*Ceistiú?* This isn't one of your colonial prisons in Belfast, Dr Dawkins. We're attempting to help the guy by getting to the roots of his issues. Something you've clearly failed to do.'

One of the orderlies said under his breath, '*Fenian scum*,' but Moore didn't seem to hear. He continued the argument with Dawkins until Albé appeared, apparently materialising out of nowhere. He glanced at Augusta and me, drifted in beside Moore and imposed his presence.

'Any problem, Dr Dawkins?'

Dawkins stiffened up at Albé's arrival. He started to rub his trouser pockets and stammered a response: 'You… you know well… know well the protocols we have in place here. The patient—'

'The patient was brought here for the protection and wellbeing of other patients in the hospital was he not? They have now been protected, and the patient is in a secure and safe environment.'

Dawkins mopped his head with his handkerchief. 'I recognise this, but you have been taking liberties with him. There was no agreement, none whatsoever, for you to carry out any type of interrog— any therapy with the patient, and yet I am reliably informed that he has twice been within your Observation Room.' He snarled the words. Albé's lip curled up.

'Our first duty is not to do evil; but alas, that is impossible. Our next is to repair it, if in our power.'

'No poetic riddles to cover up what's been going on,' said Dawkins, twitching and holding his ear. 'I demand a full transcription of the sessions. I know everything is recorded by your devices.'

'Indeed they are. We are all about total transparency here.'

'But the patient is not within your remit. There is no question of Hysterical Neurosis, and as you well know, this is… this is the determining factor—'

'Well, perhaps you need to listen to the recorded transcripts before you make any further judgement doctor. All I can tell you is that we are perhaps more able here at the TRU to apply a focussed and time-intensive therapy than you are able to at the hospital. And I'm delighted to tell you that after only a couple of sessions, the patient is showing radically improved behaviour patterns. He hasn't wanked off in front of anyone for two days.'

Dawkins glanced at me, recognising there were others present for the first time. I heard Augusta giggle below the radar.

'Your crudity of language does you no favours, my lord. Especially in front of ladies.'

I looked at Augusta. She avoided my eyes.

'All right… he hasn't displayed any socially unacceptable behaviour in two days. Either way, we're curing him where you would have had no chance. You're right—we have the resources you don't. So we are using them in the best interests of the patient. Surely that's a sensible thing to do. Do we not want to cure these people if at all possible? Is that not our duty and prime responsibility?'

Dawkins pressed his ear again. He looked around to the two orderlies, who seemed to have shrunk away, and then back to Albé.

'I would like the transcripts of your therapy sessions by tomorrow, if you please,' he said, attempting to draw himself up to Albé's height. 'And I would appreciate it if Gloop… ahem, the patient, be returned to a ward designated by me at the first opportunity. And I would like to let it be known that I am most uncomfortable at you applying Jungian psychoanalytical techniques on hospital patients… most uncomfortable.'

Moore struck up a ciggy, grinning. Albé bowed a little too low and Dawkins turned to leave. One of the orderlies stayed put, staring at Moore, who noticed immediately. He glided over, looked him in the eye from a distance of one foot and said, just loud enough for us all to hear, 'If you ever utter another racialist word against me again, I'll come into your quarters, lay a small incendiary device under your bed and blow you into kingdom fucking come. *An dtuigeann tú?*'

The orderly looked around at us quick, scrunched his face at Moore and made off behind Dawkins.

Albé clamped an arm around Moore, who still bristled.

'Come on, Thom. We're not in the Bogside now. You know what they're like.'

'Aye, I do.'

Albé moved over to us, wrapped his arms around Augusta and kissed her on the lips. There was a moment of silence.

'Hope you've both had a good day,' he said, side-glancing at me. 'Sorry about all this shouting and screaming. Dr Dawkins likes to maintain control, and when he loses it, he likes to bluster. It's the way of things.'

'Mmm. Well, we were having a lovely day,' said Augusta, inches from Albé's face, 'until we turned up here. What are you all like? Such crinkum-crankum.'

They smiled into each other's eyes. It was time for me to get back to my room.

XIX

Some days passed. Augusta disappeared without me seeing her before she left. Would I ever see her again? Would she want me to? I stared out of my window at the hardening of summer, when everything in nature appears languid and at an end of things. The window was open and I could hear some voices drifting up from the hospital grounds, inarticulate and slightly menacing. I thought I heard *annihilation* but convinced myself it was just what I expected to hear. It did, however, start me thinking about annihilated relationships. Augusta had come and gone. She'd impacted me. She'd kissed me and squirrelled into me, much as an empathetic character in a dream. Now she was no more, at least from my solipsistic perspective. What about all the others? My parents, my friends (such as they were), my fellow students… Sis. Annihilated. They existed nowhere but my memory.

My gaze reverted from inner to outer. A hundred yards away Scrope walked along a path with Gloop at his side. Gloop looked a different man than the one I'd witnessed exhibiting himself in his room. He wore a (somewhat ill-fitting) suit and nodded along to whatever Scrope was saying as they ambled along. Ten minutes later there was a knock on my door and the two of them moved from distant observation to intimate experience.

'Sorry to disturb you, Blondie,' said Scrope, ushering in Gloop, 'but Mr Clare is going to be leaving us tomorrow, and he is anxious to say a few words to you.'

It took two seconds for me to realise Mr Clare was Gloop and then another five to wonder why he would want to say a word to me. He wasn't quite meeting my eyes but I sensed some contrition, as if this were something he felt the need to do but didn't want to.

'I just wanted to say' — his eyes finally met mine but at a subsumed angle — 'that I'm quite ashamed of what you had to witness the other day. I've been in quite a bad way for some time now, and I didn't always know what I was doing. Mr Scrope Davies here and m'lord Albé have gotten to the root of the problems I had and have... flushed them out. But I didn't want to leave before apologising to you for my horrible behaviour. It must have been most upsetting, especially for... you.'

I couldn't quite get the image of the gurning, orgasmic Gloop out of my head but stretched out my hand, which he took with both of his, and extended consolatory words, assuring him I was none the worse for the episode.

'But I'm glad Albé and Mr Davies could help you out so effectively,' I said, looking at Scrope, who was fidgeting. 'They must have been able to get right inside your mind to get at all the problems.'

Mr Clare smiled and looked as if he wanted to expand on what had happened, but Scrope waylaid him with some dubious words about Jungian analyses being the cure for most of humanity's ills, before shuffling him out of the room. He hung his head back before closing the door behind him.

'Albé's got something important to show you. He's gone away for a few days with Augusta but when he's back he'll most likely show you what's going on. Only if you want to, of course.'

The door clicked shut. *What's going on*. Did I want to know what was going on? Would I be able to deal with it? As I returned to the desk in front of the window, the questions dissipated and I found myself once again ruminating on people who came into and out of my life.

Gloop... Mr Clare had exploded (literally) into my life for a very short period. I would never forget him, but I would never see him again and most likely have no knowledge of how his life turned out. Did he exist? Or was he just another part in the play of my life — annihilated the moment he stepped off the stage?

I looked out the window towards the vegetable gardens and caught a flash of a red jacket. All previous distractions became obsolete; I wanted to see Fernanda.

When I reached the gardens, she was sitting on the tree stump, eyes closed with her face to the sky. Some other inmates and a couple of nurses were a few plots along, but apart from the clink of trowel on stone, there was a still quiet, scented with something floral and indecipherable. The image of an orchid came into my mind, even though I still had no idea what an orchid smelt like. I watched her for a few seconds, nerves starting to jangle. Her black hair didn't fit in there somehow. It made her a part of something else, just as the red jacket detached her from the backdrop.

'*Hola*,' she said without opening her eyes.

'Hi, Fernanda... Hi.'

'You did not come to see me the other day. I was disappointed.'

'Ah yes — the rain, you see. I didn't think you'd be here.'

She reclined her head, opened her eyes and beckoned me towards her all in one movement.

'But you are here now. Why do you not join me?'

She patted the stump and I sat down, shuffling to the edge to nullify the intimacy. But we were close. I could see the pores on her face, a slight, faded scar on her nose and the weirdness of her eye colour, constantly manoeuvring between dark purple and black. She touched my hand and adopted a new expression: quizzical?

'We've been finding out some things about you, my blonde friend. I like your hair, by the way. We Chileans always love to see blonde. *Rubia*. Do you like to see black?'

'Um, yes, very much. What things have you been finding out?'

I fidgeted again. There was no tic, but I knew I was turning red.

'*Sueños.* You had dreams last night. Do you remember them?'

'No. Please don't tell me you do.'

She smiled, pouted and moved a fraction closer.

'A cliff. You watched a figure hesitate at the edge from a distance and then the figure leapt. You tried to shout but nothing came out of your pretty mouth. You knew you were watching yourself. In the dream, you were the only person in the world. Any other person had to be you also.'

The association clanked into place in my mind like a steel shutter opening. The cliff, the leap, the horror. But most of all, the feeling of desperation. I stared at Fernanda, twitch starting to grip my cheek.

'If… if I did dream such a thing last night… how would you know? It was my dream, inside my head.'

She laughed and held my hand. The burn in my cheeks spread to my neck.

'Where do you think the dreamworld lives? It is not part of this.' She motioned around us. 'When you are there, you are opened up to another world, another universe. We can see you there.'

'We?'

'You should know this by now. You are supposed to know about them. They think the way we feel. Your dreams are all about feelings. You are mixing in their world when you dream.'

'Who are they?'

'*Las hadas.* They want to help but you are too stuck in this world of things. You forget your dreams and just see what is in front of you. This is bad for you. You despair. Your dreams try to warn you and advise you, but you ignore them. But we found you last night.'

'How did you find me, Fernanda?'

She gripped my hand tighter and drew her other hand through her hair. She withdrew her gaze.

'When you dream, you enter another universe. You would like to think it is all part of your own creation. It is not. It is even here now. As I said to you before... you just do not want to see it.'

She gently took hold of my head and pointed it towards the vegetable patch. I quivered.

'They are here. They are just waiting to show you something more, but you will not see them. What does the Austrian say... Steiner? He says you need to lower your threshold until it is like you are in a dream. Then you will understand. There are different worlds to this one. Sometimes they meet. You just need to bring your dreams into this world. What is your word for... intersect. Ah no, it is the same word.'

'Can you see the intersect?'

She let go of me and prompted me to look at the vegetable patch.

'If you could let go of all the things you have been taught, all the things you think you know, you will start to see the things you sometimes see in your dreams. But they are here in front of you. Your education stops you from seeing them.'

I gazed for a few moments, concentrating on the rumpled spinach leaf I'd watched change form before. But I was too tense with Fernanda so close, and I lost focus. There was no intersect for me. I needed to break the tension.

'Do you see them, Fernanda?'

'You know I do. This is why I am here. The doctors think I see things that are not real and so here I am. My father insisted I was... what is the word... *Seccionado?*'

'Certified.'

'Yes. The people in my college just presumed I am insane because I did not view the world in their way. My father listened to them and not to me. My father is a monster.'

I kind of wanted to twist the conversation back to the faeries, but an empathetic drift realised she wanted to tell me something else.

'Was your father unkind to you, then?'

She looked at me sidelong, her eyes glinting purple. She was only inches from me.

'He was more than unkind to me, my blonde friend. He did this.'

She took my forefinger and ran it over the scar on her nose. It felt more pronounced than it looked. I felt some shame for thrilling at the touch.

'He likes little girls. He likes to hurt little girls. There were seven of us. He had much opportunity. *Monstruo.* But he is a powerful man. He could do whatever he liked in his home. He used to do whatever he liked in my country too… but that is all changing now. We have good people chasing out the bad people. That is why he came here and brought some of us with him. The people in charge of your country are as bad as him. He fits in. I hope I never see him again. If I do, I know something bad will happen.'

I remembered Moore's words about her father being some sort of privileged diplomat. I started to feel inferior and sheltered. But I sensed she needed to tell me more.

'Was he… was he… intimate with you?'

'*Frecuentemente.* He is the only man who has ever penetrated me.'

I baulked, hoping she wouldn't notice. She did.

'Oh, I'm… I'm…'

'Do not worry. It is in the past now. It is just a memory. I am happy I am here. I can be me and it is safe. And I get to meet lovely people like you. And Albé understands me. I think he is more like a father than my father.'

I felt the need to tread carefully. 'I'm sorry about your father. I really am. I'm sorry. But Albé… do you have much contact?'

'You will find out. You will come to the intersect someday soon. He is a good man. He wants to help people. I like to help him and he helps me. We have a little understanding of how the world really works.'

'Do you?'

She shrugged and moved away slightly, to better look me in the eye.

'And your father,' she said, manoeuvring the air between us. 'You have escaped him too?'

His image came up through the nether-regions of my mind's eye. My lip curled up at the thought.

'He disapproved of my… of my life choices. And he blamed me for my sister's death. But yes, I've escaped him. I have escaped all of my old life. But I'm not sure my new life is really where I should be. I've annihilated the old, but now I don't know where I belong. Does that make sense?'

'*Sí.* Did he ever hurt you?'

'Only with words… only with words.'

'Yes, I see that. Words can be as brutal as physical… *abuso*.'

'Yes.'

'And your sister? She hangs around you, does she not?'

Now the tears welled up. I focussed in on the vegetable garden. I stared at the spinach leaves and found there the face of Sis, forming in the folds, smiling at me and somehow telling me it was all going to be all right. I saw her face. She seemed to be there. She squinted her eyes as she always used to do and nodded towards Fernanda: *You need to love her.*

I stood up, disconcerted, prickling sweat. When I looked back, Sis was gone. Fernanda grinned up at me.

'*Hermana.* She is in the otherworld but she is keeping an eye on you, is she not? You loved her deeply, yes?'

'Yes. I loved her. I'm, err… I think I might need to get back, Fernanda. Would you excuse me?'

'I understand — more than you know. I will walk back with you. You may not have noticed, the others have already been taken back to the hospital. But they always leave me. They know I can be trusted. I will not run away.'

We exchanged a smile. I hadn't noticed all the other inmates had dispersed. My thoughts had been too wrapped up. I wanted to stay with Fernanda. I wanted more of her touches and her words. But there was a fear beginning to take hold of me. I knew I needed to extract myself and get back to my room where I could be alone with my introspection. We walked down the path. She had withdrawn and the silence made me want to fill it.

'So you have six sisters?' I asked, recognising the terseness in my voice.

'I am the youngest. I am the seventh daughter of a seventh daughter. Do you recognise the importance of this?'

'Yes. It's usually the seventh son in this country. Robert Kirk was a seventh son I believe.'

'*Sí.* I read about him. He would have had the sight. Do you believe he had the sight?'

'I guess it's easy to believe things about people in the past. He lived in different times — three hundred years ago. But I believe in his belief.'

'That is an easy thing to say. He was as real as you and I. He understood. You will understand too; I can feel it. I am hoping you can take the faeries out of your books and into your life. You are well-placed to do this, no?'

Her coded impatience with me coloured the air. She knew something I didn't. But the momentary bristling between us ended at the fork in the path. She took hold of my hand.

'I will be in the gardens tomorrow again if you would like to see me,' she said, rolling her fingers over mine.

'I would like that. I'll see you then. Fernanda… are you ok in the hospital? I mean, well, are you ok?'

'I told you, I feel safe here; much safer than in Santiago or my English college.'

She let go of my hand and made off back to her seclusion without turning once. I watched her disappear behind the chapel. I lingered for a moment, touching my hand where her fingers had been. I headed back to the TRU.

XX

Back in my room, I thought about the dream. Fernanda
had called it in every detail. All I could do was presume
she had psychic abilities. How else could I explain it? I
lit up a ciggy and noticed my hands were shaking. But
I was pretty sure it wasn't due to Fernanda's apparent
telepathy. It was due to the content of the dream. Its
memory swirled around inside me as the non-linear
scenes reconstructed themselves and formed into
vividness. It had been forgotten until she recalled it,
but now it reconstituted in vivid detail.

I had been watching myself jump off the cliff. The
high-pitched horror of the moment brought tears. The
despair, heightened by the dream reality, lived on as I
concentrated on teasing out some more of the details.
The jumper-me had been certain there was only one
option to escape the undefined fear. The watcher-me
wanted to save the jumper but could not get out the
words that may have succeeded. It was like a reversal
of the dissociative hysteric neurotics at the TRU: I'd
had one mind and two bodies.

I drifted back to suicidal thoughts. The cliff scene
was replaced by the noose hanging in my university
room. Was this annihilation inevitable for me? A cliff, a
rope, some pills — whatever awaited my consciousness
in the next life, at least I would have extracted myself
from this one, which consistently pressed me into the
ground and filled my days with a filthy guilt-ridden
hopelessness.

But I thought of the watcher-me in the dream.
There had been hope there; my avatar had wanted
to save the jumper. The voice had been silenced
though and the jumper leapt. Perhaps the watcher-
me represented how I'd been since turning up at the

TRU, filled with new ideas and some residual hope even though my voice was impotent and passive. The jumper-me was something I knew I had to avoid, was maybe even a part of my past. Scrope might say the jump was symbolic of my past, which needed to be annihilated, and there was nothing the present version of myself could do about it. The analyses could go on indefinitely. But I recognised the pull towards self-destruction starting to get a grip of me and knew I needed to release myself from it before the despondency turned into actionable intent.

I drew a line under it by getting out the packet of sleeping pills I'd brought with me. I hadn't taken one for months, but I always kept them close. There were twenty-four of them—barbiturates, carelessly prescribed for me by my doctor in London. My understanding was that half of them would put me to sleep for good. For a moment I hovered over the idea of flushing them down the toilet. It would be a symbolic rejection of suicidal thoughts. But I didn't flush them away—I tucked them back into the drawer. I needed the safety net of knowing I could kill myself effectually at any given moment.

I wandered around the room, aimless and absorbed. Gradually the light of the window drew me to it. I stared out and thought of Fernanda. Perhaps she was turning me around.

God, in the last day I'd kissed Augusta and felt the gravitational pull towards a Chilean exile who, according to the hospital certification, was insane. Maybe this speeding up of my life was what would save me. But then Sis crept back into my stream of thought. She hung there, sometimes dead, sometimes alive, until I knew I needed a blackout. I popped out a single sleeping pill, took it and got into bed, burrowing under the blankets. Sleep was always an effective remedy against my brutalised version of waking reality. I slept.

***

The faeries are here. They're in a forest clearing dancing around an orchid that looks as if it's breathing like an animal. They are small and gnarled, laughing and sinister. They glance at me, pretending not to see me, but I know they do. I look up at the sky, sure that someone or something is watching me. I am fearful. There is a menace in the air but I know I am trapped here and need to deal with it.

Fernanda appears, kisses me, and then disappears immediately. Her presence lingers though. Emboldened, I step towards the dancing faeries. They are in a circle and Uncle John is with them, whirling around to some discordant tune being played by unseen entities hiding in the gloom of a tree. There is insanity in the cadence of the music. I recognise it, but can't recall from where. It's something to do with a car, but the thought is too far away.

And now I am at the circle dance and thinking about joining in. I know that joining in would be much the same as stepping off a cliff, but I am being pulled in like a magnet. Then I'm face to face with one of them. I think of Fernanda—her pores, scar and black hair. It is her but then it isn't. I look into the black eyes of something not human but humanoid. It flickers and reaches out two spindly arms towards me. There is a subsumed sexuality in the way it wants me. I'm ready to just give myself to whatever it wants. Its hand grabs the back of my head and draws my ear towards what passes for its mouth. The words are silky smooth, whispered from some deep place:

'*I had a dream, which was not all a dream.*'

***

I wake up. I slide over in the bed and look for the time. The carriage clock is not there. But there is a faerie at the end of the bed. She is glowing. She looks like one of the Cottingley faeries.

'You're not a real faerie,' I say, feeling slightly guilty in my abruptness.

'*How do you know?*' she says, her words forming gaseous tracers in the air.

'The forest faeries were real. You're an invention.'

'*We come in many forms. We are many actors. One shade the more, one ray the less. You must not end your life.*'

'Why not?'

'*Because I say so and won't allow it.*'

'Prove it.'

'*I will.*'

I feel her goodness making me grotty. So I hide my head under the pillow, which wraps around me and begins to press against my neck. It constricts my breathing and I start to gasp for air. Voices whisper but they fade away. They leave a buzzing, which I recognise. It is someone else's mind. The realisation brings the shock that is necessary for me to transcend. There is a spiral of wind and a whoosh of perception as this reality comes to an end.

***

I woke up. I slid over on the bed and looked for the time. It was dark and my hands trembled as they held the carriage clock closer. I touched the hands; it was eleven o'clock. I pulled myself out of bed, unwilling to accept I'd been asleep so long.

I needed to get out of the room, so slipped into some clothes and crept out through the corridor and out the main door. As I walked along the path towards the chapel, the still night was disturbed by a couple of screaming people somewhere in the hospital; male and female, in different wings. The screams oscillated so one moment I could make out some words from the male, the next from the female. The male was evidently in a state of high excitement and within his stream of invective-laced ranting, the only words I could make out (apart from 'fucking') were: '*A new Heaven and a new Earth. The first Heaven and the first Earth had passed away…*'

The female was in closer proximity and although her distressed voice was masked with weeping, her words were more distinct even though underlain by the softer, muffled voices of whoever was attempting to deal with her. During a lull in the male's hysterical pronouncements, I stopped on the path in front of the chapel and zoned into her crying voice.

'He be here again. He be here again. 'Tis the buzz… the buzz. He takes me over. He is inside me making me him. I not be me… I am him… We are… We.'

She became inarticulate and then silent. I imagined the intravenous injection shutting her up. The hysterics of the male started up again as if in recognition of the interlude. This time his individual words were lost amidst screams and a manic whooping that initiated my facial tic. I sat down on the bench, head bent forward, waiting for the response of his orderly. One minute later there was a medicated silence. The tic stopped and I breathed slower. But I stared up at the hospital façade beyond the chapel and began to imagine the scenes on the two wards, reconstructing the interiors from my single visit inside. I visualised nurses and orderlies with splashing syringes at the ready.

The new silence encouraged me to seek thoughts to take me away from this. They rested on Fernanda and, for a few moments, I luxuriated in the imagery of her face and her accented words, which formed inside my mind in that magical way that's never been explained. But soon I turned to imagine her cooped up in her small, partitioned space on one of the wards; she was no better than a prisoner amongst disturbed minds. What could I do to help her? I projected a fantasy into the future, where she and I lived quietly in a secret corner of the world as comrades and lovers, free from the constraints of incarceration and prejudice. I smiled, but these types of positive, utopian thoughts never sat long with me, and within seconds I'd dispatched them into the delusional pipe-dream dustbin. I got up and walked past the chapel, up the hill to the hospital bounds.

I felt my way over the stile into the lane in the darkness and found the same space I'd sat before, so I could not see the hospital at all. This time there were no cows on the other side of the hedgerow and all I could hear were crickets chirping. The air was charged but I couldn't work out if it were a storm brewing or the result of the disordered minds in the hospital infecting me, agitating me and making me view the external world as a febrile reality, enhanced by the blackness of the moonless, cloud-covered landscape before me. In the far distance were the street lights of a town. They created a low orange haze that mingled on the underside of the clouds. But otherwise, all was obsidian and I could not make out the horizon.

The horizon. I stared into the darkness and visualised my train companion. I couldn't bring his features to mind except in a dull, generalised way, but his voice was clear: *We have nothing but our own horizon, which includes the entire universe from our perspective.* Was this darkened landscape all that existed at the moment? I had no way of knowing otherwise. I gazed upwards, where a single star was momentarily shining through a narrow break in the cloud cover. Was it really millions of light-years away, twinkling at me from the aeons of the past, or was it just me making it up from within the confines of my consciousness? The screaming inmates — were they real? I could have as many presumptions as I liked, but I could never be certain of anything, even if it were right in front of me. In my recent dreams of the faeries and of jumping off the cliff, I had been convinced this was the bottom-line reality, happening to me as a person. But the reality was fake; everything from the cliff face to the faeries and the image of Fernanda had been constructed as an artificial, simulated reality, which had totally fooled me until I woke up. Was I being fooled now? It felt like it at that moment. Perhaps being at the TRU with people who appeared to have different minds with which to interact with the world was rubbing off on me and causing me to question basic assumptions that had always been a given before. Maybe I was being infected with the insanity of this place and starting to lose myself.

The crickets seemed to increase their volume. 'Does that mean the storm is approaching?' I asked aloud, feeling around in the grass to see if any were nearby. They were keeping their distance. Perhaps I should begin to keep my distance from everyone in this lunatic asylum. Before I came I had just presumed I'd be left to my own devices, but within less than a month I had become enmeshed with the people here. I'd even kissed Albé's sister — what was I doing?

I attempted to release the tension in my shoulders and drew myself back to my dreams — they seemed to match the ambience of the low-cloud darkness. Fernanda's words about them being intersects filled me, dispelling for a while the idea that dreams were the result of ultimate solipsism. I still did not properly understand how she could have known about my cliff dream, and however many convoluted explanations I came up with, the only reasonable one was that she somehow had access to my dreamworld. Supposing that were true, how many other people had access? Then I considered the faeries in the dream. If there were truly supernatural entities sharing our universe, why should they not be able to show up when circumstances were right? If that were true then my dreams weren't my own projection but were being populated by whoever or whatever had the occult ability to infiltrate them. And if that were the case, Sis was communicating to me from her current location: dead but dreaming.

A massive sheet of lightning pulled me up. For a second it drew out features in the landscape previously unseen: a weird conical hill in the distance, bent trees on the rise before me and perhaps — just perhaps — some figures moving with stealth at the bottom of the field. The crickets ceased their chirping in unison. I knew it was time to get back.

I got to my feet and made for the lane, quicker than I wanted to. It was an approaching storm, I was safe in a field and the figures had probably been rabbits made bigger than they were by the skewed cadence of the lightning. But the ambience of the place had suddenly changed from reflection to menace.

I crossed the lane, and as I climbed over the stile back into the hospital grounds, a crash of thunder disassembled itself through the sky. I covered my head with my hands as if under fire. Recovering, I looked back to the gate in the field from where I'd come. Dark shapes were climbing over it. I squinted for a few seconds, attempting to cool my boots about this. I was being ridiculous and seeing things in the darkness. But then another cascade of lightning filled the sky and confirmed the shapes on the gate. I ran. The thunder followed close behind the lightning, but as I ran along the path through the vegetable patches, its rumble was undercut by a buzz that morphed into indistinct voices. They were behind me, laughing and manic.

I reached the side of the laundry building. The artificial light outside made me feel as if I'd crossed a threshold, and I stopped and turned. For an instant, there was a movement, ten yards away. It was a bush but it moved around in some prehensile way, black against a lesser blackness. I turned and walked with a trot past the now-comforting brick and stone of the hospital buildings, up the path to the TRU and back inside my room. My thumping heart boomed like the thunderstorm outside. I laughed.

'This is ludicrous.'

I looked at the carriage clock. It was three o'clock in the morning. I knew I hadn't spent four hours outside but didn't want to think about it. I drew the curtains and the thunder rumbled on. At least the lightning had been closed out; it flashed impotently against the shield of the curtains. I got into bed with my clothes on and reached over to pull out the sleeping pills from the bedside drawer. I looked at the packet for about a minute then pulled one out — just one — and swallowed it. Two within a day couldn't hurt me. I needed the sleep.

I turned out the light and bit by bit drifted into the otherworld to the backdrop of the rolling, diminishing thunder and the beginning pats of rain against the window.

XXI

Albé was back. I heard him herding a barky Boatswain past my door less than five hours after I'd fallen asleep. I was nervous about seeing him. He wanted to import something on me and I wasn't sure I was ready to deal with it. I'd had a taste of what it might be, and while I was becoming increasingly desperate to know what was going on at the TRU, I knew there was going to be some type of reckoning for me when it was disclosed. I didn't like reckonings.

When I made my way to the common room later that morning, I was caught off guard as I wandered in, still stuck in a stream of thought about my mini-adventure the night before. One moment, my memory dominated my reality at the expense of my immediate surroundings, replaying the scenes of thunder, lightning and pursuing beings. Then within a second, I was sucked out of it and into an interaction with real people battering on my senses. Albé was waving about a vinyl and telling some story about it to Moore, Scrope and Fletcher, all of them nodding their smiles of approval. Boatswain moved around their legs excitedly and Epsilon stood apart, lock-jawed as if he couldn't work out what was going on.

'So there you are.'

The voice came from the other side of the room. I recognised it and froze. This wasn't a reckoning I'd thought about, but it had arrived and my head lightened. I turned.

'Professor Hobhouse. I didn't… didn't know you were coming down here.'

As always, his face remained passive while his eyes smiled. It had always disconcerted me but was a preferable arrangement to the opposite state of affairs.

My tic started but I managed to shake his hand and exchange some pleasantries, which I hoped were not going to quickly transfer into questions about how much work I'd done. With luck, before we got to that, Moore came over and drew us into the melee around the hi-fi.

'So much to go through today, Hobby... and Blondie, but all that can wait,' said Albé, looking triumphant. 'Do you know what a white-label is Blondie?'

'Nope.'

'It's a pre-release vinyl cut, given out to radio stations and the like.'

'Meaning?'

'Meaning, I have here the new offering of the Floyd, which goes by the name of *Atom Heart Mother*. And having listened to it a couple of times, I can confirm it is a bit of a masterpiece.'

'No Syd Barrett?'

'No Syd Barrett, but there is a full orchestra.'

'Mmm.'

Albé slid out the vinyl from the sleeve with some ceremony, revolved it in his hands for effect and then slipped it onto the player. Moore carefully lowered the needle onto the vinyl, fiddled around with the big metallic dials on the hi-fi and then the music began to fill the room at high volume. Within a couple of minutes, the horn section was in full swing and Albé and Moore took each other by the arms and started to dance around the room — Moore leading and Albé limping — much to Epsilon's delight. Scrope nodded his approval and Fletcher flopped down on the sofa with a sceptical expression. Boatswain sat at the side of the sofa and began a low, resonant howl, which somehow matched the musical madness.

'It's not very melodic is it?' said Professor Hobhouse.

'Oh come on, Hobby,' said Albé, wheeling off with Moore, 'get in the groove. It's 1970 not 1770. These guys are laying the blueprint for the future. I predict the Floyd will provide the musical backdrop of the great decade we are about to witness. If you got out of your stuffy ivory tower every now and then, you'd know we've moved on from boring old symphonies recited ad nauseam in the Albert Hall.'

'So why are they using an orchestra?'

Moore chipped in. 'They're subverting it, deconstructing it. I mean, listen to this.'

He slipped Albé's grasp and bent to turn up the volume even louder. The choir section was just ratcheting up, intense and like nothing I'd ever heard before.

'Well, maybe,' said Professor Hobhouse, 'but it's all a bit pompous, isn't it? When's the real music going to begin?'

But the electric guitar kicked in just at that moment and Albé and Moore took up air guitars to make an answer without reply. From there the music became very esoteric. There was much collapsing on the sofa and waving of hands as the orchestra finally subsided to the pure tones of electric guitar backed up by sound effects and a choir that sounded as if they might have belonged in the hospital. After twenty-four minutes the music crescendoed and everyone found seats as Moore flipped the vinyl and we all listened to the second side, with incessant commentary from Albé and Moore, until things faded out to nothing while mimicking the extended sounds induced by a psychedelic.

'Marvellous, eh Fletcher?' said Albé, clapping his hand on the sleeping Fletcher's back. Fletcher assented in a daze.

'Well, they're gonna miss Syd,' said Moore, rolling a joint, 'but that is total genius. What say you, Blondie?'

'Better than Van der Graaf Generator?' I asked, attempting humour but failing as always.

'An impossible question to answer that, my friend. But I think they'll be selling more records.'

He took a couple of tokes from the joint and handed it to me. I noticed Professor Hobhouse cast a knowing eye on me.

Albé took the joint from me and announced, 'Right then. Enough of this excess; we have two sessions in the Observation Room today and so I'll thank you to gird your loins and be about your business. Hobby, Blondie — you're welcome to observe the second session if you like, although I'm sure you have faerie folklore things to catch up on.'

I tensed up. I guessed I was just going to have to tell Professor Hobhouse that I hadn't been doing much research since I'd been here.

***

I pulled up the bedside chair for Professor Hobhouse, and we sat down at the desk in my room. It felt awkward but he eased the passage of conversation by filling me in on some goings-on at the university and how he'd recently discovered an archive of faerie folklore collected by an obscure folklorist in Suffolk just before the war. I nodded and made eye contact, but only heard half the words.

'But now to you,' he said, settling back in the chair, breathing deep to demonstrate a turnaround. 'Don't worry — this isn't an interrogation. I know Albé well, and I know what they've probably been up to since you've been here. You haven't got much done, have you?'

'Well, it's… you see… No, not really.'

'Let me guess: Albé and Moore have had you watching patients in their Observation Room at every opportunity and buzzing around you with their damned magic orchid serum. God, they haven't given it to you, have they?'

I stuttered a reply.

'Because I've warned them about it. It's all very well with disordered patients but I mightily disapprove of its casual use, especially when it's one of my students.'

For a few seconds, I realised I was in the position to play the game and induce some insights from the professor about what might be going on at the TRU, most especially in regard to the *magic orchid serum*—Orchid-24 as I presumed. His disapproving knowledge could reveal some hidden things to me. But I wasn't cunning enough to pull it off. I guessed he would see through any subterfuge. Instead, I pulled back to safer ground, with a continued stuttering explanation.

'I have been, err… in the monitoring chamber of the Observation Room a few times, but it's been, y'know, more my own fault. I've been taking too long to organise my visits from Mr Goodfellow's list. But I'm expecting quite a few field visits in the next month and I have… um, conducted my first one.'

'Ah, good. So how did that go? Decent transcript?'

Why didn't I keep my mouth shut? I decided I needed to adopt the policy of truth.

'Well, to be honest, it was a bit of a strange experience… I mean, I don't really know too much about the working practices here or the methods. But I smoked a joint, um… Moore gave it to me and the visit was quite odd. I did get decent notes though. The Pigots' testimony has lots of good motifs.'

'But you were stoned when you collected it?'

'I'm not too sure.'

'Mmm, I'm starting to get the picture. Don't worry, I'm not laying the blame on you. But I will be discussing this with Albé and Moore. Albé has such a laissez-faire attitude to what he's up to here, and I'm afraid I cannot allow it to infringe upon what you are supposed to be doing. I'll be having words. But let me see the notes anyway.'

'I've typed them up,' I said, handing over the pages. 'And there are also some… sketches.'

'Sketches?'

'Yes, I made some drawings based on the stories.'

I opened up my notebook, regret fluttering over me the moment I did so.

'Unorthodox,' he said, flicking through the pages. 'But they're very resonant. You draw well. These faeries have something about them… they have some real folkloric character… you've captured something here.'

'Have I?'

'No doubt. Although I'm not convinced they'll translate into an academic volume. But as a subsidiary they are good. Keep it up.'

I pretended to look out the window, knowing the sketches were wholly the result of Moore's potion and that I wouldn't be able to recreate them without it. Professor Hobhouse scanned through my notes and placed them back on the table with a decisive thump.

'Now don't take this the wrong way, but I am going to need you to apply yourself to the task at hand here. Like I've said, I don't apportion any blame to you. I know you have had some difficult recent history, and in hindsight, it might have been better for the university to put you up in a local hostelry while you are down here. Albé has only one thing on his mind these days." He shook his head. "But you are here now, so let us make the best of it. You make up an itinerary for field visits for the next month, I'll have a serious conversation with Albé about your position here, and we will ensure that our alchemical friend Mr Moore doesn't, in future, spike your smoking matter with this diabolical substance they appear to have discovered.'

Diabolical substance? Again, I wanted to ask what he knew, but I was on the back foot, even beginning to nod like an obsequious servant.

'But having said that, and despite my reservations, I would be interested in witnessing another session in the Observation Room later today, so let's meet up there and you can let me have an itinerary. I have to leave tomorrow, so we do need to get this sorted out.'

He left; I slumped. I was always doing things for other people, to fit in with their objectives in life. If solipsism were true, my horizon may have been mine alone, and everything that existed, but it was heavily compromised. I could not help thinking there were forces outside of it that suggested I was nothing more than a whirlpool in a stream. And the stream was something I knew precious little about.

XXII

I moped in my room. Professor Hobhouse had been understanding, but not understanding enough. His visit had instilled a paranoia, creeping over me and making me shaky. What was I doing here? I'd swapped the intolerable isolation of university for the questionable confinement of this lunatic asylum. When I first finished my degree, I had managed, against my usual pessimism, to develop a rosy version of my future: collecting folklore, writing articles, even finding some academic position where I could disperse knowledge and give my existence some purpose. This had quickly unravelled as grief and guilt took hold of me and took me to dark places. I had dealt with this, to some extent, but now I was living with mad people and those who treated them. After nearly a month I was not doing what I was supposed to be doing. Part of the problem was that I was bored by the folklore. I understood it well enough and knew the faeries had an important part in it. But all the old stories I worked with seemed somehow fossilised, remnants of the past and a people who believed different things than we believed, in the age of moon landings and nuclear standoffs. My visit to the Pigots had brought things into sharper focus, perhaps indicating the folklore was more important than an imprint from the past, but I couldn't trust what I'd heard there as I'd been off my head on some substance that had scrambled my brain.

What I wanted was proof. I wanted to know whether the faeries existed and whether my sister was a mystic or just a deluded little girl. The folklore from the past could always be explained away. From my understanding of the subject, most folklorists were cultural colonialists whose job, it seemed, was to condescend societies previous to their own while maintaining some faux anthropological outlook, which gave them arbitrary scientific credence. I had gone along with this, which is why I was disillusioned. I needed to apply different criteria — another way of thinking about supernatural beings that might match my understanding rather than my learning.

This matching could be made here. Albé, Moore and Scrope were evidently tinkering with people's minds, even if I didn't understand how they were doing it. They all seemed quite comfortable with the idea of non-ordinary states of consciousness. They thrived on it. But they were also hiding their knowledge from me; maybe even stringing me along. How would I ever understand what they were doing?

I thought of Fernanda. She appeared to be the link. I'd yet to see her interact with anyone at the TRU, but there was a link; she appeared to hold some special, undefined position. And she seemed to be able to see into my mind. I'd yet to come up with a rational explanation for how she saw my dreams. And she made no bones about her relationship with the faeries. Maybe I just needed to accept that people like her and Sis experienced different realities from me.

But now I had Fernanda in my mind's eye, I began to forget about folklore and faeries and weird states of consciousness. All I could think about was kissing her and feeling her warmth against me. I hated myself for such smallness of thought, but perhaps it was an antidote to all the overthinking. I needed the embrace of another human. My brief foray with Augusta had made me realise how calcified I'd become without the touch of another for so long. I wanted to hold Fernanda. I went out to the gardens.

It was early afternoon. The sun should have been warm, but the wind took the heat out of it. I stopped for a moment behind the laundry building, closed my eyes and pictured her. My hands shook a little. I steadied my breathing and walked on.

She was sitting on the tree stump again, eyes closed, head bowed, her hands clasped together as if in prayer. I coughed before I reached her, so as not to startle her. She waited until I was a few feet away and slowly raised her head. She kept her eyes closed for a moment, then opened them, black and watery.

'*Hola*,' she said, continuing to stare ahead.

'Hey, Fernanda. Nice day… bit windy.'

God, what did I sound like? Why did I always make personal contact so uncomfortable? She didn't seem to notice, but when she turned to look at me, the curve of her lips suggested she was reading my awkwardness perfectly.

'It is not a good day, my friend. There is some bad news.'

I tensed up, shoulders and stomach. She observed me for a few seconds, and her words began to echo inside my head. At that moment I was quite sure she was putting them there herself, negating the need to say anything else by reinforcing what she had already said by direct, wordless communication.

'*Telepatía*,' she whispered, standing up, close to me, her black eyes still pooled with tears. 'I know you do not believe, but it is true anyway.'

'I'm not quite sure what to believe, Fernanda. Why is there bad news?'

'There has been a suicide.'

'Really? In the hospital?'

'No, here. In the *cobertizo*.'

She motioned to the tool shed on the edge of the gardens. My pulse quickened.

'A faerie has ended her life there… she did it for you. She met you in your dream. She took your place in death.'

I stared at her, looking for something that would abbreviate her words in her face. There was nothing there.

'Fernanda, please don't play games with me. I can't deal with this sort of thing right now.'

She moved closer to me and stroked my hair. 'We know you have been thinking about ending your life, my friend. We know how sad you have been. She did it so you do not have to. It was a selfless act. *Las hadas* have no ego. This one soaked up your sorrow and ended her existence so you can continue. She knew your life must carry on, but there had to be a sacrifice. The sacrifice was her life.'

A head-rush dulled my vision for a moment. My hands were shaking so much I put them behind my back instinctively.

'Fernanda, I… I…'

'You must come and see. It is tragic but it is beautiful. It is wonderful. You must come and see… Come.'

She reached round, took my hand from behind me and led me, unresisting, to the shed.

***

We walked back slowly to the main building of the hospital, hand in hand. We didn't speak, but I could hear her soft voice in my head, sometimes in English, sometimes in Spanish: *It is ok… You will be ok. It was meant to be… mantener la calma.*

In between her words, I tried desperately to rationalise what I'd just seen. But every attempt failed. What I'd seen was not rational, it was absurdly irrational, but as real as the neo-gothic walls of the hospital in front of us. I was going to have to overhaul my understanding of the nuts and bolts of this world. It had just been forced upon me. There was no choice, only acceptance.

She left me at the door with a kiss on the cheek but no words. I wondered why it was her who was going back to the ward instead of me. If I told Dr Dawkins what I'd just seen, he'd probably certify me on the spot.

In my head I heard Fernanda's voice again: *She is dead but dreaming. Soñando.*

'My sister or the faerie?' I asked out loud. There was no response. I walked, unseeing, back to my room.

XXIII

I'd grown up as a product of a secular society. There was no religion, the supernatural was baloney and only scientific endeavour explained how the world worked. Sis had once told my father about her interactions with the faeries. He eviscerated her and told her that only idiots believed in such mumbo-jumbo. She never said a word to him about them again. At university, the reductionism became ingrained and articulated in more intellectual form. There appeared to be only one way to understand physical reality and that was with a materialistic outlook. Any suggestion of something outside the reality box was effectively marginalised, ridiculed and destroyed.

I remembered a night in a bar, in my third year, stoned and drunk and having an ill-advised conversation with a guy who was getting closer to me than I wanted. He was a biologist, thought he knew everything about everything and was keen to tell me all about it. I mentioned Sis and her faeries and that perhaps there were elements of reality only certain people, under certain conditions, could experience. He scoffed, he ridiculed, he insisted on the absoluteness of scientific methods, and then he said that my sister was just a stupid, uneducated little fool. I hit him hard. He's the only person I've ever hit in my life, but the memory of him falling to the deck, nose bleeding, with his malt whiskey splashing over his face, made me smirk. A little victory born of violence — but under certain circumstances actions are needed over words. It was this episode that made me understand any theory or worldview is reliant on individuals within the belief-system, and that frequently, loud, braying individuals such as my decked acquaintance were the mouthpieces and propagators of received wisdom, which was not necessarily too close to the truth.

I'd always had my suspicions of the mainstream doctrine. But what I'd seen in the shed turned me inside out. It overrode everything. My hazy understanding of what Sis may have experienced and the unsettling weirdness of multiplying minds since I'd arrived at the hospital had suddenly found concrete form as Fernanda leant against me in the half-light. A foot-high humanoid dressed in some antiquated muslin had been hanging from the rafter; the dead facial features feminine but alien. It was unequivocal. I'd seen it from five feet away. The tiny noose was still swaying, making her dress speckle in the dull light, and her black eyes bulged as the natural motion of the rope turned her to face me directly. Fernanda had held me from behind. I can't remember what she said but her touch kept me from fainting. We were back out in a minute, holding each other and enveloped in a reality that did not allow such things. One moment there had been an impossible death in constrained, musty dullness, the next there was sunshine and airiness. It was like the difference between dreaming and waking.

I knew I had to draw away from it. I didn't need to rationalise it but I needed to subdue it. It was too much for me. The mildew scent of the shed stayed with me though. I went to the sink and rubbed the soap bar around my nostrils. I'd brought the soap from my university room—its fake scent realigned my memories with something long past and they took over from what had happened fifteen minutes ago. But the past and the present can be as one in memory, and within seconds the scent invoked the noose hanging from the cross-beam of my university room, which then became associated with the faerie's noose in the shed.

I pulled myself up, shook my head and sat down at the desk. I needed to do something practical to dispel these tides that were beginning to wash over me. I rolled a sheet of paper up in the Olivetti and locked it in position. I would start to put together my planned itinerary for Professor Hobhouse.

But I stared at the paper for a few moments, then typed: *My Sis… I'm so sorry. Please come back. I know your faeries are real. I've seen them…*

My breathing shallowed and the usual tears welled up. I yanked out the paper, screwed it up and flung it over the room. One thing was for sure; she wasn't coming back.

I put the *cobertizo* faerie into the backwaters of my mind, ducked out of the session in the Observation Room and handed over an itinerary to Professor Hobhouse next morning before he left for London. For the next week, I stuck to it. I avoided too much contact with everyone at the TRU and visited the people on my list. They were all within walking distance and there was no repeat of my visit to the Pigots after Moore's chemical intervention. My interviewees were all over sixty, mostly in their seventies, and, like the Pigots, gave me stories about the faeries that happened in their parents' or grandparents' generation. The latest date for an anecdote was just before the war; the faeries had blinded an old boy in one eye after he revealed with which one he could see them (Aarne-Thompson motif F 362.1, that one). It seemed the people willing to talk about faeries, even when they expressed a belief in them, wanted to distance themselves from the actual episodes. They were comfortable talking about other people's experiences from the past, but they never put themselves on the line.

After six visits it became clear to me these people were masking something. Vague intuition it may have been, but I recognised the tactics of projection diverting something these people might have been willing to explicate if I hadn't been a stranger, a person with some modicum of authority injected into their lives from London. They were all friendly enough and willing to talk about testimonies from the old days, but they were suspicious of me and maintained some barrier that would not be breached. By the sixth visit, I had got used to the look of incredulity on the doorstep, the gradual acceptance of me as a genuine folklorist, the softening of temperament over tea, and then the telling of tales from times past. But the final barrier was always maintained.

The stories all conformed to various Aarne-Thompson motifs but there was always a local flavour and the participants were named people, albeit from generations past. Each time I found myself comparing their descriptions of the faeries to what I'd seen in the shed; the *cobertizo*. The descriptions were never the winged Tinkerbell whimsy — they were humanoids dressed up in some archaic garb with ambivalent morals, who seemed intent on kidnapping, abducting, teasing or hurting their human protagonists. They were usually described as having black eyes. Each time I was told this, I zoned out for moments and visualised my hanging faerie; her black eyes were burned into my memory. But as I was drawn back into the stories, I always put a gap between my faerie and theirs — mine had (apparently) dissolved her existence for the sake of keeping me alive. There was no moral ambiguity in that action. She had acted very differently from the cast of supernatural bandits I was being told about by my aged interviewees. Their faeries correlated with the folklore with which I was familiar, but my faerie, while looking like theirs, appeared to represent something else.

But this disparity was subsumed by my burgeoned confidence. After the sixth visit, I returned to the hospital with a strut in my step. The awkwardness of my interviewing technique was inevitable, but I had done it. I had walked into people's houses and taken notes about their stories of faeries. I felt I might be turning myself into a proper folklorist. I was doing what I was supposed to be doing, for a definitive purpose. But underneath my temporary swagger, I knew there were things being hidden from me by these people and that these same things were, perhaps, being gradually revealed to me at the TRU.

As I collapsed onto my bed, I fell into the solipsistic mindset. Maybe all this was just an elaborate trick, conjured up by a single mind—the mind was mine. Folklore, faeries, locals with stories, Augusta, Albé, Fernanda, the hospital, the TRU, the noosed-up faerie, even Pink Floyd… where did they exist except in my own head? Where else could they be?

I spent half an hour staring at the ceiling, ruminating. The hanging faerie in the *cobertizo* obsessed my thoughts. I began an attempt to rationalise it again. Could it have been a dream? Was it an after-effect of Moore's nefarious joint? I knew it was neither. Fernanda had intersected me with an otherworld. It had been unreal, but it was real. I had no choice but to accept it. My recent folkloric visits paled into the background of my mind beside the gnostic certitude of the event. I closed my eyes and saw again her black, dead eyes. Dead… for me.

Fletcher broke my meditation with a knock on the door and the delivery of a letter. I brought myself back to the room, to the everyday. I needed to store away the weirdness and get myself back to what most people called normal. The letter was from Mr Goodfellow, suggesting I might like to visit the station-master and the Methodist chapel. The congregation were disappointed I hadn't visited since my arrival and thought I might gain something for my research by dropping in. I lay back on the bed with the letter on my chest. The guilt I felt at their disappointment did the job of grounding me. There's nothing like guilt to bring a person back to the real world.

The next day I was in a taxi, arranged by Fletcher, heading for the station where all this had begun.

I met the station-master on the platform. Everything was transformed from the night I'd arrived. The sunshine picked out the vagaries of green on the hills beyond and there were a couple of dozen people waiting on the platform, bringing vitality to the place. He greeted me and let me know he'd be with me in ten minutes once the incoming train had been dealt with. It duly arrived. There was flag-wielding and whistling from the station-master, and people were welcomed with handshakes and hugs and seen off with blown kisses and waves. I watched them, wondering how much of this was real emotion and how much was stage-managed for social expectation. But I also felt envy of their connections. My connections were all broken.

Ten minutes later, the station-master had handed over the baton of duties to another and we walked over the footbridge and onto a footpath leading from the station uphill to the town.

'Hope you did not mind me writing to Mr Goodfellow like that,' he said, walking stiff and not meeting my eyes. 'It's just that when I started talking about you and the hospital and what you're doing here, there was much interest among chapelgoers. We Wesleyans aren't as closed-minded as you Londoners might think.'

'I'm sure. I wouldn't have thought such a thing.'

'Well, I admit, there is some suspicion of London types down here. Most in the town have never been there, even though the train service from here is exemplary and very affordable. But it is a foreign world to what we know here.'

'So they know who I am?'

'There's been chatter. But I want you to meet one chap in particular. I'll explain it later when you meet our congregation. They'll all be there. We are having a children's harvest home today — not our main harvest festival; it's too early for that. But we like to give the children their own day as we reach September.'

'Children? Will there be many?'

'A few. There are some who are excited to tell you about their faeries. It's all become a bit odd, I have to tell 'ee, since young Edward was taken under the wing of your Lord Albé. But this should become clear. You'll see.'

I began to feel a prickly heat. But as we reached the first road of the small town, the station-master began pointing out architectural features and talking about the history of the place and I became a numb but appreciative receptacle of local knowledge. When we reached the chapel there were already children racing around outside and a couple of dozen adults milling around, their thick accents causing me to judge them even though I tried to resist the urge. A girl, maybe eight years old, ran up to us as we entered the gate.

'Are you the faerie person?' she asked, looking at me and then the station-master as if she were unsure if she could address me directly.

'That depends what you mean,' I said, adopting the fake tone reserved for children.

'I like to play with the faeries.'

'Do you?'

'Yes. Are you a boy or a girl?'

The station-master shuffled things along with a cough and embracing arms. We engaged in polite conversation, more people came, we entered the small chapel and I found myself sitting on a rear bench behind about forty people with the dozen or so children at the front. The station-master was evidently a minister as well. He hushed the congregation for a minute's silent prayer and then began reading some scripture. I zoned out as he recited the sonorous biblical texts. As ever, they sounded like the words of slightly deranged people from long ago. But after a few minutes, a change in the cadence of his voice brought me around and I found the rather unlikely proclamation from Revelations being voiced right in front of the children, who all sat mesmerised at the delivery from the station-master, whose plentiful moustache quivered as he grew more animated.

'Revelations, chapter four: After this, I looked, and, behold, a door was opened in heaven. And the first voice which I heard was as it were of a trumpet talking with me; which said, Come up hither, and I will shew thee things which must be hereafter. And immediately I was in the spirit: and, behold, a throne was set in heaven, and one sat on the throne… And round about the throne were four and twenty seats: and upon the seats, I saw four and twenty elders sitting, clothed in white raiment; and they had on their heads crowns of gold.'

I swivelled on the bench, a pang crossing my chest. The number twenty-four. Was this being directed at me? Was I making this up?

After an animated rendition of *Then I saw a new heaven and a new earth; the first heaven and the first earth had passed away*, things calmed down a little and the station-master's attention was drawn to the children looking up at him. They were encouraged to follow the path of righteousness through their lives and to be always thankful for nature's bounty, which was given to us by God. At a sign from a woman sitting alongside them, they dutifully filed onto the step in front of the lectern and deposited small baskets of fruit and vegetables, meant for distribution to the poor and elderly of the town, as the station-master nodded approvingly above them.

There were a couple of hymns, the Lord's Prayer and then dispersal outside, where some tables and chairs had been set up by unseen persons. The tic started to bother my eye as I realised social engagement was imminent, and I manoeuvred my way beside the station-master as a means of lessening the contact with strangers, all of whom were Methodists with what I imagined would be very definitive worldviews.

'I hope that was as uplifting for you as for us, my young folklore scholar,' said the station-master, exuberant after his leading of the flock.

'I, err… yes. I liked the Revelations. I've always thought it was the best book in the Bible.'

I caught a woman looking at me with pursed lips from across the table and made a mental note to keep my mouth shut whenever possible.

'Much wisdom, much wisdom. The four and twenty elders…'

He looked at me in expectation, but there was instead a few seconds of awkward silence, broken by the shuffling of a young man — maybe my age — into our presence. He had a spaced look about him and I'd have presumed he were stoned if he hadn't been part of this particular gathering.

'Ah,' said the station-master, raising his arms in announcement. 'This is Edward, and we are blessed to have him back within our fold.'

He sat down next to me and we engaged in the usual small talk. He still seemed stoned; his pupils were dilated and his words were far apart. Some of the children came and sat down on the grass beside us as if expecting some interaction. They were comfortable with him and so that seemed to extend to me.

'Lord Albé,' he said, shifting the conversation in an instant. 'You be with him now?'

'Yes, I'm staying at the Tertiary Research Unit at the hospital.'

'They saved me, you know.'

'Really?'

'He's a magician… an angel maybe. He sees inside a person's head. I had many problems before I went there. It seemed I were full of people. They were like demons. It be like I wasn't me. There were… different mes. Sometimes I had to rest in the dark place, and Lord knows what was happening to Edward when I be there. But they've sorted me. The others have gone and I can live again. Praise the Lord.'

I left it for a moment, conscious of the children still wriggling around our feet, but I wanted to know. 'So what did they do to you at the hospital?'

'Well, I had a time of it in the hospital. They put the wires on my head. Were a proper bad time for me, that. But then one-day m'lord came and got me. With his sister he were. She was a beauty. Wheeled me up the hill to their place, she did. And then Mr

Scrope took over for a while before m'lord came inside my head and dealt with all the people there. He was quite harsh with them. He was being cruel to be kind. It all seems like a dream now. But now I'm back here with friends and within the embrace of Jesus. I am me; I weren't before.'

'How did m' lor — Albé manage to get inside your head?'

'I don't know. He was just there. He was more real than me. It was the work of the Lord. God sent him as an angel to save me.'

'Mmm.'

The children began pulling at Edward's trousers as they got bored.

'Tell how 'ee brought the vairies,' piped up one of the girls.

'The faeries?' I asked the girl, pretending to be pleasant.

'When Edward came back, the vairies came with 'ee.'

He ruffled the girl's hair and held on a little too long to her pigtail. My shoulder muscles tweaked.

'Well, I never see them, I know that. I've heard all the stories but I never saw a faerie. But these little beauties think I brought them back with me. As soon as I was back, they all started seeing them. Maybe I brought something back from yonder hospital.'

The girl started to babble about gnomes and some kind of game she and her friends played with them down in the marshes. But I couldn't get to the gist of what she was saying. Her enthusiasm brought the other children into the fray, and in a few moments, they were all chattering about the faeries as an incoherent group collective.

Edward quietened them, only then letting go of the girl's pigtail.

'You all see different things though, don't you?' he said, turning to face me. 'Some talk about Tinkerbells, some of gnomes and such like, and then some sound like what my grandmother used to talk of.' He paused for a few seconds then said in a stunted voice, 'The coherence pattern is disparate.'

'The coherence pattern is disparate?'

He looked at me as if I were talking a foreign language.

'Sorry,' he said. 'I don't understand these big London words.'

'But you just said them, Edward.'

He frowned at me and then lost eye contact. He brought things back by asking one of the little girls on the fringe of the group to tell me what she'd seen. She was the same girl who had greeted me on arrival. She screwed up her mouth and shrank back a little but subsumed her shyness and stepped forward. I was still pondering the *disparate coherence pattern* but turned my attention to her.

'I saw spirits,' she said, her voice sounding in tune with Sis. 'They be smaller than me but not like in the films. They live in the trees and marshies. They like me but they are all unhappy about man, and him not caring about them. They told me to always save bees and insects. They do look after trees and marshies. I only see them since Edward come back.'

'What do they look like?' I asked, leaning slightly towards her.

She pondered, with a regulation finger on her lips, then said, 'A bit like you. Neither man nor lady. But their bodies can be seen through. They be spirits sent by God to look after His world.'

Her testimony encouraged the other children to come forward again with their own, producing incoherence. Their cacophony was broken by the station-master, who reared up behind them.

'Now then, now then… now then. We have a distinguished guest amidst our gathering and they don't want to hear your hullabaloo. One at a time.'

The children hushed at the voice of authority. But I coaxed out a few more stories from them, making mental notes to script them as soon as I got back to the TRU. The final testimony came from a boy, maybe eight or nine years old. He began with a rambling discourse about how he had found his way into a wood behind his house, but then suddenly jumped into an account of joining the faeries in a dance.

'I be frightened at first,' he said, getting excited. 'Because they looked all odd. They be like little old men with scruffy green clothes and caps. But they smiled and laughed a lot and some of them be tooting on whistles and pipes and making such music I never heard in my life. Then there were ladies… they be bigger. When one hugged me I felt warm and happy. I just danced around with 'em laughing. But I do not know how I got home. I was just sort of there. I don't remember how the dance ended, and I was late. I got told off for that. But I loved them faeries and want to see them again. I be feeling a bit sad since I left 'em.'

I wanted to investigate the boy's story, his feelings about it and its aftermath more but some women moved into our childish social space and dispersed the storytellers. The conversation turned around to other matters as the bubble around me transformed from juvenile to adult: the weather, worries about the harvest, rumoured talks about cuts to the train service; always laced with the Methodist reasoning that whatever happened, God would provide. One woman began to ask about the hospital, her uncomfortable demeanour letting me know what she thought of it, but in the nick of time the roar of an engine announced itself thirty yards away on the lane, making all heads turn. Moore got out the E-Type, swaggered through the gathering, stopping to exchange some aphorisms with them and then appeared at my side.

'Your carriage awaits,' he said, winking at me.

I made quick farewells to Edward and the unnamed people in my immediate vicinity. The station-master took both of my hands in his and hoped I'd be back. Two minutes later Moore and I were swishing through lanes with Led Zeppelin's exaggerated blues colouring every moment from the eight-track. The music gave me the excuse to not talk. For once, Moore seemed disinclined as well. I stared out the window, allowing the children's stories and the now unsettling resonance of Edward's pigtail-tugging to mix with the blurred greenery seen through zoned-out eyes.

Twenty-Four

Twenty-four. I was in the Observation Room with Scrope attempting to put me in some hypnotic state without me knowing it. Albé came in and set down a small wooden box on the table. I pretended not to look at it.

'I'm nervous about this, chaps,' I said, turning to the two-way mirror. 'I don't even know who is behind the mirror.'

Moore's voice came through the speakers. *'No worries, Blondie. I swear there's nobody but me here.'*

'You must trust us by now,' said Scrope. 'We're here to help.'

'I didn't realise I needed psychiatric help.'

Albé grinned. 'I think everyone probably needs psychiatric help, my friend. Most people just don't realise it. There are always blockages—usually difficult to unblock. But we think we've developed a way of dealing with some of the deep issues.'

'You *think*?'

'To say we *know* would be presumptive.'

He unpacked the box: vial, needle, petals. The tic began to take over the left side of my face and I made an instinctive turn to hide it. It levelled off and I drew my gaze to the box. The petals were moving. They shimmered and melded within their confines. They seemed like living creatures. I looked away.

'Let's cut to the quick,' said Albé. 'As a psychiatrist of many years' experience, I believe you've got a deeply embedded trauma that needs to be scooped up from within your memory and cleaned out. We're going to do this with the help of this.' He touched the vial. 'It's not a pharmaceutical. It's something that we'll need to explain to you later.

It's best we inject it this time—just to make sure we get the dose right.'

'Is it what you call Orchid-24?'

'Well, that's something for later. For the moment you just need to trust us. Do you?'

'I think so.'

'This is going to be weird for you. It will be like nothing else you've ever experienced. But you'll have me as a guide, and you will soon give over to it. You'll have me in your mind and it will be uncomfortable at first. It will probably become even more uncomfortable when you realise where we're going. The past may be a different country, and there's no way of changing it. But we can access it. We can recreate it because it exists in your mind... in your memory. And despite your flirtations with solipsism, your personal horizon is not all that exists... as you'll find out.'

'But I'm uncomfortable, Albé. I'm not sure this is right for me now.'

'You'll be fine,' said Scrope, firing up the vial. 'We've done this many times now, and you'll be back here on the couch in fifteen minutes.'

'Back from where?'

Scrope didn't answer. I looked away as he found my vein with the needle.

'There'll be a nodal point at first,' said Albé, his voice already starting to distort and echo. 'A collapse of the wave function. It's just the way it works... strange to begin with but you'll get it within a very short time. Now relax, close your eyes and I'll be with you in a moment.'

I closed my eyes and reached out to hold Scrope's hand. There was a lurch as if I were falling from the couch. A purple ambience took over my inner vision. The moving petals appeared before my internal eye and a spindly faerie in a tricorn hat stood before me, grinning and ushering me through a door that led onto a windswept hillside overlooking a road running through the valley bottom. I shivered. Something big was coming towards me.

My world is contained within a giant bubble reaching up to the stratosphere. It contains all my senses. I'm not in my body, but it still feels as if I am. I look up and see the perimeter of the bubble, glinting in the sunlight above the hill. But there is something outside it. Whatever it is, it pierces the bubble; it forces its way into my self-contained universe. A deep buzz pervades everything. It vibrates all. And then another violent lurch, which feels like the collapse of all I know. The bubble is burst. I am no longer me. The echoing, distorted voice of Albé fills everything as a stream of consciousness. He is me. At least his mind is my mind.

Row, row, row your boat, gently down the stream. The past has such an ambience, doesn't it? It's filtered through unimaginable bias and suppression until it fades into a dim hinterland with only fragments available for recall, and all of them mere fuzzy representatives of what really happened. Memory is subject to brutal assaults. Each one is adapted as it disappears into the recoiling past. You cannot trust your brain to transceive memory. It will transform it to make it understandable and palatable. But your memory is not reality—it is usually nowhere near it. However, you'll be pleased to hear that there is a collective memory. Every incident that has ever happened in our physical reality has been observed from a billion or more different angles. A car crash, say. The moment will have been witnessed by a myriad of different lifeforms, from the bacteria swarming over everything, to the cows standing in the field adjacent, to the humans in the midst of it. All of these observations are recorded, from the instant they happened, in the collective memory. Some people call this God. But that's just a name. The important thing is that we can tap into the collective. It is the Absolute Memory. It is Truth. And we have access. Sorry about the echo everywhere. It's usually like this—not sure why. It doesn't matter.

We need to start off with this cow. It's a visual field with a vertical vision of about sixty degrees. This isn't great, and the main memory here is of the grass in front of its snout. But the noise in the road a hundred yards away attracts some attention and so we can get an overview from the hillside. Its own consciousness has no conception of what's going on, but we can access its visual field to contextualise, because the bare data has been stored in the collective memory. Its wildness doesn't forbear its accuracy. There is the road as viewed from the hillside. The distractions of the snout snuffling in the grass and the olfactory sensory input are perturbing, but just concentrate on the visuals for now. We need the pandect to set things up. So, there are four cars queued behind some man holding up a STOP sign. There are works in the road; some men digging in a trench and a mound of soil piled up at the side of the road, stretching back to beside the fourth car. There's the overview. But we need to escape our bovine perspective and get into some of these human memories. This will be painful. But this will be necessary.

Here we go—feel the slide. Like slipping and falling down a slope in a dream, eh? Second car in the queue. Who have we got here? A middle-aged bloke. Oh man, all sorts of issues here. Listen to the stream of internal blather: *She's brought this on herself. She needs to realise I have my own needs, she really does. Twenty-four years I've given to her and tried my all for the kids. But all there is is nag, nag, nag. She wanders around in her dressing gown all day and pitches into me the moment I get home. What else could I do? Sheila gives me what I don't get at home anymore. Why shouldn't I? As soon as they're grown up, I'm off. Maybe Sheila and me could get together then. But she's young. Maybe she'll get bored…*

It's so predictable, isn't it? The crisis of a middle-aged man who has made the wrong decisions in life and is now looking around for external input to make him complete, without realising he first needs to look within. But we're not interested in him and his pitiful existential crisis. He sees mostly his dashboard as he ruminates on his inadequacies. But there are moments where he lifts his vision. And there she is — little Sis, sidelong, looking smiley and carefree from the distance of ten feet and the skewing of two sets of car windows. But we'll have to come back to that. The slide again. Back to the fourth and last car in the queue. Little Johnny is playing up in the back seat with his brother. The parents' resentment emanates in the enclosed environment of the car, infecting the children. These two kiddy-winks remind me why I've always been such a great admirer of King Herod. But anyway, it's his visual memory we're after… and there it is. He senses an out of context rumble behind him and looks back through the window. There is a lorry coming up fast. This consciousness doesn't understand how vehicles move on the road but he can sense, intuitively, the lorry is moving too fast. It careers on the road. Johnny sees it as a cartoon. It's his only way of comprehending it. But we can see it is not a cartoon and that there is a fast-moving hunk of metal careering along the road and approaching little Johnny's view. Time for another slide. Apologies for the intoxicated feel of this, but we're coming to the nub of things here.

Lorry driver. He's drunk. The wooziness is palpable, isn't it? And what's this? He's flicking through the pages of a porn rag on the passenger seat. There's more time looking at tits and fannies than the road in front. And here it is. The moment. One second there's an open road ahead and the next there's a queue of cars for some unknown reason. Feel the instant of realisation; the heart-gulping moment when he's moved outside the reality box and is approaching catastrophe with barely a second to think about it. You'll probably pick up that he's not a bad bloke. But he is a careless bloke. A quick glance at the speedo — 60 mph. Back to the road… swerve and brake. The lorry mounts the mound of soil with its offside wheels and takes off through the air.

Slide. Back to you, Blondie. Glinting sunlight through the side window, the STOP-sign man right in front of the car, with the first intimations of concern layered on his face. Take a glance at Sis. Such a pretty child. She carries the weight of her faerie encounter a few weeks before—you cannot ignore the downturn in her usual upcurved, laughing lips. And now the metallic clatter and dull thuds behind bring out an expression of gnosis. Oh, her eyes are adorable, but they are now wide and ready for something. She knows. For some reason we can't get inside her—it happens sometimes. It doesn't matter. It might be better for you to not know anyway.

But we can slow things down here. Let's look at this. Your memory has deceived you into thinking you got frustrated with the hold-up and pulled the car to the left to avoid the STOP-sign man and move on to the carriageway beyond. But as you can see, this was nothing more than a thought. You never acted on it. You stayed where you were. But here's the hard part. You won't want to see it, but I'm afraid you have to. Life can be brutal, and often is. Let's go back to you. I know it all seems unreal, but at the same time you know it's the true reality.

The buzz has become unbearable, mixing with the echoing resonance of all around me. I reach out to touch Sis's fingers. The dim unease of the rumble behind us sends a cold load through my abdomen. I flinch and look into her eyes. She smiles for a moment. It is a smile of knowing. There is a second of utter silence. It is the sole break in the echoed buzz.

'I love you,' she whispers.

The air shakes. There is a sound which shouldn't be a sound. I turn to look behind her but don't have time. There is a cataclysmic impact of metal and glass as something alien smashes into our existence. It is slowed down though. Why is it slowed down? The massive sound continues, but I watch the white metal inch its way through. It pulverises the offside window to the passenger seat. The implosion is mesmerising — it is the whole world at this moment. The slowness of movement makes me think I can do something. But I can't do anything. The metal intruder is unstoppable. It shatters and dismantles reality. I am stupefied. I cover my head. I am consumed by the annihilation. The word rings through me, buzzing: *ANNIHILATION*.

The metal is replaced by the muddied black of a tyre. It is inexorable. It is ferocious. The brutality of the impact is an apocalypse. The tyre and metal crash through the side window and seat into Sis and pump her through the windshield like a rag doll, all in slow motion. But I can't move so it may as well be in real-time. I cower. There is some undefined pain, but it seems unimportant. I see the lorry turn on its side as Sis disappears below it amidst the shattering of everything in front of me. There is a deluge in me; a maelstrom inside and out. I'm about to pass out, but not before I see the back of the lorry turn over, sending off a shard of sparking, dismembered metal. Slow-time suddenly becomes real-time, making me dry heave at the instant lurch caused by the switch.

The length of metal whips into the air and hits the man with the STOP sign with absolute impact. It takes his head off at a peculiar angle. The decapitated head blasts upwards, vertically from his body with a spurt of blood, arcs into the air and then thuds onto what remains of the bonnet of the car before slowly rolling up to the shattered glass of the windscreen. The roll brings it to completion two feet in front of me, blood splattering over my face. The mouth twitches and the eyes settle into position looking at me. I look into the dead eyes as drops of blood fill my own and tinge everything red. I crouch further into the seat, perhaps the only remaining part of the car intact. I crouch… I crouch.

The crunching sounds of the lorry turning over and skidding into the road in front continue but then fade like the end of a song. The detonation is replaced by the smooth buzz, which now pervades everything.

There is nothing but the buzz. The light fades. The faerie with the tricorn hat appears on the bonnet of the car and kicks the bludgeoned head off. His eyes are black but they emanate sympathy.

'*This be the end of the memory,*' he says. '*Now it be time for you to leave. We'll be seeing you soon.*'

He reaches out his spindly hand to me. I raise my own bloodied hand to meet it. But blackness takes over. All is black.

I shivered on the couch, my vision blurred and dim. Scrope put a blanket around me and held me close.

'Are you back with us?' he whispered into my ear.

'Mmm.'

I passed out.

XXV

I watched the sun go down below the distant tree line from my window. For a moment I was sure it was setting in the east. Such a subversive, unreal thought would usually have had my face twitching, but I soon correlated and stayed calm, even allowing the beauty of the scene to infiltrate me. I convinced myself I was indeed looking to the west. I watched the remnants of subdued yellow light flicker between the distant greenery. It made me not want to be alone. Somehow, I knew I wouldn't be. I sensed him gravitate towards me. How could it be otherwise? He'd been inside me; taken me over. The deep connection had been made.

I waited, coiled and ready. Sure enough, within a few moments, Albé knocked and came in. I moved to him quickly, wrapped my arms around him and buried my head into his chest. I needed the touch of another human. After a minute's silent hugging, I extracted myself and sat down on the edge of the bed without meeting his eyes. He observed me for another minute. The buzz was low but seemed to transfer into a tingle over my skin. He sat down next to me.

'Are you ok?' he asked, his voice still echoing as it had done during the experience. He took hold of my hand, squeezed it and let go. 'I should have made sure Augusta were here. She's the mistress of these post-experience chats. She's a bit of a magician.'

'Mmm.'

'But there's a need for us to make some assessments while things are fresh. Do you believe what you experienced is the truth?'

'How could I not? It was more real than real.'

'Yes. When you swap the subjective for the objective, the reality can be shocking; especially if you've never been to that place before.'

'What is that place, Albé? Where were we? I felt as if I were… as if I were you. There seemed to be no *me*. I was subsumed. How do you do it? It's as if you're… God.'

He laughed. The buzz and echo stopped.

'Don't worry, I can assure you I'm not God or even a god. We've just developed a tool to infiltrate the minds of people. I'm simply good at administering it. You must see the advantage it gives us when dealing with our dissociative patients at the TRU. We can just get in there and flush out all of the characters who are causing trouble. They don't expect it and they have no defence.'

'Yes, I think I see that. But what about me? What were you flushing out in me?'

'Well, Blondie,' he said, standing up. 'What do you think? You've been crippling yourself with guilt. You believed yourself responsible for putting the car in the way of the lorry that killed your sister. You have thought your impatience was the reason she was killed. But your memory had become distorted — there was nothing you could have done. It was an accident of fate, brought on by the ineptitude and carelessness of the lorry driver — nobody else. And as you know, you completely suppressed the decapitation. Such a horrendous thing to happen. We've found that this type of cataclysmic trauma will usually be suppressed and that there is then a knock-on effect to all the other immediate memories. In your case, you invented the story of moving the car into the path of the lorry and have more or less cast yourself as the murderer of your sister.'

I took this in. I knew I trusted the experience more than my previous dim memory.

'I've always told people I drove the car into the line of the lorry.'

'I know.'

'But I didn't.'

'You didn't.'

I closed my eyes and relived the experience. Its super-reality made my previous memories seem dumb and ridiculous. The difference was as between night and day.

'But how can I trust this experience? You gave me a drug. How do I know it's not just one big hallucination? And the faerie. What was he about?'

'Do you intuitively trust it?'

'Well, yes. It was… it was incredibly real. I cannot help but trust it.'

'Then perhaps that's the best option. We've taken you to a place arbitrated by the maximum amount of witness. It's the collective consciousness. And it would appear that entities like your tricorned friend live there all the time—they cross over between the collective and the subjective when conditions are right. It won't be one hundred per cent accurate, but it'll be much more accurate than your own individual low-resolution memory. You've had a cosmic view of an incident in your own subjective past. It's shown you how things were, not how you thought they were.'

I steadied my breathing. 'Mmm. I don't understand it, but I'm trying to accept it. I don't really have a choice, do I?'

'We all have choices.'

I ran through the super-memory, looking for chinks in its objectivity. Despite the absurdity of the faerie entity, made less absurd after my experience in the *cobertizo*, I knew it was a record of truth. I scrabbled around for other reasons to justify my guilt. 'But I took the car without my father knowing. It was his car. If I hadn't taken it the accident wouldn't have happened.'

'That's special pleading and you know it,' he said, curling that lip. 'You didn't cause the incident. And you know very well that your father was aware that you'd go out for drives in the car—there was an implicit understanding. If you'd caused the accident there might have been a problem. But you didn't cause it. You were a victim. Your sister was a victim. You were both blameless. Your father just needed to blame someone. It's a common reaction in these sorts of situations. Unfortunately, he blamed you.'

I allowed that to sink in. I wanted it to be true. *Implicit understanding.* 'How do you know there was an implicit understanding?'

Albé sighed. 'I took over your mind, remember. All of your relevant memories, however distorted, were available to me. I know how it worked between you and your father. The implicit understanding was that you could use the car if he didn't need it. So please don't try to start transferring your guilt to that trope, whatever he may have said afterwards. You borrowed the car. You took your sister for a ride and were unfortunate enough to be in the wrong place at the wrong time. You're blameless for her death. You. Are. Not. To. Blame.'

I squirmed on the bed, but Albé's words were knocking down the doors. The relief rose to the surface. I smiled and met his eyes. Then my gaze strayed to the window. The sun was higher than it had been when he came in. It was still fully above the tree line horizon. Albé followed my eyes.

'There'll be aftereffects,' he said, walking to the window and looking out. 'You can't expect magic to release you instantly from its grasp.'

'I'm beginning to realise that. But... when are you going to tell me about Orchid-24?'

'Soon... real soon.'

XXVI

The last week of August passed. Albé, Moore and Fletcher had gone off to some music festival, on the Isle of Wight of all places, leaving Scrope in charge at the TRU. I'd somehow agreed to look after Boatswain. We took to each other. He slept with me, taking up more room on the bed than me, and we quickly developed a routine of early-morning walks out through the hospital grounds and into the countryside. My father had never allowed pets in the home and this was the first time I'd been responsible for an animal. I liked it. I soon began to see his character — he was belligerent, loving, naughty, farty, protective, inquisitive, growly, insecure. He would look at me with that semi-smile dogs have, as if he knew things he couldn't possibly know. I soon started to talk to him as I went about collating my notes, allowing my blathered stream of consciousness to become externalised, with the excuse that there was another living being to listen to it all. He would lie at my feet as I typed away at the Olivetti, reading out each sentence and asking him what he thought about the faeries.

I always started our walks through the hospital gardens, hoping to see Fernanda. But she was nowhere to be seen, and it would usually end up with just me and him wandering through the lanes, surrounded by nature on the turn. It was the time of year I'd always dreaded; darkness overhauling light and dampness overcoming dryness. It was the cusp of autumn, which took on the aspect of a global consciousness, sneering at me and insinuating the coming of something bleak and cold. But having Boatswain at my side made it all a little more agreeable and manageable.

On the last day of August, we ended up in the spot where I had laid down with Augusta. Boatswain became more animated than usual, sniffing around and grumbling as if he were sensing her presence in the past.

'What's up old boy? Do you know your mistress has been here?'

Woof.

I sat down and put my back to the same log as Boatswain continued to snuffle around. I closed my eyes and remembered the kiss. Why had that happened? Did it matter? The diluted memory soon subsided, and the events of the last month flickered through my internal vision, ending on my journey into the past with Albé. My dreams had been infiltrated by what I'd experienced, warped into the usual subconscious ramblings—distorting the horror of the crash into a dozen different episodes. In one dream my father had made an appearance in the car, waving his finger at me and snarling. I had blistered at him, shouting and screaming while Sis was whirled out of the car and into the air without either of us noticing. I had told him that God had told me it wasn't my fault and he became enraged. The tricorned faerie came to intercede, holding up his branch-like hands in pacification. There were many variations on this theme and I usually awoke scrambling around in the bed with Boatswain whimpering his solidarity and moving close to me as if in instinctive protection.

I took out the small packet of weed Moore had given me, rolled it up with some tobacco, lit up and allowed it to filter into my system. As usual, it enhanced my memories—made them more direct. I once again touched her hand in the car and looked into her watery eyes. Everything that had happened before and since revolved around that moment. I had begun to accept it, but at the same time, I still couldn't accept it. Why had it happened? Why had we been there at that moment? Why had she died and I survived?

And as the weed embedded itself, I began to question the validity of the reconstruction via Albé's magic formulae. The experience he had wrapped me up in was beginning to dissipate into memory, and like all memories I began to distrust it, even though it was being made clearer by the cannabis. He'd been inside my mind, I was pretty sure of that. But that was impossible. Was it just some stage-managed trick to make me think about my past in a certain way? If it were it was a very, very clever trick. As I thought deeper, I revisited the experience and began to accept something cosmic had happened. I didn't understand it, but my solipsistic bubble had been burst by the agency of an unknown drug and the considerable personality of Albé, who, quite evidently, had worked out a method of entering other people's minds and taking them over. He'd taken me back to the moment of the crash, and however I might try to rationalise it, the experience had been so visceral and more real than real that any denial of it as a genuine participatory event seemed absurd.

I closed my eyes and put myself into the zone of memory. I allowed the memories of the past month to layer and take me over: the madness of the dissociated TRU patients, the overbearing characters I found myself with, the disengaged faerie folklore, the insane ambience of the hospital, the hanging faerie, the compelling lure of constantly thinking about Fernanda, the cataclysm of Albé's enforced, intrusive experience dredging up the clarity of the crash. I ended up visioning the noose in my university room. The noose then filled with the faerie in the shed and I had to shake my head with some violence to get rid of the absurdity of the image. But even as I dispatched it, I knew it had been real. It may have been absurd, but those black eyes had been as real as anything I'd ever experienced.

I sank back against the log. Why was I living this life? Despite the categorical pricking of my solipsistic bubble during my experience with Albé, I began to drift back to thinking I was all there was. I was just making all this up. I was all that existed and everything that happened was contained within my all-seeing horizon, which was, perhaps, capable of producing anything.

The lick of a slobbering tongue brought me back to consensus reality. Boatswain plonked himself onto my lap with force and held his snout to my face, looking into my eyes as if he might know what I had been thinking.

'Augusta's kiss was better than yours, sunshine.'

He replied with another tongue slapping. We headed back to the hospital.

***

I climbed the stile into the hospital grounds and Boatswain wriggled through the gap in the hedge, which we'd discovered on our first excursion. After only a few steps I saw Fernanda's red top in the distant vegetable gardens. A flush crept over my face and chest but there was no hint of any tic. That was some progress. Maybe the residual effect of the weed was keeping me calm. Boatswain strutted along the path in front of me. I'd found him a little nervous of people over the week—he usually grumbled and retreated when faced with a stranger. But as we neared the gardens, his ears pricked up as he heard Fernanda singing to herself, then he trotted quicker and bounded up to her, burying his head in her embrace, thwacking his tail and whimpering as I'd only seen him do with Albé and Augusta.

'*Hola, mi amigo*,' she said, ruffling his snout as she spoke some soft Spanish into his ear. She looked at me from her crouch, her black eyes catching the watery morning sun. 'And hello to you, my friend. You both seem happy and beautiful today.'

She finished with Boatswain and stood up. She stepped over and hugged me. I hesitated before returning it, but only for a few seconds. I clasped her and held on for longer than I should have. But she didn't retract, and I found myself smelling her hair as I held on. It had the peculiar floral smell that for some unproven reason I still identified as orchid. Eventually, Boatswain forced his body between us and we separated but continued to hold each other's hands.

'I'm so glad to see you, Fernanda. I've missed you this week.'

It was my usual awkwardness. But it didn't seem to matter too much this time. Our eye contact remained. Our smiles were mutual. She pulled her hands away and gave me a knowing, coy look.

'And I have missed you too. I sense you are happier than when last we met. I am sorry about the faerie. It had to happen. It was in some ways *simbólico*.'

'Symbolic?'

'In some ways. You must know this. The death was your death. She was a part of you.'

'Was she? It's disturbed me, Fernanda. How can it have been real?'

'How can it not have been real?'

'I… I…'

'She did it for you. You know this. Perhaps you just need to accept it.'

'Yes, maybe I do. I just don't understand it.'

'Understanding will come with time. *Las hadas* have their ways—they will do things we consider outrageous and unacceptable. They do not see death the way we do. They know more than we do.'

'But the hanging… how did it happen?'

'It just did. I am sorry you are upset. I am upset. But again… we just need to accept it. A faerie has sacrificed herself for you. She saw herself as a part of you… a part that needed to die. The moment has been and gone. It has dissolved. It lives nowhere but in our memories. As soon as we walked out of the *cobertizo*, she would have disappeared from this world. She was more of an event than a thing. It is the way things work.'

'Mmm.'

'But there is more, is there not? I am guessing that his lordship has been at work on you with our flower.'

She moved back close to me and squinted. Her irises seemed to glint purple for a moment as she looked at me. My natural reaction was to look away, but her gaze held me.

'You now know what happened, do you not?'

'Explain.'

'Your sister. Your beautiful little sister. You have been reprieved... is that the right word? You understand?'

'I think I do, Fernanda. But how do you know?'

She just smiled and diverted her attention to Boatswain, who had started to display some canine jealousy at being left out and was muzzling at her hand.

'I see you do not know all things. I am sure you will after the boys come back — their heads ringing with Jimi Hendrix.'

'Jimi Hendrix?'

She looked at me as if I were joking. 'You Brits and gringos and your music festivals. Your culture is taking over the world.'

'Hendrix is playing at this festival?'

She laughed and nodded in confirmation.

'How do you know this, Fernanda? You're in a psychiatric hospital. How do you know so much? Forgive me if that's rude.'

'Not rude, my lovely friend... just a bit naive. You must know by now that Albé and I have a connection.'

I felt Boatswain's jealousy transfer to me. I lost eye contact for the first time.

'Come on now,' she said, taking my hand again and compelling me to look back into her eyes. 'You need to gain some acceptance of certain things. I can read your mind, remember?'

Her smile and wink infected me and we moved closer. Just as our bodies were about to touch, she turned and led me by the hand over to the tree stump.

'Look at the rings.'

'The rings?'

'The rings in the stump. They tell the story of a hundred years. Some are thick, some are thin. Good years and bad years. Those near the middle are from years when your Queen Victoria was around. This tree witnessed all of the souls who came and went in the hospital. It has a memory. Its memory adds to the total memory. The stump is dead but dreaming. The faeries live in that memory. This is why most people cannot see them. They have lost the connection. But you know you have seen them. You know you have been to that place.'

I touched the stump and tried to feel some resonance. I couldn't. I wanted to kiss her, but I knew I couldn't do that either. She drew away and began stroking Boatswain, who had stayed close to her side.

'You have some visits this week to people who have seen the faeries, have you not?'

I nodded, not even bothering to ask how she knew.

'May I join you?'

'Join me?

'I might be of some help.'

'But is that allowed? What would Dr Dawkins say?'

'They do not care too much about me. They know I am not ill like most here. And if I have a responsible person like you from London escorting me, they will see it as therapy. *Rehabilitación.*'

'Um, I'd love that. Yes, I'd truly love that, Fernanda. Are you sure?'

'*Sí.* Day?'

'Friday is probably best. Friday the fourth. I've been invited back to the Shervage Arms — that's a pub — to interview some people. If you can and would like to, I'd love you to come. It would be great... yes.'

I knew I was gushing and smiling like a fool, but the sudden prospect of a day out with Fernanda was starting to make my head spin.

'*Es un trato.* Mister Davies will arrange it.'

'Scrope? Yes, I'm sure he will.'

My bubble of fragmented joy was broken by Boatswain letting out a grumbled growl. Epsilon trudged up the path towards us. He stopped five feet away, looking nervously at the dog and then at us in his usual bewilderment. Fernanda covered her mouth with her hand, her eyes smiling. Epsilon quivered for a few moments.

''Ee Mister Davies... Mister Davies...'

'Mister Davies?'

'Mister Davies... yeah, fuck. He'd like to see 'ee.'

'Now?'

Epsilon ran a confused look over his face and nodded. Boatswain continued his protective growl.

'Until next Friday then,' said Fernanda, touching my arm and running her fingers down to mine. 'I am looking forward to hearing all about these people's faeries.'

She ruffled Boatswain's head then turned back to the gardens. I watched her go and made off with Epsilon back to the TRU, Boatswain sticking to my side and baring his teeth whenever Epsilon got too close.

XXVII

Scrope was smoking, sat on a low wall outside the entrance.

'Thank you, young Epsilon. That'll be all.'

Epsilon skulked off and Scrope stood up and handed me the joint.

'Is everything ok?'

'Nothing we can't handle, but I am going to require your assistance if you'd be so kind.'

'Right.'

'I know you'll want to talk about what happened the other day, but if you can put that on hold for the moment, I'm afraid Caroline Lamb has taken a bit of a bad turn and we need to get her into the Observation Room pronto. And as Albé and Moore are in absentia on Vectis, we're going to have to improvise. We can't have any nurses or hospital staff at the consul in the monitoring chamber, so you're going to have to do it.'

'Err, I don't think that's a good idea, Scrope. I'm not very technically minded. I wouldn't know what to do.'

'Don't worry about that. You won't have to do all the knob-twiddling Moore does. I'll set the recording monitor up and then all you have to do is make sure the sound keeps coming through. I'll run through it with you. But I do need to ensure this conversation is on record. So put Boatswain in your room and I'll see you there… as soon as you can.'

I inhaled the rest of the joint, and in we went.

In the monitoring chamber, Scrope set things up. I shook a bit, partly due to the cannabis in my bloodstream but mostly because I had a feeling I'd balls things up.

'Right,' he said, standing back with satisfaction. 'It's now recording. All you have to do is make sure the sound continues to come through and that this little gauge keeps showing spikes as we talk in the Observation Room.'

'And if it doesn't?'

'Press this button next to this red light until it does. Don't worry about anything else, volume or feedback. We simply need to make sure everything is recorded. If you need to talk to me, the mic is on too. So keep quiet unless you really need to say something.'

The door swung open in the Observation Room and an orderly and a nurse brought in Caroline. In an instant, I recognised the scowling face of Caro as she struggled between them. They made her sit on the couch as she cursed at them. Scrope looked at me and raised an eyebrow.

'This is going to be a holding exercise,' he said, scratching his stubble. 'This particular character is proving troublesome.'

'Have you taken Orchid-24?'

He grinned and gave me a confused look. 'I did it once, months ago; that was enough for me. These days only Albé takes the magic formula. You were privileged. But we can discuss that later. I know you want to know all about it. For the moment I'll just need to do this the old-fashioned way.'

He made his way out and a few seconds later appeared in the Observation Room and ordered the hospital staff out. He sat down in the armchair at a safe distance from the patient. She bristled but remained seated.

SCROPE: Coming through loud and clear, Blondie?
Yes. All ok.
CARO: Who the fuck is Blondie?
SCROPE: None of your business really. Let's concentrate on you. Why have you come back?
CARO: I never went away.

SCROPE: Caroline has been doing well. She's had a peaceful time of it this last week and —

CARO: Fuck Caroline. She's useless. If you send her back into the world outside here she'll be all over the place. It's tough out there. She's better off in the dark place. I'll deal with things… especially *men*. Men like you. She'll be taken advantage of — raped and impregnated by some bastard like our father.

SCROPE: But we can't send *you* back out there.

CARO: Why not? I know how things work. I'd take no shit from anyone.

SCROPE: You're psychotic.

CARO: Ha. Is that your word for it? A strong woman is what I call it. And I'm in control so there's nothing you can… hold on. Where's m'lord? He's not here is he? I can sense his absence. He's been brutal with me. He's a fucking magician. But he's not here. So there's nothing you can do, is there?

SCROPE: You're right, he's not here just now. But he'll be back very soon. And do remember you're in a secure unit. You're not going anywhere until we have your situation dealt with. It's not fair on Caroline, is it?

CARO: It's not fair on me more like. Who the hell do you think you are making judgement on a person's character? Why is she right and I'm wrong?

SCROPE: You are destructive.

CARO: I am strong. You just don't like it because I'm a woman.

SCROPE: Are you always this angry?

CARO: Only when I have to deal with fuckers like you.

SCROPE: Where is Caroline?

CARO: You know where she is. She's safely put away with all the others. They're all useless. They just need to stay where they are and let me get on with it here. I won't harm them but they can't be out here.

SCROPE: But Caroline was the first, wasn't she? She had this body before you and the others turned up.

CARO: Why don't you just get lost? I'm in charge now and there's nothing you can do about it.

SCROPE: Maybe, but Albé will be back in a few days. I

think he'll be quite annoyed at your taking over. I have a feeling he'll be giving you a bit of a hard time.

CARO: I guess he will. I've no fight against him. He's not like other men, is he? But I want to stay in charge. I need to stay in charge… in charge…

Caro slumped into the couch, her bluster suddenly turned soft. She closed her eyes and began talking to herself, all indecipherable. Scrope sat in silence watching her, motioning to me to keep recording by twirling his finger. Her rambling continued for about five minutes. Eventually she slumped again, straightened up, opened her eyes and stopped talking.

SCROPE: Caro?

CAROLINE: I guess she's gone back. I sensed the shift. I never know whether it's a dream or just what happens in the dark place. Why am I like this? Are other people like this?

SCROPE: Some are. Are you all right?

CAROLINE: I'm sad. I want to be ok like you. Being in the dark place is like dreaming… dead but dreaming. Sometimes I wish that I were dead.

SCROPE: But life can be golden, Caroline. I think a little more time here with us and you'll be better. You'll want to be alive.

CAROLINE: Maybe. But I know I'm not one person. I don't really know the others. They feel like people in my dreams. When I'm here, I'm just me. Do they really exist?

SCROPE: Probably. But I think we need to concentrate on you right now. We need to get you in control. Then things will be better. Would you like to be in control of your life?

CAROLINE: I think so. Is Caro very bad?

SCROPE: She's just angry. She's the part of you that's angry. We'll help her. But she'll need to stay in the dark place, otherwise you won't get better. Do you trust us?

CAROLINE: I think so. I trust Albé the most. He comes in and soothes me. I still think he is a god.

SCROPE: Well, you can see him in a few days. It'll all be ok. But we'll take you back to your room now. We can play your favourite music there on the record player. Would you like that?

CAROLINE: I would like that… yes, I would. Mr Moore gave me some Beatles records. They make me cry sometimes, but oh I love to listen to them. May I listen to them?

SCROPE: You can listen to whatever you like, Caroline. Whatever makes you happy is good.

The nurse came and took Caroline away and Scrope came back into the monitoring chamber and allowed himself a large exhalation.

'I'm glad Moore didn't give her any Van Der Graaf Generator records,' he said, sending me a knowing look.

I chuckled. 'Yes, I think that would be more up Caro's street. But I think everything is ok here. The monitor spikes continued throughout.'

'Good, good.' He pressed a couple of buttons on the console and allowed a pregnant pause before speaking. 'I realise we've dragged you into all this. Probably not what you were expecting when you came here.'

'Definitely not.'

'But before Albé gets back, perhaps I can run through a few things with you. I think you might need some insights about what's going on here. I realise you'll probably be working things out of your own accord after the other day, but what we're tapping into is something important. I'd like to just clarify some philosophical and metaphysical concepts with you before anything else happens. Is that ok?'

'Cool.'

'Excellent. Join me in the common room about one. I'll get Epsilon to bring us lunch.'

I returned to my room, took Boatswain for a short walk and braced myself for some *philosophical and metaphysical concepts*.

XXVIII

Scrope and I ate our sandwiches and then settled down at either end of one of the sofas, cups of tea in hand. He had a way of looking through me as if thinking about something else while he talked. But he had always been easy to engage with. I couldn't put my finger on it, but he seemed less *predatory* than Albé and Moore.

'So, what do you think of patient Caroline?' he said, in his best psychologist's tone.

'I feel pity for her. The change between her and Caro is… extraordinary. The first time I saw her I thought she was playacting. But she's not, is she? It's obvious. Do you know how long she's been like this?'

'It's difficult to get the complete records of most patients. They tend to come here with a bit of a foggy history, but probably several years.'

'How has she coped in the real world then? I can't imagine her being able to deal with the everyday when she seems to switch personalities so quickly.'

'Well, in terms of what she's been through, it might have actually saved her. She's a timid character. Her father sexually abused her and Caro turned up as a defence mechanism. You've seen what *she* is like. The problem is, once the abuser was taken away, Caro stayed. That's almost certainly when her other personalities came into being. They all seem quite weak characters but they will all have a role to play. They all provide certain things Caroline needs.'

'But are they real?'

Scrope pursed his lips and lit up a ciggy. He gave me one and we spent a minute filling the room with smoke as he considered what to say.

'That depends who you ask,' he said. 'Dr Dawkins back in mission control will confidently tell you that she is schizophrenic and that, although she's not faking her other personalities, she is simply operating under a delusion. Something within her psyche has acted to protect her from an external threat. The result is that she manifests different characters to help her deal with those threats. She has no control over these personalities and eventually a psychosis forms, even when the threat has gone.'

'But you don't believe that, do you?'

'No.'

'You think the dark place is real and that these personalities exist there as distinct minds?'

'Yes.'

'You'll need to explain that, Scrope. What is the dark place?'

He blew out some smoke rings and settled back into the sofa. 'Do you know Carl Jung's theory of the Collective Unconscious?'

'Vaguely.'

'Well, he developed it to describe concepts of humanity, stored in a metaphysical landscape, mostly by using archetypes: Anima and animus, father and mother, the trickster, the maiden, et cetera. It contains all the attributes of humanity. It's where all consciousness ends up and then feeds back into individual minds in a myriad of ways: dreams, faerie stories, numinous experiences.'

'That doesn't sound like the dark place to me.'

'Maybe not. But the important thing to know is that there is a world of consciousness that is not reliant on our material physical reality. In fact, consciousness per se is not physical in any sense. We usually experience it through our physical senses, but it is immaterial. Jung's Collective Unconscious is one way to describe its form at an overarching level, but as soon as you accept that consciousness is not tied to the material universe then there become many other places in which it can exist. Dreams are the most obvious. Where are you when you dream?'

'Usually in bed.'

'Are you sure about that? Your dreaming mind is in its own self-created universe with its own rules.'

'But it's dependent on me being in bed doing the dreaming.'

'How do you know?'

'Because when I wake up I realise it was just a dream.'

'What if you continue dreaming when you die?'

'Dead but dreaming?'

'Indeed. The most important point here is that we have access to altered forms of consciousness. And it would appear as if these forms exist in various types of autonomous locations. Dreams, the dark place, your visit to the car crash… they are as real as the room you and I are sitting in. And they contain a range of beings usually deemed unreal. So all the characters in your dreams, the different personalities of our patients, people from your past memories… faeries. They all exist. We just need to find out how they exist and how they interact with what we usually term as reality.'

I shuffled on the sofa, but once again my tic was absent. I was becoming more comfortable here. Scrope's refined intellectualism made me feel a bit thick, but the message was starting to come through and it was ringing bells inside me. How could it not after my transcendent episode, which had suggested my reality box was constrained and inaccurate?

'How do *you* know about the car crash? Don't tell me you were there as well.'

'Albé and I do talk, you know,' he said, eyes glimmering. 'Have you assimilated the experience yet?'

'I'm working on it. It was… super real. I can't help thinking it's closer to what happened than my previous memory.'

'We've found that to be the case time and again.'

'Mmm. But even if it is close to the truth, and I'm not to blame for Sis's death, I'm now finding myself wondering why she died and I didn't.'

'Would you rather she had survived and you died?'

'Yes.'

'Is that because of your suicidal tendencies?'

'No, it's just because… hold on. How do you know about my suicidal tendencies?'

'As I say, Albé and I talk.'

'But how does *he*… eugh. This is all so hard to get my head around, Scrope. How can he possibly have access to my mind? To my memory?'

'Do you really want to know?'

'Well, I think so, but I'm scared. What has Fernanda got to do with it?'

'She's the lynchpin.'

'Meaning?'

'Meaning, she is a special person. She has access to places we don't and she brings us things we would otherwise not have.'

'You're riddling me, Scrope.'

'It's not intentional… well, maybe a little. But Albé's back tomorrow morning, so I'll have a word with him and we can let you in on what's happening here.'

'Orchid-24?'

'Orchid-24.'

***

I returned to my room. Boatswain was sprawled over the bed. He didn't bother getting up, but his tail started swishing when he saw me, and I flopped down next him as he elicited grumbly excitement.

'What am I going to do, fella? I'm supposed to be collecting faerie folklore from old people, but your master's been inside my head and I'm starting to question reality. This isn't what I came here for. Have you got any answers?'

He whimpered and slobbered his tongue over my face. I held on to him, smoothing the fur on his head and gently fell asleep as orchids, Fernanda, the hanging faerie, the crash, and ultimately Sis drifted through my internal vision before seeping into my dreams, where they all intermingled and became different, distorted versions of their usual reality.

XXIX

The weather had turned. It was only the beginning of September, but the sky was bruised with ominous intent and a yellow hue began to appear on some trees. It was the time of year Sis had been smashed to pieces. I loathed September and the darkness it heralded.

As Boatswain and I came back towards the hospital grounds from our morning walk, the drizzle turned persistent, and by the time we got back to the TRU, it was lashing down and we were both soaked. Inside, he shook himself off and then saw Moore coming down the corridor. He greeted him as if he knew this meant Albé was back.

'You're wet, Blondie,' said Moore, winking and ruffling Boatswain. 'Looks like you need a good rub down.'

'Yeah, thanks. How was the festival?'

'Oh man. A mixed bag to be honest. The sound was awful, conditions were atrocious and there was a persistent scent of urine everywhere. But we were near the stage for Hendrix and there was some potent acid doing the rounds, so we got through it all. Don't ask Fletcher what he thought though—he spent most of the time in the tent moaning about being forced to live in a refugee camp with hundreds of thousands of people. But Albé got to hang out with Miles Davis backstage, so he's happy.'

'Miles Davis? I hope Albé hadn't taken the orchid.'

Moore looked at me with a slanted eye, 'Not that I know. I've heard Scrope has been talking to you?'

'Yes, a little bit.'

'Well, it's probably time you were introduced to our alchemical means of operation. But I also hear you have a hot date with Fernanda at the Shervage Arms on Friday. I might join you in order to reacquaint myself with the charming Miss Dyke, if that's all right. Don't worry, I'll leave you two to it. I wouldn't want to interrupt anything.'

'How do you know about that, Moore?'

He just winked again and made off towards the Observation Room. I went back to my room with Boatswain, towelled him off, stripped, dried and lay on the bed staring at the ceiling, waiting for the next intrusion into my existence.

Ten minutes later, it came. The intrusion was Albé. He came into the room more reliant on his cane than usual and I guessed the festival experience had taken its toll. Boatswain was all over him, standing on his hind legs and almost knocking him off his feet. After a few minutes of excited repatriation, Albé sat on the chair, Boatswain locked to his legs.

'The poor dog; in life the firmest friend, the first to welcome, foremost to defend. How have you been doing, Blondie?'

'Up and down. Moore tells me that you met Miles Davis.'

'Indeed. He's a nice bloke. But these famous musicians live in a different world… and talking of different worlds, I think it might be time for you to come and understand what we're about here. Would you like that?'

'I'm scared, but I do want to understand. I'm not going to like it, am I?'

'Well, you need to keep your mind open. There are many mysteries in this world and we need to maintain a gnostic attitude: if you experience something directly, you sometimes just need to take it at face value. Your experience the other day should have taught you that. The nuts and bolts world is just one world. It intersects with others. What's the William James line… *Our normal waking consciousness, rational consciousness as we call it, is but one special type of consciousness, whilst all about it, parted from it by the flimsiest of screens, there lie potential forms of consciousness that are entirely different.*

A wise man, James. Come on, let's go. You're safe with me — you must know that by now. Come.'

He commanded Boatswain to lie down with a raised finger, and off we went.

***

I hadn't been in the lab before. It was pervaded by the peculiar floral scent and I felt high in an instant. Albé shuffled me past a table with some clunky machine and test tubes resting at angles. He stood behind me with his hands on my shoulders, massaging them and bringing his lips to my ears.

'So this is Orchid-24,' he whispered. 'Don't try to look at it for too long.'

The plant appeared to hover above the sill of a sash window. Its form was in a translucent bubble, rotating, glistening. It didn't look like an orchid, but then I couldn't be sure as it kept shifting like light through a kaleidoscope and I was unable to focus on it. It seemed to be making a low buzzing sound, but I couldn't tell if this was coming from somewhere else in the room. It kept changing colours, and after morphing through some blues and purples, it transitioned into pure white and then... and then, a colour which was not a colour. I jerked and looked away. A sudden nausea drew up through my stomach.

'As I say: don't try to look at it for more than a few seconds. We're not used to gazing into its world. It is here, but it's also not here.'

He left me and went over to it. I watched from my peripheral vision. His hand passed through the bubble, which became momentarily diffuse, and he skimmed a finger over what appeared to be a petal. It dripped over his hand and he licked it. Then he did it again and brought the liquid substance to his lips. He came back to me and held me close.

'We don't need to inject it. It is potent in its original form.'

He kissed me and stood back. His lips tasted like nothing else I'd ever known. I quivered, still nauseous, as a purple cloud drew down to obscure my sight. I looked into his eyes behind the mist and then at the orchid, now shimmering and formless.

'Albé… I… I….'

'Just stay calm. Allow it to do what it does. We'll be together again in a moment. I promise there'll be no car crash this time.'

The moment passes. The bubble that contains everything I know is once again penetrated. I'm overwhelmed with a sudden tidal wave of understanding from elsewhere. But I can make no sense of its otherness. It is transcendent. It is Albé. His every thought and memory wash over me for an instant — a confused babble of love, poetry and patients — but he's in firm control, and in another instant he's taking everything from me and giving me nothing in return.

We are in a dim-lit circular enclosure. It is as substantive and real as the lab we'd just been in. I think it is underground, but I don't know how. I am seated next to Albé, and there is some kind of celebratory feasting going on nearby. There is a gathering of entities. They are nearly human but not quite. They are singing in a foreign, alien tongue and they seem to meld into the background and back again as if they don't quite belong within my visual range. There is music, such beautiful music, coming from I know not where. The entities skirt around us, aware of our presence but reticent. Their thoughts go through me, like wine through water, and alter the colour of my mind. They speak to me in whispered, half-recognised tones, filling up my experience as if they are my own memories. My folklore and their real presence drift into the same thing, the same memories, even though what they are inserting is alien and ancient.

One of them finally approaches us and offers us a silver goblet to drink from. It has massive, black, almond-shaped eyes that take up half its head. I think of a hanging entity with the same eyes, but I cannot make the connection.

'My lord,' it says, bowing and turning its tiny mouth into what might pass for a smile.

Albé holds up his hand in rejection. It bows even lower and then drifts away back to the celebration, which seems both close but also an immense distance away.

'We can't drink or eat anything here,' says Albé, his words echoing in my head as though they are my own. 'If we do, we'll have to stay. You might like that, but I don't recommend it.'

'Where are we?' My words come out in slow motion. I can see them moving from my mouth into the thick atmosphere like smoke trails.

'Halfway between life and death. You might like to call it Faerieland. This lot are the handmaidens of the eternal. Their reality is not like ours. Their space-time is different, but there is an overlap. The overlap is where we are.'

'Why are we here?'

'Because here I can communicate to you with meaning. Think of it like a dream where the feeling and direct knowledge is everything. If I tried to explain to you back in consensus reality using words as metaphors, it wouldn't mean as much. Here you'll just get it. It's just my mind connecting with yours. Notice how we don't talk.'

This is true. Albé is putting the words in my mind without talking. But no… it's more than that—the words are not words but images that form the communication with utter resolution. The nuances and ambiguity of language are bypassed.

'Are you ready?'

'I think so.'

The meaning comes with a deep symbolic residue. The meaning is transcendent. Language does not convey it, but it translates with this accord:

'The orchid is a gift. These entities, faeries if you like, live in a larger consciousness. They are creatures that exist closer to the collective unconscious and operate accordingly. They have no material reality as we think of it, but under certain circumstances, they can manifest in our reality. They've been doing it for a long time, which is why we have all the folklore about them. You know all about that. But their modus operandi is different from ours. They have a different morality. They don't care about many of the things we care about, which is why they sometimes appear as immoral bandits. But they do know that consciousness is everything. They aren't stuck in the materialistic, reductionist thinking prevalent in our world. And, ultimately, they want to help us. They want to help us understand our minds. So when a special person like Fernanda comes along who is willing and able to take them at face value, they react. They've given her the orchid to pass on to humanity. In the right hands, it can be used to access people's minds and to cure them of all the insanity our modern world has infected them with. The orchid is metaphysical. It's not real in any sense we understand. But it has manifested in our reality — alchemically — and we can use its attributes to cure and heal. Like I say, it is a gift. And like all gifts, it needs to be fully appreciated and used wisely. It requires reverence. The faeries gave the orchid to Fernanda. She gave it to us. We have a responsibility. You've seen our patients. They need help. The orchid allows me to get inside their minds and to get to the bottom of things. It works.'

'Mmm.'

'We're here because of you. All that faerie folklore rattling around inside your mind; it's brought us to an archetypal faerie place.'

'Yes. How did you know about not drinking or eating here?'

'Because I have access to your knowledge, Blondie. That's just how it works.'

'Mmm. I guess this puts paid to solipsism. I don't think I'm me. I feel quite ill.'

'I know.'

'Yes, of course.'

The enclosure begins to spin and an extended vision shows some orchids gesticulating in alcoves. The faerie entities begin to mimic this and form a circle where they dance to the music, which now has a sitar added to it. The Indian ambience is out of place but also in place. They come close to us and want us to join in. I manage to look at Albé, although the optics are skewed and melting into the background. But he looks nervous. I am amazed to see this.

'Time to go, Blondie.'

'How?'

'How do you get out of a dream?'

'Force of will through fear?'

'Yep.'

A faerie breaks the circle and slithers over to me. It is female, I think. Her body writhes and moves in an impossible way. Her elongated fingers touch mine and her black, bulbous eyes come to within a few inches of my face. She forces out Albé's thoughts and transfers something to me. Again, they are not words. They are images of Sis reclining on a flower bed, surrounded by some type of energy pattern, winding around her. The imagery refocusses and I see the energy is a myriad of creatures; more faeries I guess.

The vision is now accompanied by words, real words, whispered into my ear: *'She is with us. She awaits transference to the infinite. She waits for you. Shall you come now?'*

Albé grabs my arm and grips hard. There is a heaving lurch and I slide downwards… no, upwards. I vomit. I pass out to blackness.

The blackness is nothing but it is everything. I stay here for a long time. No body, no memory, no thoughts, just emptiness. It is peaceful. Oh, it is peaceful. Why do I not just stay here? But what is *I*? There is nothing. There is only void.

XXX

I come to. What is the difference between past and present? Are they the same thing? For now the present must again become the past.

I came to. There was a blanket wrapped around me and someone was holding on to me from behind, spooning me. I captured the surroundings; it was the Observation Room and I was on the sofa. I shuffled around, a headache coursing through my brain. When I'd turned enough, I looked into Fernanda's eyes, glinting purple as always. She put her cheek to mine and whispered some soft Spanish I didn't understand.

'How am I here?' I croaked.

'You needed some help,' she whispered. 'Albé has been taking advantage of you. I have told him off. *Las hadas* are not too happy. But now *shhh* and let me hold you. You need it.'

I slumped into her arms. I wanted to turn around and kiss her; feel her. But I knew I couldn't, so I just luxuriated in her embrace. She caressed me and carried on whispering Spanish words in my ear. I drew down and passed into sleep.

***

When I woke up again the headache had cleared. I sat up on the bed in my room. Boatswain was gone and I was on my own. I had no idea how I had got there. There was an ambience of twilight, which I confirmed by getting up and gathering in the dusky aspect from the window. I thought I could hear the faint sound of a sitar. It drew me back to the faerie enclosure. I closed my eyes and attempted to piece it together. The memory of Albé's voice echoed in my head, but when I tried to visualise the faerie gathering, I started to feel nauseous again and I sat back down. The floral scent lingered and I assured myself of the concrete reality around me by getting up, touching the desk, the typewriter and then myself. This brought Fernanda's touch to mind. It aroused me.

***

And then I was sitting on the sofa in the common room. Again, there was no linear memory to tell me how I'd got there.

'This will be the residual effect of Orchid-24.'

Albé's voice echoed, but after a moment of disorientation, I clicked back into a solid state and looked around. The next time he spoke, I appeared to have reached an equilibrium. There was no echo.

'I think the dose may have been a little high, Blondie. We should have administered it intravenously again, rather than directly from its being—always impossible to measure what we're getting that way. I must apologise. And turning up in a faerie hollow hill might not have been the best way to get some of our ideas across. But your mind is stronger than you probably think. You've soaked yourself in the folklore for months… and because of your sister… so we kind of got dragged there. And because I'm part reliant on these entities as arbiters of a metaphysical realm… well, that's where we went.'

He was sitting on the other end of the sofa. I focussed in on him. He didn't look right. He was even paler than usual and was not meeting my eyes. I followed his gaze across the room. Fernanda and Augusta were sitting on the other sofa. I gaped for a moment and blinked hard to make sure this wasn't another *residual effect*. It wasn't. Augusta got up, swaggered a little, and came over to me. She sat down and hugged me, ensuring her breasts pushed into me.

'Albé's had a telling off from Fernanda.'

I glanced over to Fernanda. She was pouting. Was she jealous? I realised this was the first time I'd seen her and Albé together.

'My dear brother thinks everyone can deal with this mysticism as well as he can. He should have been more gentle with you.'

She shot a look at him and then kissed my cheek. I tried to collect myself but the tic came back to my face and I attempted to cover it with my hand.

'I don't… I don't think it was Albé's fault. I was willing. I kind of knew what to expect after last time. It was just so… dramatic… so real, but also unreal.'

Fernanda got up and came over with us. I found myself squeezed between these two beautiful women, holding on to me for different reasons.

'We need to be careful with otherworlds,' said Fernanda. 'It is not a game. *Las hadas* do not trust us. They know what we want but they are jealous of their gifts. They will only allow intrusion into their realm with conditions. You were both lucky to come back.'

Augusta appeared to sense the connection and moved over to Albé, who suddenly seemed to have lost his usual overbearing presence.

'Well, as a punishment,' said Augusta, tweaking Albé's forelock, 'Fernanda, Blondie and I are going to take a walk out into the countryside together, and you're not invited. And just to make it clear that we're all angry with you, we're going to take Boatswain too. I would ask Moore as well, but he'd probably think I were suggesting some sordid sexual transaction, so it'll just be we three and the woofer. You can stay here and ponder your indiscretions.'

She sidled up to him and kissed him on the lips. They exchanged a knowing look.

'Are you ok walking into the dark?' asked Fernanda.

'I guess… yes, why not?'

The impression this was all stage-managed was strong, but the chance of strolling off into the gloaming with these two overrode any suspicions of previous collusion. Augusta produced a torch from nowhere and off we went, as Albé settled back into the sofa, curling his lip as always.

***

The darkness was complete. The dusk was long gone and the sliver of a first-quarter moon illuminated nothing, so we were reliant on Augusta's torch. By the time we reached the grove, she was labouring and Boatswain was tight by her side as if he realised she needed protection. Fernanda took her arm for the last stretch and we sat down by the log, now rendered into a different form by the blackness and the occasional beamed sweep of the torch.

'Are you all right, Augusta?'

'Yes, yes. This might have been a little impetuous, but Albé needs to have his wrists spanked every now and then. He'll hate the thought of us out here in the dark talking about him.'

Fernanda laid down a blanket she'd brought and the three of us sat down close to each other, Boatswain going down in instalments beside Augusta.

Augusta found our eyes for a moment in the torchlight. 'You should probably know that I'm pregnant.'

Fernanda had her in an embrace in an instant and began to whisper Spanish into her ears. To my surprise, Augusta replied in Spanish. I felt suddenly locked out. I expected the tic but it didn't come. After a minute, Fernanda drew me to her side and the three of us held on to each other. Augusta began to sob.

'It wasn't planned,' she said through the tears. 'I hope you won't judge me.'

'Why would we judge…'

I realised in a second what she meant. Fernanda stroked her face and kissed her.

'We would never judge you, sweet lady. *Niños* are always a blessing if they come through love.'

I envied that kiss, and I disliked myself for doing so.

'Thank you, Fernanda. I appreciate that. But some people will not see it that way if they found out… most especially my husband. But what is done is done. And please — no word to Moore or Scrope, or anyone else. And before you ask, yes, Albé knows.'

Some minutes passed in silence. Augusta's hair fell over me and I luxuriated in the closeness of Fernanda's body. Augusta gained control of her tears and stiffened up a little as though to announce the moment was over. She shone the torch on her face and screwed up her nose. We all laughed and Boatswain whimpered along with us.

'I wasn't going to tell you, but I think you two might be a bit special, so what the hell. And anyway, this isn't why we're here, is it? Albé asked me to come because he knows I can talk people down after difficult experiences. For all his intellect, he's clumsy when it comes to the aftermath of a numinous adventure. He just thinks we're all as clever as he is. His compassion leaves something to be desired.'

'And you are *compasivo*, sweet Augusta,' said Fernanda. 'We know this.'

'Well, maybe. And please put aside what I've just told you. Let's leave that for now.'

There was a movement of acceptance, imperceptible but real. We all got it and shifted accordingly. We held each other's hands and allowed the moment to die. One minute of communed silence allowed Augusta to compose herself and speak as if her previous declaration had sunk.

'I do know he took you back to the car crash with your beautiful sister, Blondie. And now he's been taking you to other places. I see why he does it with the disordered souls in this place, but I'm uncomfortable with him taking people like you back to traumatic moments and then slipping you into these unknown realms just to make a point. And giving you Orchid-24. It's intense enough when it's a one-way trip from his side, but when two people take it at the same time… well. Do you understand what happened?'

'Sort of. I'm still trying to work it out. Can I ask you if you've ever been under the influence of it… the orchid?'

'Yes, once,' she said, breathing out a sigh. Her tears had dried and she was refocussing. 'Albé took me back to our childhood; showed me the connection we had there in order to explain how we are now. I've talked to Scrope about it. He likes to see us as animus and anima—the blood connection provides a deep understanding of each other… makes the love more intense and spiritual. It allows us to understand each other at a… at a transcendent level. There must be something in this. I love Albé more than anything… even my children. That sounds awful, doesn't it? But it's the truth.'

'Mmm.'

I glanced at Fernanda, her eyes somehow still purple in the darkness. 'Can I ask you what this is, Fernanda? What is the orchid?'

She wriggled on the blanket and looked between us. She was almost like a faerie herself. She stroked our hair in turn and paused in stillness, only the leaves above us rustling in the gentle breeze. Augusta switched off the torch as if in recognition of the need for her words to be spoken in obsidian blackness.

'*Las hadas*… the faeries. You must know by now that they exist. They are in another world though. Their world is different from ours, but it is a real world and they are real. I have known them since I was a little girl. When my father took advantage of me, they came to help. Nobody else did. When I told people they laughed and brushed me off… how do you say…'

'Ridiculed you?'

'Yes, ridiculed me. But I knew they were real because I talked with them and they were the only ones who cared about me. They were in my mind but also outside my mind. When I came here to England they were still with me. They were different somehow, but I knew they came from the same place.

Over the years we grew trust. Do you know how hard it is to trust anyone or anything? I think you probably do. And once here, in the hospital, they have been my friends… my only friends. When I saw all the madness and sadness around me, I asked them for help; what could they do? Some of them dislike humans, but others are more *compasivo*. They gave me twenty-three gifts. Small gifts. They helped me. But then I asked for something to help all humans with an illness of the mind. Their twenty-fourth gift was the orchid. It has been grown upon the soil of their world with thirsty roots. I took the gift and gave it to Albé. I recognised him as someone who could use it to cure people. People need to be cured. The faeries let me do it. I realise most think me mad, but Albé and the TRU people do not. And they have benefited from their trust. They have something from another world, which allows them to see into the minds of others and cure them. They have overcome their prejudices because they know it works. I am pleased about this. That is all.'

I gravitated on this for a minute. I knew she had insights I didn't, just like Sis. But I felt the need to say something. 'What is it about the twenty-fourth gift? Is the number important?'

'I know not. Humans have twenty-three pairs of chromo…'

'Chromosomes.'

'Yes. Maybe the gift is the extra pair… to make us different. To give us something from another place. Why are there twenty-four hours in a day? And twenty-four elders in the Bible? There are twenty-four major and minor keys in our music. The maths of it are important; nonagonals and Harshads… but I forget what I have been told of this. *Las hadas* know the answers. I do not. They just gave me the twenty-fourth gift and I was grateful.'

I tried to take this in, but her words were subsumed, redacted. The twenty-fourth moment slithered into the nether regions of unknowable things.

There was a minute of silence, broken only by the distant hoot of an owl. I looked at Augusta for her reaction to Fernanda's words, but the darkness hid her face. I'd had two cosmic journeys dosed up on the orchid—three if I included the visit to the Pigots—all of which had formed more intense memories than anything else in my life. Another person had penetrated my solipsistic consciousness and taken me to places that should not exist in any physical framework: the past and another dimension inhabited by non-human intelligences. But still, my rational instincts would not give way. The faeries did not live in an alternative reality, Orchid-24 was some kind of impressive hallucinogenic trick being played by Albé and co., and Fernanda was suffering from a delusional psychosis instigated by some childhood trauma. The world was just a collection of matter and, as Dr Dawkins would suggest, our experience of it relied on an epiphenomenon produced by our brains. But… but I could close my eyes and see Sis's face after one of her communions with her faeries. She had known something I didn't. And now her place had been taken by Fernanda. However much one part of me wanted to put her in a box—made easier by her being a patient in a psychiatric institution—I couldn't get away from a creeping truth that she, just like Sis, knew more than me. I'd been duped by my society, by my culture. She was outside of this indoctrination chamber. She was connected to things I was not. And knowing I was falling in love with her made everything more difficult.

As the silence atrophied, I sensed both Fernanda and Augusta were on the verge of needing to say something. Me too. But we were spared any forced words by Boatswain letting out a noisome, rasping fart. It broke the moment and we all laughed. Boatswain looked up, unaware of any indiscretion, and received pats and cuddles for his trouble.

'You speak truth, Boatswain,' said Augusta, still chuckling. 'I think it's a sign we should get back.

It's getting chilly and I think Albé's been punished enough. I feel the need to go to him. And as for you two… you'll need to help each other, I think. You seem to have a lot of freedom in the hospital, Fernanda. I'm pleased. You can help our friend here, even though you're the one with the diagnosis. I think you do need help don't you, Blondie?'

'I guess I do.'

'I'm sorry if I haven't expended any great words of wisdom to help you down from your orchid trips. But maybe a walk out into the darkness with a flatulent woofer was all that was needed.'

'Ha. Yes, maybe.'

She switched the torch on, the blanket was folded and we made our way back, arms in arms, Fernanda and Augusta chattering away, sometimes in English, sometimes in Spanish, me silent and coaxing Boatswain along whenever he disappeared behind a hedgerow. When we reached the hospital, Augusta hugged Fernanda.

'I hear you two have an appointment at the Shervage Arms on Friday,' said Augusta, holding her back at arm's length.

'We do. I have never been in an English pub before. Alcohol and faerie stories. It will be of interest to me.' Fernanda came to me and lingered a kiss on my cheek. 'See you Friday.'

She turned quickly and vanished into the building. Someone was wailing within and Augusta stood for a moment, her concerned face dimly illuminated by the lights of the hospital.

'I hope she'll be ok,' she said, taking my arm again. 'That place frightens me. But she seems to deal with it with aplomb, and she's certainly allowed more freedom of movement than the other patients. I guess that's what happens when you come here with a lot of money behind you… I hope her, and your, faeries are real.'

'So do I.'

She looked at me and took my face in her hands.

'I know you are in love with her… please, don't dissent. I know. Just be careful. Love can cross any boundary. I should know. But those boundaries are well constructed. Most people don't like them to be breached. You two were meant to be, but that's not how others may see it. So be careful.'

I allowed her to caress me for a few moments.

'And what of you, Augusta? Will you be ok? The boundaries in your life must seem… well-constructed right now.'

'Don't you worry about me. I'm stronger than you probably think. I know the score.'

We walked up to the TRU arm in arm and in silence. She kissed me goodnight, dragged Boatswain off, and I slunk into my room to attempt to put my mind in order.

XXXI

Friday came and my mind was still not in order; quite the opposite. The memories of my orchid experiences had become dissolved and confused with subsequent dreams. In one I had been in the faerie enclosure and Sis was their prisoner. They were more maleficent than during my experiences, and there was the dreamlike understanding they were torturing her and would continue to do so for an indefinite period, perhaps until I died. The dream ended with transference to the car (E-Type or my father's; I couldn't tell), which was packed with faeries, who whispered in unison in my ear at the moment of impact, before shouting the last words: *It should have been you. It was meant to be your ANNIHILATION.*

I woke from this amidst screwed up sheets and sweat. I wondered whether these intense dreams were another residual effect of the orchid, and if so, how long would they continue?

As the afternoon drifted on, I began to sink into the thought I might be losing my reason. I'd been in this place for over a month and been confronted with varying levels of insanity and gnostic events at every turn. What had I expected? It was a psychiatric hospital and I was in the part of it that dealt with an insanity I had never even contemplated as possible. And the treatment involved mind control powered by a non-physical substance. Christ — I'd even taken it. Was I descending into the arena of the unwell myself? I'd come to all this after months of relative isolation. If I were to be viewing my situation from an external, objective position, I might think an ensuing madness was the most likely possibility.

As the carriage clock chimed four o'clock, I knew I needed to extract myself from the unrestrained self-analysis before the planned meet up with Fernanda and Moore for our trip to the Shervage Arms. I hadn't even collated my notes on the people we were supposed to meet. I looked at the clock. It was a modern digital clock. Its red illuminated numbers showed 4:24. I stared at it and attempted to stay calm. I blinked. It was the carriage clock again. The time was 4:25. Its sound took over the room: *tick-tock, tick-tock, tick-fucking-tock*. I walked over to the bedside table, took it in my hand and flung it against the wall. It smashed and fell apart. No more tick-tock. Immediately, I felt guilty, as if I'd killed a living being. I picked up the shattered pieces and started apologising to them. This was an all-consuming process but at some point, I turned around and realised Moore was standing at the open door. We looked at each other. He had an expression on his face I hadn't seen before. I dropped the remnants of the clock on the bed.

'Moore... Moore. I'm sorry. I'm not feeling too good. I think I might not be able to make it tonight.'

He came over to me and put a tentative hand on my arm.

'Just stay calm, you'll be ok. There can be some side-effects to the orchid. We should have prepared you a little more, maybe. I'll get Fletcher to make you some tea. And Fernanda will be here in a minute. She's probably the best person to help you out right now. Sit down and we'll be back.'

He left. I cleared up the remnants of the clock and sat down on the bed, staring at nothing. I don't know how long passed, but my reverie was broken by Fletcher holding a tray with a steaming teapot, and Moore and Fernanda behind him. Fletcher put the tray down to one side and Fernanda sat on the other, taking me into an embrace.

'*Mantener la calma*,' she whispered, stroking my hair and kissing my cheek. 'You are with friends.'

'Am I?'

'You know you are.'

Moore nodded to Fletcher to leave and off they went without a word. Fernanda drew me up the bed and we held on to each other. I had longed to hold her like this, but now it felt somewhat frozen. I was embarrassed. She was supposed to be the patient here, but now I felt as if she were protecting me from my inabilities to deal with existence. We held each other close. She whispered Spanish I didn't understand. I nestled into her and felt sleep coming. I held out for as long as possible, wanting to make the most of it, but after a few minutes, I passed out.

When I came round she was still there, her eyes only inches from mine.

'You are a twitchy sleeper,' she said. 'Your dreams must be exciting.'

'Yes, sometimes.'

'Do you still want to go tonight? We do not have to. It is your decision.'

She drew away from me and smiled.

'We should go. I don't want you to miss out on a Friday night at the Shervage Arms with old English people talking about the faeries. And Moore has his barmaid to attend to. Yes, let's get up and go.'

We pulled apart, but before she extracted herself from the embrace, I held on a little tighter.

'Thank you, Fernanda.'

'For what?'

'Just thank you.'

***

We found Moore out the front of the TRU ordering Epsilon about. He was trying to fix the mechanism that drew the passenger seat back in the E-Type.

'Fuckin' thing won't fuckin' fuckin'.'

'Well, give it a bit of a bash.'

Epsilon looked wide-eyed. 'Lord Albé though. If I bash 'ee car, 'ee'd bash me. Fuckin' right 'ee would.'

Moore pulled him away, took over and managed to crank the seat back a little. He stood up, brushing his hands, and saw us.

'Ah, here you are. The two best-looking individuals in the hospital. You're gonna have to share the seat, so Epsilon and I have been trying to provide the maximum legroom. I think this is as good as it'll get.'

'I'm sure it'll be fine,' I said, trying to give Epsilon a smile. 'It's not far. But Moore…'

'What?'

'No Van der Graaf Generator, please. I'm not in the right frame of mind for it.'

'To be sure. I knew you'd say that. And so, in honour of our recent trip to the Isle of Wight, I've managed to procure some Miles Davis for the eight-track.'

'*Kind of Blue*, no doubt?'

'Come on, Blondie. You know me, I'm always bang up to date. You can listen to his most recent offering: *Bitches Brew*. It's a bit out there and free-form, but I promise to keep the volume down, and there'll be nothing like Peter Hammill's Dalek impersonation.'

'And you won't drive too fast.'

He held his hands up. 'As God is my witness. I'll drive us there as carefully as my Aunty Méabh would.'

'Can your Aunty Méabh actually drive?'

'Well, not officially,' he said, smiling and slapping Epsilon on the back. 'But when she does she never exceeds 30 mph, and so neither shall I. Come on, get in.'

Epsilon held the door open for us and stared wide-eyed at Fernanda as if she were a supernatural entity. We climbed in and wrapped our legs together in the enforced proximity. Moore got in and started up the chunky engine, headlights illuminating the frontage of the TRU. Epsilon slammed shut our door and stood to wave as we backed up, turned around and headed for the lane.

'What's Epsilon's story?' I asked, as Miles Davis's polytonal saxophone and trumpet wrapped around us and the headlights brought out the trees arching over the lane in the early-evening gloom.

'He's a local. He was homeless. Brought into the hospital about six months ago with a mania. He'd totally lost it. All over the shop. They dosed him up of course, but Albé took an interest and managed to extract him from their clutches. You can probably guess the rest by now. After some sessions with us, he became calm and has been at the TRU ever since. I don't think he's got anywhere else to go. You've seen what he's like – Fletcher's always moaning about him. But he's harmless and as long as you can accept his constant f-ing and c-ing… well, he's ok. He's useful. And we like to think we've saved him from a pretty awful existence.'

'Indeed.'

'But what about you, Blondie? Are you all right? Albé only lets certain people take the orchid. It can be… unpredictable.'

Moore glanced at Fernanda, who remained silent and impassive.

'I'm ok. I think I'm ok. There's just some strangeness, some weirdness that I can't quite work out. You know about what happened to me; my sister. Having it all exposed makes me feel… vulnerable. And you must understand that the way this drug, this orchid works… it's unreal, but it's also super-real. And I never came here for this. I came here to take notes from old people talking about their grandparents' stories about the faeries. What's happened has made me a bit out of sorts. I never expected it, and I'm not sure I can deal with it.'

I felt Fernanda's hand on mine. She stayed silent, but I realised she was the hub of all this. Moore knew it and I knew it. And she knew it.

'I get that, and I'm sorry I slipped you a Mickey a few weeks ago,' said Moore, giving me a sidelong glance. 'We can get a bit ahead of ourselves here sometimes. But the bottom line is that we just want to help people, and Fernanda's gift is of potential cosmic significance. We want to utilise it to help those who need it. But, of course, if the secret gets out then things will come crashing down pretty soon, because in this world people aren't gonna accept any type of alchemical solutions to psychiatric problems. If Dr Dawkins got wind of what we're really doing, he'd probably call in MI5.'

Fernanda squeezed my hand harder and placed it on her thigh. Moore noticed and rolled up his lips into a grin.

'And it's not to be taken lightly, as you've found out. Albé's got the psychic strength to use it unilaterally but for others… well…'

Fernanda spoke for the first time. 'I just hope you have not been using my friend as a pig guinea.'

'A guinea pig?'

'Yes. *Las hadas* know what we do, you know. If their gift is abused, they will take it back… and I may be the one to be punished. I do not mind punishment, but the gift needs to be kept sacred. It is magic. We should not abuse magic when it is given to us freely and with generosity. I have talked with Albé about this.'

Moore stiffened up and frowned. 'I know, I know. Albé, Scrope and I have had a few words today and we'll be tightening up protocols. I promise. I'm sorry, Fernanda. You know how we appreciate you.'

For a moment I saw something like anger sweep over her face, a new expression for her, but in a second she lightened and reached over to squeeze Moore's knee.

'Ooh madam, don't do that, I'll lose concentration and we'll end up in a ditch. And if I put Albé's Jag into a ditch, I think I'll need to leave the country immediately.'

Fernanda laughed. Her laugh penetrated me and broke the tension that had begun to permeate the enclosed environment of the car. Moore picked this up, gabbled some more and slithered the conversation over to our impending interviews at the Shervage Arms.

'So who have you got lined up, Blondie? Lots of old folk?'

'Well, yeah. Mr Goodfellow sent a letter saying there's been a bit of banter about the Londoner wanting to know about faerie folklore, and I think they're queuing up. I don't think I'm quite in the right zone to deal with it, but this is what I'm supposed to be doing and I know Goodfellow has been in contact with Professor Hobhouse, so I guess I just need to get in there and take the notes. I'm glad you're both with me. I wouldn't have been able to walk in there on my own.'

'Don't worry, you'll have our full support. Got your notebook?'

'Better than that; I've got the Olivetti.' I held it up from the car floor. 'Get everything straight into type.'

'Blimey, they'll think you've beamed down direct from the Starship Enterprise with that bit of technology.'

'Ha, maybe. But Goodfellow did mention one person who sounds genuinely interesting—a young girl with a recent experience. We'll see how that goes.'

Miles Davis had got into some echoing trumpet sounds, and Fernanda swayed along to it.

'I like this music,' she said, garnering an appreciative nod from Moore. 'He is a spiritual person. I think he knows things.'

'I think you're right, my Chilean friend. But we'll have to leave him until later, cos we're at our destination. Are you feeling ok, Blondie?'

'I'm ok. I'll have to be, won't I?'

'You'll be fine. They'll love blathering out their stories to you.'

We parked up and got out into the damp, chilled night air. Fernanda took my arm and Moore strutted in front of us to the door.

Mr Goodfellow was outside smoking his pipe, evidently waiting for us. 'I'm so very glad you are here,' he said, taking my hand with enthusiasm but with the usual brief look of bafflement. 'Your presence has aroused much interest in the community, and there are quite a few for you to meet tonight. And thank you for going over to the town and meeting the Methodist congregation. And…'

He went on for another minute or so, gesticulating and tangenting off onto a subject about which I soon lost the thread. Once he'd calmed down, he tuned to Moore and Fernanda, shaking hands formally with the former and laterally with the latter.

'Come in, come in. It's a chill evening. Come in.'

Moore was straight to the bar with his eyes and mind on Elizabeth Dyke. Fernanda held my hand—I couldn't work out if it were to support me or to protect her. Goodfellow took on an air of authority and waved us over to a table with the promise of drinks.

'Is there a plug socket here?' I asked. 'I'll need to plug in my typewriter.'

'Plug in?'

'I have an electric typewriter. I'll need a socket. I need to take my notes on it.'

Goodfellow looked at me without an answer, but Moore slipped in and suggested he'd sort the issue. After a conversation with Miss Dyke, we transferred to another table where I could plug in the Olivetti. Goodfellow, still looking confused, brought pints of cider to us and then invited some locals over, who had evidently been hanging back in the recesses. The pub was less than half full, but as per our previous visit, there were a couple of guys at the far end of the barroom plucking out some ambient folk tunes into the smoke-filled atmosphere.

After getting the typewriter set up, I zoned in to the half a dozen or so old people who had gathered around the table. Goodfellow bustled around and sorted out seats for them, and after some pleasantries, he drew into a monologue about the importance of local folklore and how it needed to be kept alive, and how this was facilitated by the local folklore society. He then introduced me as a pre-eminent university folklorist from London. I baulked and glanced at

Moore at the bar, smirking and watching proceedings. Fernanda gripped my hand tight.

'But our young folklorist is a serious person,' said Goodfellow, waving his hands around. 'The research being done here is important. I want you to know that whatever you can convey tonight will be treated with absolute discretion. Our friend here is recording a country folklore that is being forgotten as modernism takes us all over. Everyone here at this table knows something about our faerie traditions. We need not be ashamed of this. This fine young... person, realises this and wants to ensure our regional folklore is not lost. So please, tell what you know, without fear or shame.'

The group made a small round of applause, and then, emboldened, started to open up with stories about the faeries. They appeared to have discussed their approach beforehand and so each spoke in ordered turn while the others sat back a little. I just needed to smile, encourage, and attempt to project an air of authority, which I didn't have, but which they thought I had. This was enhanced by me sitting with an electronic typewriter on the table and Fernanda at my side conveying wordless looks at them. We must have appeared an exotic pair. Whenever I shifted my peripheral vision to Moore at the bar, I could see his smiling eyes. I was sure he was thinking the same thing.

First was a woman of about seventy. She spent a few seconds trying to focus on me, knitting her brow in the usual bewilderment, and then gave a sweet smile to Fernanda who, despite her foreign dusk, seemed easier to assimilate. She looked around at the others for encouragement and then began a story about her mother at some indefinite point before the First World War. It was the usual thing: the faeries appeared and drew her into a dance, which she felt compelled to join in. A few hours later she was found dishevelled and delirious and thinking she had only been there for five minutes. The testimony was honest and valid, but I quickly realised this was where we were going, just as in my previous field visits. The stories were going to be from the past, disconnected from the present and safely placed into an indistinct memory of previous generations. It was folklore, but it was transported into the past, where it became acceptable and palatable.

The other interviewees conformed to the trope. The faeries were real and appeared in reality in different forms, but the testimony was always removed by one or two generations. By the time I heard the last story — a father being lost on the moors, after being lured there by a band of faeries, and then being saved from sinking into the bog by a luminous female — I realised this was all far removed from my own gnostic experience of supernatural entities. The sincerity of the stories could not be doubted, but what did they *mean*? Whenever I glanced at Fernanda, she just gave a knowing smile.

I typed away at the Olivetti with diminished enthusiasm. I kept smiling, always smiling, but I knew this was adding little to understanding what the faeries were about. I tried to maintain the thought this was all grist to the mill of what I was supposed to be here for. But after looking into the black eyes of real faeries, alive and dead, it all seemed a bit tame. Perhaps I should have smoked another orchid joint, enabling the stories to become lucid and present, as at the Pigots.

The last chap wrapped up his story and I sat back in the chair. But I'd forgotten about the girl. Goodfellow appeared from the background and ushered her through the congregation. One of the old guys who had given a testimonial made way for her and she sat down. Fernanda immediately perked up. So did I. She looked a little like a younger Caroline Lamb: maybe sixteen, blonde, furtive eyes, distracted.

'This is Mary,' said Goodfellow. 'She's got a story to tell. I'm sure you'll take it seriously.'

'Of course.'

I glanced at Fernanda, already stiffening up in her chair, and then at Moore, resuming his interest in what was going on after drifting away to the bar and Miss Dyke, uninterested in supernatural stories from long ago. I plugged into the resonance of Mary's potential. She bristled with it. She flicked her nervous eyes to me and then around the gathered group.

'Do you have a story for us, Mary?' I asked, putting on my most soft-toned voice. 'You can trust us. We very much want to hear what you've experienced.'

Christ—I realised I sounded like Albé or Scrope talking to a patient. Maybe I'd picked up the technique. Mary looked at me blankly for a few seconds, then at Fernanda. As soon as she'd met her eyes, there was a softening in her face. She relaxed into the chair and began to talk, her local accent distinct but iterated into a cadence almost hypnotic.

'I want to tell you about something that happened about a year ago. Down on moors. I been told I dreamed it, but I know it weren't a dream. And I need to tell you something first.'

'Of course, take your time.'

'My sister, my little sister, and my dad died two years ago. They were killed in a car accident.'

A wave rushed through my head. The blood pumped in my neck and I clutched the seat, hoping the tic wouldn't take over my face. Fernanda took my hand under the table and stroked it. I sipped the cider, part to appear calm, part to wet my suddenly dry mouth. One of the women held on to Mary's shoulders in support. Mary gulped a bit and recomposed herself, smiling at Fernanda, maintaining eye contact.

'I'm so sorry to hear that, Mary.'

'I thank 'ee for that. But I been much upset. Mum has had such a hard time since it happened. I'm sorry to bring it up but it has much relevantness.'

'We understand, Mary,' said Fernanda, speaking for the first time. 'We understand these things. We really do. You poor thing… and your *Mamá*.'

Mary reached her hand over the table and Fernanda took it. She retained her hold on my hand under the table.

'So, since they died I been having lots of dreams about them. At least I think they be dreams. Me and my sister always loved faerie stories and dad would always be telling us about the faeries hereabouts and their goings-on. Sometimes Sis and I would spend hours at the bottom of our garden playing games... faerie games. She always saw them and danced about with them, but I could never see them. It always disappointed me, but I never doubted her. And anyways, this all stopped after they died... obviously.'

She welled up for a moment. So did I. The woman holding her shoulders bent down to hug her and Fernanda continued to grasp her hand. After a minute she came back.

'So... so, during that first year after the accident, I kept dreaming about Dad and Sis. They always be with the faeries. But the faeries didn't have wings and suchlike, they be like you and me, only different. They were strange. I was always frightened of them and afraid for Sis and Dad to be amongst them. In the dreams they, the faeries, always played this music and danced around. The music was beautiful but it was also scary. There be a word beginning with S... what is it?'

'*Siniestro,*' said Fernanda.

'Yes, yes. Sinister it was. It made me afeared. I always woke upset. This carried on for a long time. I always thought they be trying to tell me something... something important. But I never remembered it.'

Moore had joined the table, glinting at me and Mary. I had the feeling he knew what was coming.

'So then a year or so ago,' continued Mary, 'I be down on the moors. I got into the habit of going there. It's quiet and peaceful and I would sit resting against my favourite tree looking out on small lake. I sometimes fell asleep there, it being summer and warm. But this time I swear I was awake. There was a change in the air. It was like before a thunderstorm but there was no storm. And I heard the music like in my dreams. But this was not a dream.' She took a breath. 'There were creatures there. They seemed to crawl out of the earth… but others came from the water and then there were others in the air and some seemed to come from the sun itself. They were of different looks but all seemed like humans, only changed into something weird. Only the ones from the sun were different—they were like lizards or snakes. I was afraid but I couldn't move. Then one of the airy types came up close to me and comforted me. She was the most beautiful thing I've ever seen. She told me to *look deeper*. She seemed to be in my mind. And when she touched me I saw Dad and Sis. They were with these faeries, hovering over the water, although I could not tell how. They were sort of altered to be the same as them. Same as the faeries, I mean… I got the feeling they were trapped and I didn't know how to contact them. But within a moment they were brought to me by the faeries. I could see the light in their eyes. And this be the strangest part. I still cannot think it was real, but I know it was. My dad looked at me as he always used to and smiled a sad smile. He said: *we are dead but we are dreaming. We are dreaming of you.*'

I bit my lip and breathed hard. I hoped nobody noticed.

'I passed out then. It had been too much for me. When I came round all was still. No faeries, no Sis and Dad. There were just the lake, the reeds and the tree. But those words were still in my head. Many people won't believe me, but it's what happened. It wasn't a dream. I know it wasn't. I've had some dreams about all this since, but they are weak. There has been nothing like this since. It feels like Dad and Sis have faded, though I still see them both so clear in my memory of that day. And Dad's words… and the faeries. They comfort me when I think on it. So… um, that's it… that's my story. I hope you don't think me so odd.'

There was a silent resonance. Even the folky guitar noodlings had ceased. I looked at Moore and then Fernanda and then at Mary. I knew the ball was in my court. I realised I'd typed almost nothing during Mary's testimony. I attempted to pull together an air of authority through the whirr of my distraction.

'You are a star, Mary. Believe me, I know you are telling us the truth and we don't think you odd at all. I really do understand what you've told us… I really do.'

Without words, she stood and came around the table to us. She hugged me.

'Thank you, thank you. I knew you would as soon as I see you. You have a special look, and your London voice… I'm sorry, I don't mean to be rude.'

I laughed and kissed her cheek. She then drew over to Fernanda, who had stood up.

'May I hug you too? Apart from the faerie by the lake, you are the most beautiful person I ever seen.'

They embraced. Fernanda held the sides of her head and drew her back slightly, staring into her eyes. A silent instant passed and Mary nodded as if a message had been conveyed.

'Thank you,' she said, tears welling up. 'I know, I know.'

There was a dispersal, genial words from the old folk, some more platitudes from Goodfellow, and then I was left with Fernanda and Moore, who brought more cider, even though our first pints weren't half-finished. He clinked our glasses with his.

'*Sláinte mhaith.*'

'Cheers.'

'A successful night I'd say. Lots of material for Hobby, happy locals and a story of some dynamism from young Mary. You conducted yourself well, Blondie. I know her story must have touched a few nerves.'

'Indeed.'

'And as an added bonus, I have contrived to arrange a trip to our local spa town with the increasingly delightful Miss Dyke on Sunday. Things are looking up.'

Another hour and we were on our way back through the night, Miles Davis in the air, a joint passing between me and Moore, and Fernanda's hand stroking my thigh.

XXXII

We get out into the frigid misted evening. Moore bids us goodnight and slinks off.

'Would you like me to come with you?' asks Fernanda.

'To my room?'

'To your room.'

'But isn't there some sort of curfew at the hospital? Do they know where you are?'

She just smiles and touches my lips with her forefinger. Two minutes later, we are in my room with our lips together. Our tongues slide around, and our hands are all over each other's crotches. My mind revolves, and her soft Spanish seems to be directed straight into my head without the need for spoken words.

'*Telepatía,*' she whispers.

'Mmm.'

We are quickly naked, bodies locked together. She is stronger than I would have thought and pushes me onto the bed then climbs on top. She kisses me deep and moves down, rubbing her breasts against me and lingering over my nipples and belly with her mouth. When she reaches my genitalia, she looks up for a moment, eyes flashing big and purple. I put my fingers through her hair.

I spread out my legs further, and then lickety-split, she licks my clit. I come like a steam-train.

XXXIII

I woke up and rolled over. Fernanda was gone. I was disappointed and relieved at the same time. I hadn't had sex since Sis was killed and making morning-after small talk may have been beyond me, even with Fernanda. I sank my head into the pillow and luxuriated in the drift into and out of sporadic dreams.

Before the dreams came, I dwelt on the sex; the exquisite touch of her nakedness and her deft way of making me orgasm again and again. I'd never known anything like it. But I'd never known anyone like Fernanda. I was wet again at the thought of her. Then I drifted into a light sleep and was once again in the Shervage Arms, where Mary became a more forceful personality, marshalling the old folk into some type of mesmerising dance as she told me again about her faeries.

I transcended from the snapshot dream and looked to the dull morning light coming through the window, but fell asleep moments later. This time there was a noose dangling before me, and the faerie from the *cobertizo* was putting her head through it. As soon as it tightened, she transformed into Fernanda and then into Sis, who was smiling but crying and reaching out her hands to me. I tried to get up but couldn't. This faded and Caroline Lamb was with me, seducing me and telling me us girls must stick together. I asked her who she really was, and she told me she was many. She merged back into Fernanda and I woke up again with the feel of her tongue rolling around my mouth. I wished to be back in that dream. I calmed my breathing and a minute later I was. But Fernanda had become Albé. I felt him penetrate me. He was deep inside me, and as I rocked back in surprise I realised he'd reached to my brain. When this happened I suddenly found myself in the E-type, with Sis at my side holding a melting orchid and Albé still inside me. We were in the faerie hollow hill and something momentous and disastrous was about to happen. I gasped, pulled Albé out of me and once again transcended back into waking reality. It was like coming up from underwater and suddenly being able to breathe again.

My heart thumped. I sat up in the bed and assimilated the dubious nature of the last subconscious rambling. The details soon began to fade, but the essence of its message remained. It upset me, but I soon put that to one side and fantasised once more about Fernanda. The imagery of the previous night was strong in my mind's eye, and I brought myself off again, shivering, moaning and grasping on to the bedstead. At that moment I wished she'd stayed the night.

I relaxed back into the bed and thought I'd drift back off into sleep. I looked for the carriage clock but realised I'd smashed it up. I had no idea what time it was. But I still thought I heard it: *tick-tock, tick-tock*. The ticks turned into footsteps and the tocks turned into a knock on my door; at first soft and then loud. I manoeuvred in the bed.

'Can you give me five minutes?'

'I'll come back in ten.'

I hadn't come to. I couldn't quite work out who it was at the door. For a moment I considered whether it was part of an extended dream. But I sat up and satisfied myself this was reality. A few seconds passed. A voice, which was not my own but which was inside my head, punched out the words: *What is reality?* I stiffened for an instant and wondered whether this was the voice of insanity.

'Fuck off.'

There was no reply. I got up and dressed.

***

Ten minutes later Fletcher came knocking. He asked if I'd like to come along to a conference in the common room at noon at Albé's request. I assented and asked no questions.

Before I headed off I scanned through my notes from the previous evening, slowing down when I reached the few sentences I'd typed from Mary's testimony, which ended abruptly due to my wanting to listen rather than take notes. I closed my eyes and visualised her face. This became mixed with my dream version of her, and within seconds her story was convoluted, vying for space in my mind with the image of Sis and the faeries who seemed to swarm behind my eyelids. I rolled the sheet of paper into the Olivetti and typed: *Dead but dreaming*. Why was this phrase haunting me? What did it mean?

I jittered off the chair and stood to look out the window. Clouds were low and the ash tree was bending in a strong wind, which was taking off some of its browning leaves and whipping them about in the air. The gloom of the morning leant an oppressiveness to the scene and I could only take it in for a few moments. What was Fernanda's word? *Siniestro*. Yes, there was something sinister about this day. It was beginning to dull the glow of the previous night's sex. I was in full-blown love with Fernanda. I knew it, but it was starting to be buried under the usual malignant disquiet. I closed my eyes again and saw the noose. For a moment, the faerie swung within it once more. It appeared more real than a memory. But if it weren't a memory, what was it? Was the orchid still in my system, dictating alternate realities?

I kicked the chair and slammed down the lid of the Olivetti in an attempt to ground me back into normalcy. At least my face wasn't ticking. I watched myself in the mirror and then got out the small bottle of mascara I hadn't used since being here. I flicked it, inexpertly, over my lashes and then decided to put on eye shadow as well. The small container had lasted me two years and still wasn't half empty. I applied it and stood back to inspect in the mirror. What did I look like? How did others see me? Did it matter? I took in my reflected image again, then the swirling tree outside, and finally my beige room. Things had changed. This was a moment of change, even if I couldn't discern why. I spent a minute to calm my breathing then left for the *conference*.

***

Moore was outside the common room ruminating with a joint. He saw me at the last moment. His face turned into a grin.

'Blondie... blimey. You're looking very good. Very, err... *gnéasach*. Is this the Fernanda-effect?'

'Thanks, yeah, maybe. What is this all about?'

He drew back and offered me the last of the joint. I took it and ensured it was inhaled deep.

'Well, I don't really know yet. This is why we're here — to find out. But from my brief chat with Scrope, it's not good I'm afraid. There's some news of a previous patient. You've met him... Edward.'

'From the Methodist chapel?'

'Indeed. He's been caught kiddy-fiddling and so the vultures are circling us, as we treated him recently.'

'Kiddy-fiddling? Oh man. Who are the vultures?'

'Who do you think? Dr Dawkins et al. But come on, this is why Albé's called us in for a conflab. You probably don't need to be here, but it's perhaps best you are. Polish off the smoke and we'll join 'em in there.'

In the common room, Albé and Scrope were sat at the table in discussion, while Fletcher and Epsilon bustled around pouring out coffee and arranging sandwiches. The hospital sister who had been with us that first morning with Caroline Lamb was also at the table. She looked at Moore and me as we came in. As her gaze fell on me, she coughed and put her hand to her mouth. I repeated her gesture and stared at her for a few seconds. I didn't feel great for doing it, but hey.

'Thanks for coming, Blondie,' said Scrope, lingering his look for a moment and glancing at the impassive Albé. 'You're under no compulsion to be here, but as you are resident here at the TRU, we thought it the right thing to do to invite you along.'

'Thanks, yes, sure.'

Epsilon completed his sandwich arrangement and retreated to the sofa, never taking his bugging eyes off me. Fletcher took a chair at the table but drew it back a few respective inches and put his chin to his chest.

'Ok,' said Scrope, joining his hands together. 'Help yourselves to coffee and sandwiches' — we did — 'but also brace yourselves, because the news isn't good.'

I stiffened up and attempted to ignore the nurse and Epsilon still staring at me.

Scrope continued. 'I'm afraid that Edward T. has been arrested for the rape of a minor. We don't have all the details, but it appears to have happened three days ago and involved a girl, age eight, in the town. He's in custody.'

I pictured Edward at the chapel holding on to the little girl's pigtails. His face took on a demonic aspect as my cannabis-enhanced memory worked over the scene.

'Now just to give a bit of relevant history, for you, sister… and you, Blondie, and to refresh our memories,' continued Scrope, reading from some pages before him. 'Edward was admitted to the hospital on twenty-fourth March this year after what were called *minor indiscretions* with two children in the town. He was certified under an unknown psychosis. He then came to the TRU on the first of April after it was suspected he might be suffering from Hysterical Neurosis, Dissociative Type. ICD-8 300.1. We carried out the usual observational assessment and subsequent therapy, which appeared to demonstrate he was subject to multiple personalities, one of which was a male with a sexual predilection for children. This personality took the name of Jimmy and appeared manipulative and unapologetic about his desire to sexually abuse children. It was discovered that Edward was sexually abused as a child by an uncle and that this personality was most likely a representative of this person, who had been able to take control of Edward at various times, which had increased in frequency over the previous year.

'As is usual in these dissociative episodes, Edward had only a vague recognition of Jimmy and no knowledge of the episodes, although he admitted to an attraction to young girls. We undertook five intensive therapy sessions, all recorded, at the end of which we were satisfied that Jimmy had been... expunged from Edward's personality. At the end of his time here, Edward seemed calm and resolute, although there continued a persistent sub-character within his consciousness — a nameless young girl, who would appear only for a few seconds at a time. I believe we have recordings of this, Moore?'

'We do.'

'But we were satisfied with his condition, and so he was returned to the hospital for a further five days of monitoring and then discharged back to his home on twenty-fourth April.'

'So,' said Moore, wriggling in his chair. 'Are you saying that the Jimmy personality had not been dealt with and that he's reappeared in the last few days to commit rape while in control of Edward?'

'That may be the case.'

'But that's not something that can be laid at our door, is it? I mean we have the tape recordings of the sessions, and it was the hospital that discharged him, satisfied he was ok.'

'The thing is, Moore,' said Albé, piping up for the first time, 'he was, as usual, sucked out of the hospital by us and given his primary treatment here. Therefore, there is going to be some further investigation of our techniques. And although the tape records will record our sessions in the Observation Room, there may be some questions asked about those *techniques*. And as you may imagine, Dr Dawkins will be wanting to shine a spotlight on us rather than accept any responsibility for discharging a child abuser from his hospital. I'm sure he'll be very keen to divert any police investigation from the unimpeachable wards of the hospital to the shadowy goings-on in our unit. And if that happens we will have some questions to answer about our… procedures.'

'This is bullshit,' said Moore, getting up from the table and waving his arms about. 'We did our best to treat a severely ill, mentally ill, patient and then the hospital discharged him after they'd had him there for five days. The fact he's reverted to fiddling with some young girl after a few months can't possibly be our responsibility.'

'He raped her, Thom. She's eight.'

'But that's not our fault, is it?'

'Maybe not, but the main point here is that, because of the seriousness of the case, there will be some closer scrutiny of our methodologies here at the TRU, encouraged, no doubt, by Dr Dawkins. And not to put too fine a point on it, if there is a police investigation that penetrates the TRU, there will be some questions asked about the transcendental narcotic we've been using to carry out our therapy. You may imagine what the local CID might think about Orchid-24 and how quickly they would pass it on to some higher government authority. I don't think I'm being paranoid here… I'm just attempting to view our procedures from an outside perspective. It is unlikely to go down well.'

Moore slumped back in the chair and scowled. I glanced to the sister, who was creasing her face in discomfort. Albé must have seen either her grimace or my look. He allowed a few seconds of silence and then asked her what she thought.

'I don't know,' she said, wringing her hands. 'I have no idea of your methods here. Only that they have had remarkable success. This is just an exceptional case, is it not? I will certainly suggest to Dr Dawkins that your willingness to invite me here today shows a desire for transparency. He's not a bad man, you know. He just wants the best for the hospital. He'll just be concerned that situations like this will reflect badly on us at a time when there is much pressure on our institution. You know this.'

She and Albé exchanged an inscrutable look before he gave her an appreciative nod.

'Thank you, sister. We're grateful for this. I hope you'll take back this conversation to the hospital in good faith... *sans* the rather direct descriptions of the good doctor obviously. But I think we've covered the matter at hand, and now there is something else I need to discuss with my colleagues in private, so please excuse me if I ask you to leave us now.'

She smiled, flicked a final glance at me, and allowed Albé to walk her to the door. Before she left, he whispered in her ear and she returned an earnest nod. There was something stage-managed about the act but I couldn't get under the skin of it and so pretended to ignore it, sinking into my chair amid the uncomfortable silence in the room. Scrope and Moore looked at each other knowingly, Fletcher twiddled his fingers and Epsilon rocked about on the sofa, still unable to take his eyes off me.

'Don't worry comrades,' said Albé, limping back to the head of the table. 'She's on our side... well, mostly.' He looked at me, lips twitching. 'And I think you saw Edward T. more recently than any of us, Blondie. What were your impressions?'

I blushed. 'Yes, a few weeks ago, at the chapel. He was a little creepy... but that might be nothing more than hindsight after what I've just heard. He was tugging on a little girl's pigtails. I didn't like it. I hope it wasn't her who he abused. I was more interested in the children telling me that they all began having interactions with faeries after his return from the hospital. That was... odd.'

Moore and Albé exchanged a look. I felt I'd said enough and kept my mouth shut.

'Yes, that is rather odd,' said Albé, averting his eyes and causing a pregnant silence. 'But we'll have to leave this for now. There's not too much more we can do until we receive further word on the matter. Perhaps I'm being unreasonable about the possible consequences. We shall see. But I wanted everyone here in the picture in case things start to happen, and I wanted our nurse friend to take the news of our awareness back to the hospital.' He sat back and sighed. 'Meanwhile, I fear we have a second issue. Fernanda's father is about to pay a visit to the hospital.'

I tightened up. Scrope blew out a minor-key whistle and Moore slumped.

'When?'

'I'm not sure but it's imminent.'

'Why?'

'To see his daughter, Moore.'

'Well, yeah, but why now? He hasn't paid much interest for the last year or so.'

'I don't know.'

'Does Fernanda know?' I asked.

'Well, Blondie,' said Albé, getting up from the table and coming to stand behind me. He put his hands on my shoulders. 'She doesn't, and I was thinking it might be best for *you* to break the news to her. You two have become quite close. She'll trust you more than any of us.'

'Even you?'

'Even me. I think she'll be unhappy at the news. She'll need consolation. Is this all right with you?'

'Well, I guess. Yes, ok. When do you want me to tell her?'

'I'm afraid it might have to be right now.'

I swivelled around. Some mascara had dusted into my eye and I blinked as I stared at him inches away.

'Right now?'

'She's in the vegetable gardens at this very moment. When she gets back into the hospital, the news will be awaiting her there. Much better to come from you.'

The buzz began to fill my head along with Albé's unspoken words: *You need to earn your keep, Blondie. You're not just here for your faeries.*

***

I walked past the laundry building, the wind tunnelling through the gap between it and the hospital. I squinted and lowered my head into it. Nausea ran through me. The last time I saw Fernanda, only hours ago, we were clinging on to each other naked. Now I was the messenger of something that felt like doom. Things were going to change, and I easily catastrophised this into various negative endgames. I wanted to look into her eyes so much, wanted to hold her. But our beginning now felt like an end. A phrase entered my head, I knew not from where. Was it Albé putting it there or some dim-remembered schooling? A Greek author… Sophocles — how did I know that? Wherever it came from, he spoke truth: *No one loves the messenger who brings bad news.*

I saw her red jacket. I stopped and watched. She was feeding the ravens from her hand. It should have enchanted me, but there was instead an ominous quality about it, as if she had at that moment become separated from me, confirmed as something beyond what I was. I steadied my breathing and marched towards her. When I reached the vegetable patch, the ravens took off and she turned to me and smiled. I hesitated for a moment and then moved quick to her. We held each other and kissed. I smoothed her face, ran my fingers through her hair and felt like Judas.

'You have painted your face. You look lovely with or without, you know.'

'Thank you. Fernanda, I —'

'You have something to tell me, do you not? But first I need to tell you: *te amo*. Whatever happens… *te amo.*'

The tears gauzed my vision but I held on to her a little longer and whispered, 'I love you too… I do… I know I do.'

She kissed me again and ran her fingers over my cheeks. A few seconds of silence passed. There was just the wind exercising its remit from who knew where.

'Albé has sent you to tell me some news, no?'

'Yes. He wants me to tell you… he wants me to tell you your father is coming to the hospital.'

She drew me into a tight hug. When she moved back, the tears were running down her face but she maintained her smile. Her watered eyes glinted the usual purple. It was a juncture of moment. We were entwined — our minds were entwined. I realised this was the first time love had utterly taken me over. The first time I was blending into another. I began to whirr through how we could run away together; just take off and get away from the storm we both knew was coming.

'Fernanda, why don't we just —'

'Shh.'

She kissed me once more and I tasted her tears.

'We could only run away so far, you know. Life would catch up with us. It always does.'

'And you always read my mind.'

'It is just something I am good at.'

We held on again, kissing deep as her soft Spanish words passed into me and mixed with all the racing thoughts in my mind. But as with all moments of intensity, it slackened after a few minutes and we dried each other's eyes. I calmed my breath.

'What do you think your father wants? May I ask that?'

'Of course. You can ask anything of me. He will want something for himself. That is all he ever wants. And he is used to getting it. He cares nothing for me. But there must be something about me being here that is causing him problems. That is why he comes. He is brutal, cruel… *despiadado*. But what can I do? I must accept it.'

'But why don't you and I just—'

'He is a powerful man, my friend, my love. We would soon be *moscas* caught in his web.'

'What about Albé—could he help?'

'Maybe, maybe not. But first I need to find out why he comes, what he wants. You need to trust me in this. Do you trust me?'

'I do. Of course I do. But this makes me so anxious. I feel you're in danger. I want to protect you, but I know I can't. I don't even know when he is due. All I know is that it'll be soon.'

She stroked my hair. 'Shall I come to you tonight?'

'Um, yes… yes of course. Can you?'

'I will con… con… What is the word?'

'Contrive?'

'Yes, I will contrive it.'

A nurse started up the path from the hospital with a cordon of female inmates, huddling against the squalling wind. We put a foot or two between our bodies, hands lingering for a few seconds.

'Send Fletcher over to the kitchens tonight,' she said. 'I help out there sometimes, and he is always there looking to be with Miss Rood. He will arrange my passage. We can talk more tonight in private. And we can make love.'

My heart pumped. But the arrival of the troupe from the hospital obliged me to bow and be gone after a final lingering eye contact. The wind swished around me. It matched the delirium rooting itself in me.

XXXIV

The noose is before me but it swings from nowhere. Outside its elliptical confines, a perverted version of my university room resides in peripheral vision. Within the noose, a spectrum of reality makes itself known. It is some kind of review. There are faeries everywhere, somehow latching on to everything that is happening. My father shouts at me, Sis hugs me, girls kiss me, Albé swishes around like a god, the car smashes into smithereens, Edward pulls blonde pigtails with awful relish, Caroline Lamb splits into a hundred selfs, Augusta cries out in childbirth, Boatswain froths at the mouth as Epsilon approaches him, the black-eyed faerie swings from her noose, Moore and Scrope drive the E-type at 100 mph along a country lane (but the car is also the Observation Room), Gloop ejaculates and apologises, a train pulls into a station and the station-master recites some deranged version of the twenty-fourth psalm, ending with the phrase: *You are God*.

The scene calms. I am by a brook, which I recognise and don't recognise. I am a little girl and I am frightened. There is menace in the woodland. There are things moving in the undergrowth and I don't like them. As I cover my eyes, I am hugged from behind. I know it is Fernanda. She brings much love and compassion. She whispers in my ear. I don't understand what she says, but the words comfort me. I turn to look at her but she is gone. And now the hospital is before me. It shimmers as if in a heat haze. The shimmer turns into a shadow. The shadow morphs into a man. The man is a threat; an unhealthy threat. He approaches me slowly. But I look down and see an orchid growing at my feet. I reach down and rub its petals between my fingers then put them to my lips. The faeries dance around me, then come to a standstill. They put their mutating arms in the air and shout in unison: *Transcendence.* I waver, trying to focus on their ever-transforming faces. They laugh and then shout again, so loud their voices become distorted vibrations: *ANNIHILATION.*

I wake up.

I woke up and shifted myself to sit in the bed. The dream shuffled around, fading away bit by bit. The elements of it drifted, but the image of the noose and the shadowy man remained strong. I closed my eyes and attempted to bring it back. I knew it meant something deep, but I couldn't get hold of it. Why were dreams so abstruse? Why did they not just give me their messages in direct fashion?

I looked for the carriage clock. It wasn't there, of course. I had no idea what time it was or whether Fernanda would come. I sank back down into the pillows and began to drift again. I wanted to stay awake and be a part of what was about to happen. The thought of Fernanda's touch made me long for her presence. But there was a greater movement within me. I wanted to sleep and dream. My dreams were chaotic and sometimes terrifying. They became quickly violate. But something made me realise they were more real than real. They contained the same intensity of my contact with Fernanda. The love we found ourselves in was everywhere in my dreams — they were drenched in it, even when they were laced with horror. I slunk off into sleep again, pondering the possibility of Fernanda being with me in person and also in my dreams at the same moment. I wanted all of her: body, mind and dreams.

I'd been up for ten minutes when there was a knock at the door. I bit my lip and shook a little.

'Come in, it's open.'

Albé came in with Boatswain at his heels. My disappointment must have been all over my face.

'Good evening, Blondie,' he said. 'I know you probably didn't want to see *us* right now.'

Boatswain came over for some fuss. I gave it to him half-hearted. Albé sat down on the bed and patted beside him. I joined him at a distance, and Boatswain settled down on the floor below.

'I told Fernanda about her father coming. She was upset.'

'I know. Fletcher's been over to the kitchen tonight. Fernanda wanted to give him a message for you. She's been curfewed. She's been locked up. Her father is coming tomorrow evening.'

'Tomorrow?'

'Yes. And as predicted, we're also getting a visit from some CID inspector tomorrow afternoon regarding Edward T. Looks like it'll be an interesting day.'

'Is Fernanda ok?'

'I don't know. Fletcher didn't see her. He just got the gossip from Miss Rood.'

'Can't you find out? Use some influence?'

Albé sighed and rested back on his hands: 'We're not magicians, Blondie. Despite what you may have come to believe, there's only so much power to be wielded. Orchid-24 is an incredible gift, but it doesn't make me, or anyone else who takes it, omnipotent.'

'It seems that way. You can get inside anyone's head you want to. Can't you just override anyone in your way and free Fernanda?'

'Free her to do what?'

The heat bristled over my neck and face. For the first time in over a week, the tic began playing at my eye.

'I'm just... just worried about her. She cried when I told her about her father coming. She's been abused by him.'

'Oh, I know. He sounds like a nasty piece of work at every level. He'll most probably want to take her away from here. She may be an adult, but she is under a certificate, and as her father, he's going to be able to call the shots and do whatever he wants with her. Nobody in the hospital knows about their past history.'

'Even if she tells them?'

'She's diagnosed with a psychotic neurosis. She tells everyone about seeing and interacting with faeries. She will be believed by no one. He is a wealthy, powerful man with lots of influence. He will win the battle.'

'But can't you do anything? Can you not just get inside his head and stop him?'

Albé curled his lip and moved closer to me. I expected the buzz, but it didn't come. He smoothed back my hair.

'Maybe. But it might make matters worse. It would be a Pyrrhic victory. We could probably make a monkey of him, but then he'd come back with renewed vigour.'

'But what about the orchid? Without Fernanda, you wouldn't have it anymore. How would you do what you do at the TRU without it?'

'That's a prescient point, young lady. Perhaps we just need to accept our time here is done. I don't like it, but all things must have their day. We started here without Fernanda or any access into metaphysics. We just began with Scrope's Jungian psychoanalysis and some ideas how that might be applied to people with many minds. Fernanda's presence here was synchronicity, as Jung would say, and we just plugged into it. Do you think I want to relinquish the power this magic has given me? Of course I don't. It's helped dozens of people who would not have been helped in any other way. We've saved them from annihilation. A couple of years ago, I would have laughed at any notion of a non-physical world existing alongside our own and containing a bunch of characters like the faeries. But as soon as you have direct, gnostic access to it and find out their presence can be transferred to our own reality by something like Orchid-24... well, you simply accept it, as you accept anything previously unknown which becomes known. Most people, and certainly the psychiatric fraternity, would find it unpalatable. But that's just because they haven't experienced it. If they took Orchid-24 they'd quickly change their minds. They'd have to.'

I squirmed around. Albé had seemed like a god since I'd been here. Now he appeared degraded somehow — stripped of his powers. His reasoning was sound and logical. But I didn't like it. I wanted him to be in control. But all the while my mind slithered back to Fernanda.

'And what about Fernanda? You can't just allow her to be taken away. She'll suffer… and she's… she's done so much for you.'

Albé sat up and placed his fingers together. 'Are you sure this isn't just your own feelings for her making a special proposition? I know you're in love with her.'

'Do you?'

'Come on, Blondie. Even without magical alchemical processes, anyone could see you two are in deep.'

'Is that why I was really brought here? To fall in love with her and continue your connection?'

'Maybe.'

'Mmm. Well, I'm feeling pretty shit about it now. I just want to see her and talk with her. She must be feeling afraid and alone right now. I hate to think of her wrapped up in one of those cubicles.'

'Me too. Do you want to go to her?'

'How…? Ah, right.'

'Well, you know how it works by now. We don't need any weasel words. I give you a sip of the liquid from the bottle in my pocket — Moore's made it into a tincture — and you'll be with Fernanda in her beautiful mind in seconds. You would usually need to be closer to the subject, but you two are connected by love, and that trumps physical closeness. I'm confident that you'll be with her in an instant. If it were anyone else, I wouldn't do it — too risky. But as it's Fernanda, and it'll be you turning up, I don't think there'll be any problems. Your choice of course. But there's a distinct chance she'll be taken away tomorrow and you'll never see her again. I know what I'd do.'

He removed the little brown bottle from his pocket and handed it over to me. I took it, looked at it and saw the swirling purple liquid speaking to me from inside its glass confines. I popped the tiny cork, looked at Albé for a few seconds and then swallowed the lot.

'Happy trails,' he said. 'Remember, love is the only reason we are here. Love is all.'

After a minute the room swirled as if I were stoned. I looked into Albé's eyes. They were kind and cruel. But they faded. The buzzing took over and the purple descended over my vision. This turned into spangling lights, which overwhelmed the room. I was on my way somewhere else.

XXXV

Where is somewhere else? Where is my mind? It appears to hover in a ward of the hospital. I can't be sure of this because everything is so spectral. There is a base light; an illumination that seems to come from nowhere, but I know I'm not seeing with my eyes. Is this a dream? No, it's too concrete and I can control the environment around me. I sense Fernanda and go to her. She is waiting for me — she knows I am coming. I breeze into her mind, and we are at parity. I now have access to her memories and she to mine. We recognise what is going on and decide to abscond somewhere else. The orchid has freed us. We know it will not last long. We need to make the most of it, and the cubicle is stifling.

Now we sit with our backs to a rock beneath a Queñua tree; a shrubby bulbous thing, which seems to grow out of nothing. The mountains make their distant form against a pristine cyan sky.

'I used to come here in the summer as a girl with my mother and Maria, one of my sisters. It was a refuge.'

We put our minds together, and in an instant, the background is made clear. The mountains and the tree become special, imbued with meaning and purpose. We think about the brutality we have left behind and the way this pristine landscape heals all that has gone before. We understand — together.

A creature peers from behind a rock, only a few feet away. It takes the form of the Queñua tree but steps toward us. It smiles. Or is it snarling? We reach out to encourage it and ensure it knows we are friendly. It stalks around, looking at us with suspicion.

'*¿por qué estás aquí?*' It asks.

'Why not?' We ask.

'This is the past,' it says.

'So you speak English,' we say. 'Do all faeries speak English?'

'*Táimid go léir.*'

'Now you sound like Moore.'

'*Español, Irlandés, Inglés…* it is all the same. Our cousins have given you something special. They have given you the twenty-fourth moment, have they not? That is why you are here. The past is the present. Your love is strong. Me can tell. How else could you be here? You have been helped by the orchid, but love brings you here. However, you have seen enough of this memory. You will now move on.'

Sis embraces us as we shiver amidst the autumn willows overhanging the brook. The damp fills our head, and we have a longing for the mountains and the open spaces. But the love warms the gloom. We hold on to each other. Are we two or three? It doesn't matter; we are really one. We kiss and embrace. We manifest.

The faeries turn up, of course. They join in. They can't resist a group hug. They then break off and start dancing and singing, and in moments they begin to meld into the willow trees so that soon they are indistinguishable. Sis looks at us with black eyes.

'I'm with them. You're not. Not yet… despite your magic orchid. Off you go. You'll be back. You'll come across the brook when you're ready, but for now… farewell. I love you.'

'We love you too.'

And now we are back in the cubicle. It is restrictive, but we are able to hold on to one another, whilst knowing we are one. The warmth makes it ok. But after a while, there is a split. Things are coming apart. Fernanda is now Fernanda.

'Whatever happens,' she says, her lips quivering over mine. 'Whatever happens, you need to know I love you. *Te amo.* I cannot love you as your sister did. But whatever happens to me, I need you to know I did everything I could. Sometimes life is too over… how you say?'

'Overwhelming.'

'Yes, overwhelming. I am glad you came to me tonight. I knew you would. Our bodies are weak, but our minds are strong. We will always be at one here.'

'Fernanda.'

'Yes?'

'Is this real?'

'It is as real as you want it to be.'

'Well, I want it to be. But I can feel it fading. Can you?'

'For now. But this place will always be here. We will always have it, even after death.'

'Even after death?'

'We may be dead, but we will be —'

'Dreaming.'

'*Sí.* You need to go now. I can feel it.'

'Me too. I don't want to leave you.'

'You never will. We should kiss.'

We kiss. The kiss moves somewhere else… somewhere else. I am back in my lumpen self. It's not where I want to be. I'm in my room. I sink into the pillow. I'm exhausted. I move directly into dreams. But they are dim and unremembered. How could they be otherwise on the back of such numinosity?

I woke up a few times in the night. Each time I tasted tears.

XXXVI

I got up late and made straight for the common room. Moore was outside the door, smoking a ciggy. He was agitated.

'I'm afraid you can't go in, Blondie,' he said. 'Albé, Scrope and Dawkins are in there with a couple of coppers.'

'About Edward?'

'Ai. I've just been discharged. Not that I had much to offer the conversation… actually, that's probably why I was asked to clear off.'

'What are they asking?'

'Oh, it's all quite preliminary, and Albé's all over them of course. But I get a bad feeling about it. Dawkins seems intent on clearing any blame from the hospital and seeding the idea that we might be to blame for incorrect procedures, et cetera.'

'Can I ask if —'

'Yes, he's got the orchid working for him. I advised against it. It might raise their hackles… make them more suspicious. But Albé does what he wants. You must know that by now.'

'Indeed.'

'Come on. I need some air and a joint. Let's get Boatswain and take a walk. I believe we have some September sunshine.'

There was September sunshine. The wind had turned to stillness as we walked up the same lane we had taken to the Shervage Arms a month before. The late morning contained the heat of a summer day. Boatswain liked to always be in front of us, but whenever he sensed too great a distance, he would circle around and come back for reassurance with his canine smile exaggerated by his lolling tongue.

We exchanged the joint back and forth, and as its effects made themselves known, we moved from everyday chatter to matters of greater moment.

'You realise this is a big day, don't you?' he said, polishing off the joint and flicking the roach into the hedgerow lining the lane.

'Yes, I think so. Which is most important — the police visit or Fernanda's father's visit?'

'Good question. Both have the potential to terminate what we've been doing here at the TRU.'

'How so?'

'Well, if the police decide we're worthy of further investigation, they're gonna find out about our... unorthodox techniques. And while they might be unwilling, or unable, to take any legal action, you can rest assured it'll get into the press and then we'll have journos crawling around asking questions. You may imagine what they'll do if they get their hands on any of our session transcripts. There's already an accumulating agenda demonising psychiatric hospitals on the back of Enoch Powell's machinations, so they'll have a field day with us. Letting out a kiddy-fiddler after we'd apparently cured him of his neuroses will just be the crack in the door. And if they discovered Orchid-24... well, you can guess the headlines in the *Daily Mail*, can't you?'

'Do you not think you're... what's the word... catastrophising?'

'Maybe, but to be honest, I'm more concerned about Señor G's descent upon us this evening.'

'Señor G?'

'Fernanda's father.'

I buckled up and couldn't help halting my step. I envisioned Fernanda in the hospital and drifted back to my hallucinogenic trip with her last night. I'd been stifling it since I got up but now the imagery cascaded and overtook my immediate reality. I closed my eyes and saw her eyes. The mountains were behind her. I attempted to plug into all the memories of hers that I'd had access to. But they had drifted like a dream. Had it been a dream? I knew it hadn't been.

'Are you ok, Blondie?'

I zoned back. Boatswain licked my hand.

'Yeah... yeah. I'm just worried about Fernanda. She's told me about her father. He's bad news, isn't he?'

'You bet—for her and us. If he's coming to take her away, the orchid goes with her. I'm pretty sure of that. And all our progress here has been mostly dependent on it. I don't like to admit it but it's true. We've been imbued with magic and she's the nodal point. She's special. Without her and her cosmic gift, we will lose much of our ability to treat these patients. And despite Edward T., we've been fantastically successful so far. It's tragic.'

'Tragic for her most of all.'

'Yes... I'm sorry. I don't want you to think we're just using her. I know you two have become close.'

'Mmm. I think Albé knew that might happen when I came here. But maybe it's backfired now.'

'Well, I can't speak for Albé... I'm sorry. I'm sorry you've been dragged into all this. After all, you were supposed to just be here for a few months collecting stories about the faeries from old folk, weren't you? Maybe we shouldn't have involved you in all this—left you to your own devices.'

'What's happened has happened, Moore. We can't change it, can we? Even the orchid can't change the past.'

'No, it can't.'

We walked on for a bit in silence. Boatswain made some half-hearted attempts at chasing squirrels and Moore rolled and lit up another joint. When we reached a junction of lanes we took a natural break and sat down on a grassy bank with a view back to the hospital, its bulky architecture made miniature and partially obscured by the tree-lined distance. We finished the joint and both laid our heads down. Boatswain sprawled between us, panting away.

'So, you and Fernanda,' Moore said, staring at the sky. 'You're… y'know… into each other?'

I kept my gaze on the single cloud crossing the sky. It took on the shape of an elongated dragon with a snout and wings. Its snake-like body writhed but kept its shape, and I thought of the Shervage Wyrm, and then the Shervage Arms and being there with Fernanda listening to Mary's faerie story. The cannabis made this all a little more than it would otherwise have been. I closed my eyes.

'Yes. I've never known anyone like her. Last night clinched it… but I think I've been in love with her since the first moment I saw her. Foolish maybe… I don't know. I just know that I care for her. I hate to think of her frightened or in pain.'

'Yes, although I think you'll find she's a pretty strong character. She's in touch with herself. She's probably the sanest person in the hospital… including the staff… and us.'

'Indeed. But what will become of her? She's subject to the whims of others, is she not? She can be as strong as she likes, but if her father pulls her then she'll have to go.'

'I don't know, Blondie. I wish I had some answers for you, but I'm afraid I don't. But… and I hope you don't mind me asking…'

'Go on.'

'Have you always been, ye know, into girls?'

'*Into girls.* I suppose so. I've always found men so… abrasive. I've never had sex with a man, if that's what you mean.'

'But you have with women?'

'Yes, some.'

'If that's your bag, then why not? But when did you know…'

'Know I was gay?'

'Well, yeah.'

I wouldn't have believed I could make Moore uncomfortable, but he was squirming a bit. For some reason, this was something I had no problem with. Of all the things in life that made me an anxious wreck, this wasn't one of them.

'I fell in love with a girl at sixteen. Her name was Isabelle. It just seemed totally natural. I didn't see any problem with it. But my father did. He just couldn't comprehend it. I guess I made the mistake of announcing it one day to him: *I'm homosexual and I'm in love with Isabelle*. He flipped. He was born in 1919. He served in the war. For him, the world worked in a particular way and any divergence was dangerous. The idea of his daughter having sex with other women was anathema. So after I discovered his entrenched disgust, I hid it. I kept it away from the family. But as always happens — anything you try to keep hidden rises to the surface eventually. For a while we skirted around it, pretended everything was all right. But he knew what I was doing. I never brought girls to the house of course, but he'd hear about me being with whoever. News always got to him. And then after my sister's funeral, he finally lost it and confronted me. Told me to get out. So I did. I've never seen any of my family since.'

'Well, I get that,' said Moore, gaining equilibrium. 'Things have changed and an older generation hasn't. I'm sorry about your father. But there's also your look. I mean, you're quite androgynous… a bit *kiki*. I couldn't tell whether you were a bloke or a bird for ages. And Albé took great delight in not confirming it one way or the other. You do realise that's why everyone gives you the bewildered look, don't you?'

'Oh, you've noticed.'

'Of course. And I know I did it myself.'

'Yes, you did. But I've had that for a long time. Ye know, I've got short hair, flat tits and an ambiguous voice. Fernanda has a Chilean word for it: *machorra*. I always presumed people were just confused about my sex and so widened their eyes on first contact.'

'But?'

'But, that changed the night I came here. I told you about the guy on the train when you gave me the lift on that first day.'

'Yep, I remember. You got involved in a conversation about solipsism.'

'Right. And since then, and please don't laugh at me, I've had the overwhelming feeling that the reason people gawk at me is because…'

'Because?'

'Because I am the sole arbiter of reality. As far as I'm concerned, the entire world and universe are viewed from my perspective… my horizon. Everyone within it is just a subject. And those subjects gawk at me in the realisation that they are momentarily in contact with the only thing that actually exists. And yes, I know that sounds utterly insane, but I cannot quite get behind it. After all, as far as I'm concerned, my consciousness is everything. Nobody comes in and I can't get out. I have no neighbours.'

Moore had been rolling a joint. He lit it up.

'I get this. I really get this,' he said, inhaling deep. 'But don't you think what you've experienced at the TRU suggests that there are disparate minds and that they can interact with each other? After all, once you've been penetrated by another personality… once they've come into your bubble… doesn't that prove you're not the only consciousness in existence? Does that not dispatch solipsism to the gutter of disproved ideas?'

'Maybe. But it's one of those ideas that cling on. Whatever happens, it can always wriggle out of the explanation. Even after being penetrated by Albé's mind, I still wonder if that is not just a trick of my own all-seeing and all-knowing solipsistic mind.'

'But…'

'But, I am willing to concede that perhaps the most likely explanation for people gawking at me on first meeting is that they don't know whether I'm a male or female.'

'Well, solipsism has always sounded like a deranged idea to me, but at least you're thinking about these things, Blondie. I may have Albé and Scrope to chew the cud with, but I sometimes wonder whether the rest of humanity has become intoxicated with conventional behaviour; never asking the bigger questions. I guess this is why I'm so fascinated with our patients. They're not part of normality. They are different. They're damaged but their experiences are *out there* — and they might be able to shine some light on the human condition. I think we need some more light shining and less closing everything off in reality boxes.'

'Mmm. Me too.'

We relaxed into our prone positions for another ten minutes, staring at the sky in silence. The cloud morphed through various shapes before settling on a vaguely humanoid form with frilly, curly hair. I thought of Augusta. I wondered if she ever thought of me. Did it matter? Did anything matter?

Boatswain broke the thought by grumbling and getting up for a stretch.

'Ah, to be a dog, eh,' said Moore, lifting himself up. 'Given affection, shelter and food; they must think we are gods. Come on, we should get back.'

We walked back to the hospital in near silence. Moore was preoccupied and I didn't want to disturb him. As we reached the bottom of the lane towards the hospital, the wind returned and some black clouds made an appearance to the west. They quickly took over the sky, and by the time we were approaching the TRU, they'd darkened the afternoon and closed off the sun. We got inside just as the first patters of heavy raindrops began to splash. By the time I was in my room, the rain was lashing against the window. I stared out. The omen was not lost on me.

XXXVII

My mind was dominated by Fernanda. Her world was about to come crashing down; I was certain of it. The shadowy, malevolent male figure in my dream was a representation of her father. I was certain of that too. My inability to do anything that might help her clawed away at me. When I closed my eyes, I reimagined our orchid-induced, magical time together. At first, it was a beautiful memory. But without any confirmation it was real, the re-imagination began to sink into thoughts of her being constrained in her cubicle, with no knowledge of what I was thinking. Perhaps the orchid just induced a dream state — no real connection of minds. The experience contradicted this, but the hardwired rationalist in me couldn't quite let it be true. Despite everything I'd been a part of since coming to the TRU, I was unable to shift the suspicion that it was all a delusion. Perhaps everything was just a solipsistic trick. Even the love may not have been real. Why, after all, would anyone love me?

I opened my eyes and watched the rain wash over the window, backdropped by the blackness of the sky and the ash tree, which appeared to migrate its position through the globular lens. I needed to get to her. My first thought was to find Albé and beg him to let me take the orchid again. I could once again drift into her mind and be with her there in that special place. But my second thought was to go to her in the hospital. She'd put aside my idea to run away together, but maybe I could convince her it was a possibility. Would Albé and Moore help me? Wouldn't it be in their best interest?

I started to pace around the room, attempting to put a plan in place. If Albé came with me, surely we could extract her on some pretext before her father arrived. Perhaps we could be whisked away to his seat in Nottinghamshire. Not that I knew anything about this, but Albé appeared to have wealth and power—if he cared anything about Fernanda and her gift, would he not do this? He may not have cared about me, but I knew he needed Fernanda. I segued off into thoughts of living a secret life with Fernanda in a cloistered refuge in a stone cottage amidst rolling countryside and permanent access to her supernatural world. I lingered on this for a minute; luxuriated in it. Then I snapped out of it. I realised I needed action to bring even a modicum of this fantasy into reality. I readied myself. I put aside the omen of the black sky and rain, pondered on Sis's watery eyes for a moment and then left my room with purpose. There had to be a solution and I needed to find it.

I went to the common room—it seemed like the obvious first port of call. I burst in, alive with nervy energy. Albé was on the sofa with Caroline Lamb. He was holding her to his chest as she wept. I froze. I tried to get some words out, but they wouldn't come.

'Blondie,' said Albé, readjusting himself. 'I thought you'd be walking anxious corridors at present.'

'I... I...'

'Come and sit down with us. Caroline's leaving us tomorrow, after her final therapy session yesterday. You're a lot better now, aren't you?'

Caroline just sank deeper into him. I wished I weren't there but took up a seat on the empty sofa opposite them.

'I don't want to leave,' she whispered, barely audible. 'I feel so safe here.'

'I know you do. But Mr Davies has talked to you about the safe place we've arranged for you to go to... and it will be safe. One of us will come and see you often to make sure you're ok. And we both know you're better now, don't we?'

'Yes... yes. I feel like me now. I feel *complete*.'

She sat up and dragged her eyes away from Albé to me. After a few fidgety seconds, she got up and came over, sat down and hugged me. I caught Albé's eye over her shoulder. I thought he had tears, but I may have been wrong.

'I remember you,' she said, brushing her cheek against mine. 'You were there on that first morning in the hospital. I wondered if you were a boy or a girl then. But I know you're a girl now. Can I kiss you?'

'Umm... kiss?'

I looked at Albé again. He grinned and glinted a nod. Caroline seemed to pick up on the vibe. She held my head and kissed my lips.

'I need to take love and to give it wherever I can. I hope you will come and see me in my safe place. You are lovely. You have a good soul. I can feel it.'

Her innocence was in the air. I got it like a scent. I clasped her and kissed her back, gently, but our noses touched and I could feel myself wetting up. I pulled away and smiled.

'I'll try to come and see you, Caroline. I think you have a good soul too. I'm hoping you'll have a good life.'

Albé came over to extract her from her extended grasp as she began to cry again. As he pulled her up from the sofa, Scrope came in. As on so many occasions since I'd been at the TRU, there was a sense of things being stage-managed; timed for my solipsistic benefit. But I only had moments to ponder that as Scrope took hold of the teary Caroline and escorted her out after a last hug with Albé. He sat down on the sofa next to me and eyed me up and down.

'You're popular with the ladies, Blondie.'

'Mmm. Does she really have a safe place?'

'She does. Friends in town have agreed to give her lodgings for twelve months. They're reliable and will look after her—let us know if there's a relapse. But the last session seemed conclusive. Caro has gone... and the others. Caroline will just need to spend time coming to terms with being herself, and herself alone. We'll keep an eye on her, although…'

'Although?'

'Well, she's the last patient at the TRU. Jacob's been removed to the hospital prior to discharge, and the two other patients you haven't seen likewise. All with a clean bill of health of course. All healed, if that's how we should term it.'

'Are you saying the TRU is closing?'

'It would seem so.'

'Is this because of the police visiting today?'

'No. They weren't making any deep connections between Edward's crime and our procedures. They were just going through the investigative motions. However, their presence might be viewed as a symbolic synchronicity, using Scrope's language. They were portents of terminal conclusion. And anyway, Dr Dawkins is now refusing point-blank to refer any more certified patients until the investigation is complete. Our raison d'être has thus been nullified for the time being.'

'But… but…'

'But nothing, Blondie. There may be a future for the TRU, but we're going to have to take a break for the time being. Come on, I'll show you something.'

He took me by the hand and led me through the corridors to the lab. We stood in front of the container on the sill. It was grey. Within it was a mulch of brown dead matter.

'Orchid-24?'

'Orchid-24.'

'And you can't continue without it?'

'Maybe, if we ever got any new patients. But it's become the essential element, allowing us to do what we do. Some might say we've become addicted to it. Now it's been withdrawn.'

I looked into the container and a wave of nausea broke over me. 'Why has it been withdrawn? Is it Fernanda?'

'Probably. Her father is here. The connection has been broken. She's lost it… and we've lost it.'

'Her father is here? But we can help her, can we not? Surely she's not just at his whim? She's connected to an otherworld. I know she is. That can't just be snapped off.'

'Are you sure about that, Blondie? After all, we're talking about supernatural entities here. Do you have any idea what might really be in their cosmic hive-mind? Fernanda is probably at this very moment sedated with a big dose of Chlorpromazine. The connection is gone. And you know more than me about how these faerie entities are an ambivalent lot… quick to withdraw their favours. I'm as certain as anything that they exist in their metaphysical space — we've met them, haven't we? And I have Orchid-24 to prove it, but without Fernanda, they may as well be fossilised relics of folklore. She brought them, and their gift, into reality and now she's being taken away. Perhaps they didn't care about her as much as she thought they did.'

I ran my fingers over the container. The tic was all over my face and there was bile rising in my throat. I reached out and took Albé by the arm.

'But Fernanda. We have to help her, Albé. She's given you something… something…'

'Transcendent.'

'Yes. Transcendent. Something magic. She needs your help.'

Albé blew out a sigh and pulled me over to a range of small bottles suspended on a metal frame. They all contained a dull, brown liquid, except the one on the end of the rack. This one glistened with the moving purple essence inside it.

'For whatever reason, and I don't pretend to understand it, this seems to be the only tincture still active. The rest are dead, like the plant. This is the last active Orchid-24. Now, we have a choice here. Either I can take it and talk to Señor G, maybe persuade him to allow her to stay, or you can take it and attempt to find out how Fernanda is. There's not enough to do both. I'm giving you the choice, Blondie. You need to make that choice.'

My vision swirled. The bottle did indeed move with some supernal purple energy. It seemed alive. I gulped back my nausea and pulled up the thought of this all being a test for my all-knowing solipsistic mind. The universe existed nowhere but here and now, and I was being offered a choice between an external agency sorting out a problem via another person or taking control of my destiny and transporting myself to Fernanda.

I took the bottle from its stand and held it up to the light. I thought I saw within it writhing beings. There were eyes there, but I could never focus on them. I handed the bottle to Albé. He took it as if he knew this is what I'd do. I looked into his purple eyes. All I could put through my mind was how I'd failed Fernanda. Was this the best I could do for her? If so, I should be ashamed. She needed me and I hadn't been there. It was a dereliction of love. I was a fraud.

XXXVIII

I sat on the bed and stared at the dusk bleeding life from the day. My self-pitying tears had passed, but I rocked backwards and forwards with my hands on my lap, as I imagined hundreds of patients in the hospital and TRU had done over the years as they tried to come to terms with the unfathomable consequences of existence. My stream of consciousness flickered over the last two months—the folklore, the faeries, the numinous, the dreams, the patients of many minds, the cosmic but sinister states I'd found myself in and the people with who I'd become so enmeshed after my previous solitary life. At the terminus of each non-linear stream, I pictured Fernanda. Her image wavered into Sis as their eyes became one and the same, but her accented voice swam in my head as a distinct but amorphous form. I had no idea how memory could conjure up sound within the mind when in reality there was only silence. Perhaps it was just more evidence of her telepathic abilities. But her voice was clear and as bewitching as if she'd been sitting next to me. She wasn't sitting next to me though, and the tears came again. I knew I'd never see her again, or hear her again, or touch….

Three quick knocks on the door brought me back to the present like the violent waking from a dream. Fletcher burst in without waiting for a reply.

'I'm sorry to interrupt… ma'am,' he said, his agitation filling the room. 'But Mr Moore has asked if you could get along to the monitoring chamber with immediate effect.'

'Right now?'

'Yes, right now.'

I didn't bother asking any more questions. My worst-case scenario proclivity told me what was happening. I pulled on my baggy jumper and followed Fletcher in quick-step through the corridors.

Mantener la calma I heard in my head. It was a tough instruction. We slipped into the monitoring chamber. Moore and Scrope were on the edge of their chairs.

'Lock the door, Fletcher,' snapped Moore. 'Have a seat, Blondie. I'm guessing you know what this is about.'

'I'm guessing I do.'

Albé was in the Observation Room, standing and swaying with a peculiar gait. Moore twiddled some knobs on the console. We waited in silence. When the Observation Room door opened, there was a suspension in the air. I gulped hard. A nurse ushered in two men and disappeared.

'Señor G,' said Moore, biting his lip.

'And henchman,' added Scrope.

Señor G was exactly as I'd expected. He swished into the room like a Latin version of Albé without the limp. His immaculate long-coat seemed to add dramatic effect as he looked around; suspicious, derisive. But his eyes were Fernanda's; just the cruel version.

'Christ,' whispered Moore. 'This looks like a Sergio Leone standoff. Any second now one of them's gonna get out a Morricone musical pocket watch and set it off.'

SEÑOR G: Your lordship.

ALBÉ: Señor. I had requested a private meeting with you.

Señor G scanned the room again and then waved his man away. He left with a bow. Señor G locked eyes on us and moved towards the window. He knocked it hard with a clenched fist. We all made an instinctive move backwards in our chairs. He seemed to be looking straight at me, even though I knew he couldn't be.

SEÑOR G: This is a two-way mirror. We have them in our facilities.

ALBÉ: I bet you do.

SEÑOR G: Mmm. Do I have your word there is nobody on the other side?

ALBÉ: No.

SEÑOR G: Ha. Well, it is no matter. I do not intend to spend much time here, as I have only come out of courtesy to your request. Nothing more. I am informed my daughter has spent some time here… with you.

ALBÉ: Fernanda has been invaluable to us. Her abilities have aided our programme of therapy… very successful therapy.

SEÑOR G: I am sure. I have heard a little about your *programme*. Although I fail to see what she has to offer you. She was sent here in refuge. Her mind is weakened: *la lunática*. This was the only place for her.

ALBÉ: She has indeed thrived here, señor. But I can assure you, she is no lunatic. Although I am concerned you intend to take her away.

SEÑOR G: You seem to know my mind very well, my lord.

ALBÉ: Well, it's a talent I have—an invaluable skill for a psychiatrist.

Señor G lost some of his languid complacency for the first time and flicked his head to one side and then the other. I imagined the buzz in his ear.

SEÑOR G: Be that as it may. It becomes *inappropriate* for her to stay here now that I am to take up residence in London. And so she shall be coming with me tomorrow.

ALBÉ: In London? Will this be due to your new president — *La vía Chilena al socialismo*? I would say this is a positive move for your country. I'm surprised you don't want to be part of it.

Señor G's face darkened. He took a step towards Albé and lowered his voice. Moore twiddled a couple of knobs and his words came through, heightened, more accented.

SEÑOR G: I am surprised to hear a peer of the realm talk in this way about such filth. *Socialismo* is communism. But many of my countrymen are fools. They have been seduced by Allende's false promises. Fortunately, your own new government contains many who see this for what it is. I will be working with them to correct this disease. And mark my words, we will. A cancer needs to be cut out... ruthlessly.

ALBÉ: Yes, but he who surpasses or subdues mankind must look down on the hate of those below.

SEÑOR G: Meaning?

ALBÉ: Meaning what it means, señor. I'm sure you will find out as you pursue what is best for you. But I suggest, in my professional capacity, that Fernanda's wellbeing would be best served by her staying here.

SEÑOR G: That is impossible. My new position will not countenance my daughter being shut up in an asylum. She comes with me tomorrow.

ALBÉ: I must advise you, again, in a professional capacity, that this may harm her.

SEÑOR G: I fail to see how being with her family would harm her more than being in... how do you say... a looney bin.

ALBÉ: All I can confirm is that she has been happy here and has made much progress. And she is of an age in this country where her consent would be needed to take her anywhere if she is discharged from her certification.

SEÑOR G: Her consent is my will as her father. I am amazed that an esteemed person such as your lordship would think being here, living in a cubicle, is better for her than being with her family in a Mayfair townhouse.

ALBÉ: Other family members are with you?

SEÑOR G: I do not see that is any of your concern. Dr Daw... Daw...

ALBÉ: Dawkins.

SEÑOR G: Yes. He is perfectly happy with the discharge. As far as I am concerned that is the end of the matter. I presume… presume you have no ulterior motive for keeping my daughter here. You have not explained your *relationship* with her.

ALBÉ: She has helped us in a therapeutic capacity. Many of our patients would not have received the treatment they have without Fernanda's unique perspicacity.

SEÑOR G: How so?

ALBÉ: She has a refinement of vision. Standard psychiatry deems her insane. Her condition is termed Delusional Psychosis. But her ability to understand and make connections with… with unusual forms of human consciousness, has convinced me that she just has a different take on consensus reality. She is not mad, but simply antithetic to orthodox belief systems. It is an ability we have utilised both for her own benefit and for those of our patients.

SEÑOR G: Mmm. You use your language skilfully. But your patients are no concern of mine. And having seen her living conditions here, I have no hesitation to take her away with me. She will be afforded every convenience of wealth as is her birthright and may be able to return to… *consensus reality*, which to my mind is the only reality. I respect your opinion but her time here is done. Dr Daw…

ALBÉ: Dawkins.

SEÑOR G: Sí. Dr Dawkins and I will breakfast tomorrow in your quaint local market town where I am staying, and then my daughter will return to London with me. This is how it will be. Now unless you have any further business, I will bid you goodnight… and… just for your information, my *valet* will spend the night in the hospital to ensure my daughter's safety. Goodnight.

They stared at each other for a few moments and then bowed, never losing the eye contact. Señor G held his hand to his ear for a few moments, then swirled away and was gone. Albé returned to his peculiar gait, and in the monitoring chamber we looked at each other, Moore and Scrope putting their hands through their hair and Fletcher letting out an extended huffing sigh.

'Give the señor a couple of minutes to make his way off the premises and we'll get in there,' said Moore. 'Find out what's really going on.'

When we did get into the Observation Room, Albé hadn't moved. We stood in silence for a moment as he scanned us in slow motion, his eyes finally resting on me. The buzz came on. I felt compelled to close my eyes as some deep memory of my father hitting my sister surfaced from nowhere. It was vivid. I opened my eyes and looked at the others. Something was being done to them too; looks of confusion and revulsion at some past events dredged up from suppressed places.

'Sorry,' said Albé, his voice echoing somehow. 'It's a residue. I'm picking out some bad memories from you all. It's an accident. I'm sorry… it's the last of the orchid and it's become infected by what I just found in *his* mind. I've become accustomed to finding corrupt personalities hiding in the minds of relative innocents. But what is in his mind is… is…'

He took an awkward step back and slumped onto the sofa. I wasn't used to seeing Albé vulnerable. My face started to tick like a clock. Scrope joined him, but I knew he was still thinking about something else. Fletcher remained staring into the middle distance.

Moore was first to come out of the stupor. He started pacing the room, putting aside whatever grievous memory had just had a light shone on it and forcing himself back to the present.

'So what is it?' he asked. 'The guy never called Fernanda by her name once. I noticed that. He seemed sociopathic. I got that too. But what's in there, Albé… Albé?'

'What's in there,' repeated Albé. 'I don't know how to tell you.'

'Try.'

'Well… well, he's raped them all. Fernanda, her sisters… and others. And he's killed a lot of people. It flashed by quicker than I'm used to, but I can assure you it was very real. There was a lot of blood and torture. He's not sociopathic... he's psychopathic. You don't want to know the details.'

I flicked my tongue around a dry mouth.

Moore spoke, his accent rooting itself. 'Psychopathic? Oh, God. Well, then we can't let him take her to London. We need to get her out of there tonight. We owe her.'

'We're not the Special Air Service, Moore. We can't abseil in there and smuggle her away under the nose of Señor G's man... who'll be in the car park... and probably armed.'

'So what do we do?' I said, taking a seat next to Albé and holding his arm.

He sighed and rolled his head: 'We'll have to wait. Let him take her to London — I know the address — and then see if we can intervene.'

'Intervene?'

'It's a better option than trying to do anything here. When she's in London she'll be technically free to do whatever she likes. Her consent will be her own.'

'By the sound of it,' said Moore, losing some spark, 'I don't think Señor Fascista will see it that way. She'll probably be locked up... and God knows what else.'

I pulled back, a tear rolling into my mouth. I closed my eyes and visualised Fernanda — it was a vision of despair.

'Well,' said Albé, his voice as dusk, 'I'll make sure I'm there in the morning... see if I can speak to her. At least let her know we know what's happening. There's no more to be done.'

There was an end of words. I got up and left, shrugging off Moore's attempt to hold my arm. Something in the pit of my mind told me I was going to see Fernanda tonight. It was irresolute, shaded, but I knew it would happen. I just didn't know how. I slammed the door behind me and went back to my room and got under the covers. I was shaking. I was ashamed of such a retreat but felt I had no other option. If I went dashing over to the hospital, I'd be stopped somehow. It would be useless. But Albé's plan of waiting frightened me. What would become of Fernanda?

I continued to tremble. I presumed sleep wouldn't come, but soon the hypnic jerks began. They contained a delirium; a falling loss of control. I was heading out of waking reality. Part of me was glad about this, despite the shame. I needed the escape. But there was something awaiting me. What was it awaiting me? The hypnagogia told me but I couldn't pin it down. I drifted between sleep states; one moment watching the black silhouette of the ash tree moving outside the window, the next moving into dreamt otherworlds.

Tonight is an ANNIHILATION.

The whispered words were clear in my head, but I couldn't allow them to be real. I thought I was getting up from the bed, but this was just a trick of my sleep-state. I was sinking into a dream. My avatar was taking over. I just had to go with it. I went with it.

XXXIX

The noose is before me, swinging in the weird, redacted moonlight. For a moment I'm in my university room, but it soon becomes the shed — the *cobertizo*. The faerie appears with her neck in the noose, but she opens her big almond-shaped, black eyes and manoeuvres in the air in an impossible way. She has an orchid flower in her black hair.

'I thought you were dead,' I think.

She grimaces and speaks without words: *'Only in one world. You are dreaming. You are in another world now. I live here. Would you like some poetry?'*

'Mmm.'

'Our life is twofold: Sleep hath its own world,
 A boundary between the things misnamed
Death and existence: Sleep hath its own world,
And a wide realm of wild reality.'

'Byron?'

'You know him?'

'I suppose I do.'

'Death and existence are misnamed. And you are at the boundary.'

'Is this really a dream?'

'A dream but not a dream. I'm afraid you will not like it, but it's the only way we could show you. Otherwise you would have found out from others. But this is the truth filtered through some layers of reality. A change is about to come o'er the spirit of your dream...'

There is a change; the passing of something. The rafters of the *cobertizo* extend to a great height and Fernanda swings in the noose. I panic and start looking for something to stand on to get her down. But she smiles and sends me back with a wave of her hands. She seems unharmed by the strangulation. She puts thoughts into my mind.

'This is my last gift from las hadas. *I am with them now. They help me to cross over from flesh to spirit. It had to be this way. I could not go with him. And you must not be sad about it. I could not see you before I left. But I am here now to tell you I love you.* Te amo. *All things have an end. But the end is always followed by a new beginning… forever.* Terminus et exordium… te amo.'

I feel her kiss and sink into it. But soon it is gone and I crawl around in the dust of the *cobertizo* floor, not daring to look up. Finally I do. She swings in the air, lifeless. I try to move but can't. The faerie reappears, slithers over to me and strokes my hair with elongated fingers. She is inside my mind, playing about with my memories. She invokes first Fernanda and then Sis. There is a tidal wave of love. I cry.

'Their annihilation is not really annihilation. They exist and their love remains within you. You need to go now. You have a life to live. They both want you to live that life. They are dead but dreaming… they are dreaming of you.'

She extracts herself from my mind as wind through a tunnel. I am dragged through the tunnel, ever upwards towards something outside of where I am….

***

I wake up with a ratcheting, as if my head is being slapped. I scramble out of bed, pull on some clothes and make for the door. There is a distant siren and an insidious movement outside. Boatswain is barking. I pause for a few seconds before opening the door. The dream is still with me. Something is speaking inside my head: *Oh! She was changed as by the sickness of the soul; her mind had wandered from its dwelling, and her eyes, they had not their own lustre, but the look which is not of the earth; she was become The Queen of a fantastic realm; her thoughts were combinations of disjointed things.*

I clamp my temples with my hands to shut out the voices. They dissipate. I open the door and run out.

As I reached the entrance, Moore was coming back in at a rush. His face was white as snow.

'Woah, Blondie. You can't go out there now. Please.'

'It's Fernanda, isn't it?'

He said nothing and just held on to me until I lost some tension. I pretended to relax, and as I stepped back he released his hold. As soon as he did, I darted past him, out the door and ran down the path, past the hospital buildings and up to the gardens. It was dark but the moonlight allowed me to see there were a number of people bustling around outside the shed. The siren was getting nearer. I ran up the path straight into Albé, who seemed to emerge out of the darkness from nowhere. He clasped me. He held me tight.

'She's dead, Blondie,' he whispered in my ear. 'I know you know this. You don't need to see it.'

'Dead,' I repeated. 'Dead?'

I looked at the moon over Albé's shoulder. It spangled and broke into pieces. Raised voices came to me. The siren became louder. My vision wavered into darkness. I became limp. Albé picked me up into his arms and carried me somewhere. This was the last I remembered.

XL

I had a dream, which was not all a dream.
The bright sun was extinguish'd, and the stars
Did wander darkling in the eternal space,
Rayless, and pathless, and the icy earth
Swung blind and blackening in the moonless air;
Morn came and went — and came, and brought no day.

The words repeat themselves. They are formed within darkness. I'm delirious but I cannot get out of the loop. A clock ticks beside me — *tick-tock*, *tick*-fucking-*tock*. Had I not destroyed it? It is probably a dream, but I can't tell anymore. At times I'm given water and food and taken to the bathroom. But I don't know who is doing it and I fight against it. I'm convinced it's the faeries trying to make me eat their fruits and pretend they are on my side only to lure me into their otherworld. At one moment I am sure I'm in a red-lit room in the Villa Diodati. I think I know where this is and what it is, but it is infused with unknowing. The people around me are as shadows and there are orchids crawling over my bed. They sometimes get hold of me and I cry out against them. They reply with whispered words, sometimes in Spanish and other times in an unknown language. I am sure there is someone attempting to get inside my mind. It's a girl. She has black hair and a red cloak. She pours a wave of love over me. But I can't return it. I am passive to all intrusions. Once she is gone I am nothing but a conduit for so much I do not understand. My brain ceases to filter out things. My memory becomes actualised as the present. It washes over me: car crash, Sis, creeping faeries, a train carriage compartment, a station-master, iron grave-markers, one-way mirrors, a bookin' E-Type, Peter Hammill

screaming, lunatics made of more than one person,
a dismembered head, my father's scowl, Uncle John,
Flossy the injured horse, Gloop ejaculating, Boatswain
grumbling, Goodfellow seen through a pint of cider,
Mary and Caroline combined as a single person in
white linen, dark-shaped humanoids chasing me
through a field, soft feminine kisses, Richard Burton,
a typewriter with reams of paper, Lord Byron holding
on to me… and then a noose with a faerie hanging. I
try to clear her out and get my head into the noose but
it becomes too small. There is a rumble of thunder.
It is accompanied by a floral scent and then the deep
bass of some music spelling out an apocalypse… an
annihilation. A gnarled, emotionless faerie ushers me
through a door into darkness. The darkness takes over
and brought no day.

***

There came a time when I woke up and found myself
back among physical objects. The pillow seemed
real—the linen against my face made me think
I'd come back to a world I knew. The light seemed
harsh but I grabbed on to the sheets and was glad for
their grounding reality. I turned over, touching my
belly and genitalia to ensure I was still existing. As I
revolved I tuned into an immediacy — Augusta's eyes
were inches from mine.

'*Hola.*'

'Are you real?'

'I'm real. Are you back with us?'

'I guess. How long have I been here?'

'A week.'

She pulled her body to mine and we held on to
each other. Her perfumed hair fell over my face and
I gritted my teeth for further corroboration of my
return. She kissed me, then drew away to get focus.

'You've been ill, Blondie. Things have taken their
toll on you. We've been looking after you. You're
worth looking after.'

'Am I?'

'Yes.'

'Fernanda is dead, isn't she?'

'Yes.'

'She hung herself?'

'Yes.'

'I don't think I want to live in this world.'

'Oh yes you do. We'll help you to deal with this. We're on your side.'

'Are you?'

'Yes. The TRU is closing. You're coming back with me and Albé. You need some recovery time. He has a lot of money and much property. You'll be looked after until you get over this.'

'Is he a lord?'

'You know he is.'

'Is he Lord Byron?'

She smiled, stroked my hair and kissed my forehead. I slumped back into the pillow. More sleep was coming. But the delirium was gone. A heavy tide of darkness flowed over me and I slept. It was deep and dreamless.

XLI

The station-master met us outside the station with averted eyes as Fletcher and Epsilon unloaded our luggage from the two taxis. I was still visualising my last glimpse of the hospital as we had drawn away — as gaunt and foreboding as the day I'd arrived, only now with the weight of desiccated memories. Scrope had retained a stoical restraint as he waved us off, but Moore had burst into tears as he hugged us all. He'd also taken the opportunity to squeeze my ass, but I allowed this as a friendly gesture and squeezed his in return with a smile and a quick kiss. Boatswain had stood looking desolate at the desertion. His loyal canine brain just saw betrayal with no idea that plans were afoot to soon reunite him with his master. He ran after the taxis as we left, barking and whimpering. It was, perhaps, an appropriate send-off.

'I'm sorry about Edward and all the trouble,' said Albé to the station-master.

'Aye. It is a most troublesome situation. Most troublesome. Our community has been much disturbed by it. But I would like to say that no blame rests with 'ee. You tried to help him but things turned out not so well.'

'How is the girl?' asked Augusta.

'She is… she is doing as well as could be expected. She has a good family to look after her, and we at chapel will be asking God to help her. The Lord will always help when asked, especially when it comes to young innocents.'

Albé nodded and curled his lip. The station-master took my hands and wished me well, then we made our way on to the platform. Fletcher and Epsilon sat on the cases while Albé, Augusta and I took our place on the bench as the station-master bustled around the platform creating busyness where none was needed. Ten minutes later the train rolled in, the smell of burning diesel bringing the association of my arrival over two months before. Another ten minutes and we were ensconced in our first-class compartment heading for London. Ten minutes more and Fletcher was already snoozing in his window seat and, opposite him, Epsilon was transfixed by the passing autumn landscape. I didn't know, but I guessed he'd never been on a train before.

There was half an hour of silence, just the clickety-clack of the train infiltrating my wandering thoughts. I was brought out of them by Augusta running her hand over my thigh.

'So we need to get you to Hobby once we're in the Smoke,' she said, moving her touch to my arm. 'He knows what's been going on.'

'Does he?'

'Yes. He'll understand. You must have quite a lot of material for him.'

'I guess I do. I don't know whether it'll be what he wants, but it'll have to do. I feel he might be disappointed.'

Albé came out of his trance: 'He'll be fine. I'll have words. And anyway, there are plenty of faeries up north. You've still got work to do for him.'

'Once she's recovered,' said Augusta. 'After what has happened, Blondie does not need any more pressure put on her. She needs time.'

Albé bowed his acquiescence and another half hour of silence ensued. *Clickety-clack… clackety-click.* I diverted my gaze to the bronze landscape flashing by outside. Fernanda still flooded my thoughts. I closed my eyes and pictured her. I imagined her purple eyes, her hair, her body… her spirit. Then I imagined her dead body, dragged out of the noose and interned somewhere. We had loved each other for a short time. Now she was gone for good. She had spoken to me in my dream, but that wasn't enough. I wanted her touch. I wanted her mind. But it was gone… gone.

'And what about the faeries?' asked Albé, after we pulled out of a station. 'Did we really meet them?'

I brought myself up from my introspection with the images lingering. 'Um, yes, I think we did. But I'm… I'm starting to have the feeling they are perhaps arbiters between this world and the next. They are in-betweeners; trying to give us messages that we barely understand. Fernanda understood it, but we don't. I think maybe Orchid-24 was just a symbol. It wasn't really part of our world. It fooled us. I think it might have lured you into… into a false metaphysics. It was like a trick being played on us.'

'But it enabled me to help a lot of patients. I would not have been able to do this without Orchid-24.'

'I know… yes, I know. But the price, Albé. The price has been high.'

'Indeed it has. But Fernanda's choice was made because of her father's return, not because of her relationship with us… or you.'

'That's right,' said Augusta, taking my hand. 'You've been released from one guilt trip and we won't allow you to start gestating another. And once we get back to the estate you'll need to work with Albé, and me if you like, to help you get over this.'

'Will I?'

'Yes. There's a cottage I'm thinking of that has your name all over it. We'll set you up with the Olivetti and you can recover… Albé?'

'Yep. You'll just need to put your pride to one side, Blondie, and let us help you. You need to be among friends, and don't take this the wrong way but… well, you don't have anyone else, do you?'

'No. I don't suppose I do.'

'And maybe the cabal will get back together. Moore is going back to Ireland for a while — with Miss Dyke, I hear — and Scrope needs to wrap things up at the TRU, but before the end of the year, they'll both be coming for an extended stay with us, with the E-Type and Boatswain. We might even get Miss Rood to join us for Fletcher's convenience. We'll plot our next move then. Maybe even set up a new unit. There will continue to be people with dissociative disorders and they will continue to need understanding from within the psychiatric profession. And after fifteen months of treatments at the TRU, we probably know more about the condition than anyone else... anywhere.'

'But no orchid?'

'No orchid. We'll just have to cope without supernatural help.'

'Mmm. But you'll be staying on your... *estate*?'

'For the time being. I go to Greece for a conference in April—Missolonghi. But I'll be back in May for the... the, err...'

'Birthing,' said Augusta, placing my hand on her belly. 'Someone will have to be around because my husband almost certainly won't be. I hope you like children, Blondie, as mine will be with me, and when this little lady appears there'll be a brood.'

'Mmm. I've not really spent much time with children. They always seem a bit... alien to me. How do you know this one's a girl?'

'Oh, just a feeling.'

She and Albé exchanged an intimate glance. I broke from it and spent more time looking out the window at tractors ploughing up fields of dirty yellow stub. Fletcher snored on and Epsilon was still in a trance as he stared at the ever-changing rurality. I joined his gaze until pulled back by Albé.

'And what about your flirtations with solipsism, Blondie? Has this all been just a figment of your all-encompassing imagination?'

I laughed a nervous laugh.

'How would I know? I have no neighbours. Maybe I'm God after all.'

'Ha, yes. But your experiences with the orchid... with other minds. Has that not put it to bed?'

'I guess. It should have, shouldn't it? It should have.'

'But it hasn't, has it? You're still wondering whether any of us or *this* exists.'

'Still reading my mind?'

Albé smiled and curled his lip. 'Maybe. But perhaps you need to put solipsism to one side... for your own health and wellbeing. It's an insidious concept that has the potential to drive you to insanity. You might be advised to direct your energy elsewhere. I would humbly suggest there are only four questions of real value in life: What is sacred? Of what is the spirit made? What is worth living for and what is worth dying for? The answer to each is the same. Only love.'

'Love... yes, love.'

I started to tear up but controlled it and we fell back to silence, broken only by the clickety-clack. Time passed. Albé and Augusta read and I closed my eyes and pretended to sleep. Then I pretended to awake and rolled a ciggy, excusing myself to go smoke it in the passageway. As I closed the compartment door, Albé and Augusta shifted together. I moved down away from them, slid open a window in the vestibule and struck up.

The patchwork fields gave way to suburbs. The lowering autumn sun gave them a golden glow they probably didn't deserve. The wind-stream blew out the ciggy before it was half finished, but I leant on the window frame and watched the passing world. Were there really people here in these houses, living out their lives? Did it matter? From my own perspective, there was nothing but the immediate confines of the train carriage, the blustering wind and an amorphous vista that changed every few seconds. This was all I could know. But Albé's words lingered. Love trumped solipsism. I cried. But then I drew myself up and wiped away the tears. I re-engaged with the present. What would become of me? I still felt weak from my illness and now I was about to put myself into the hands of others. They were kind—Augusta was perhaps the kindest person I'd ever known, and our moments of intimacy touched me and stayed with me. Albé still scared me but they both seemed to have my best interests at heart. And yet, should I be doing this? What other choice did I have? This prospective new life with them was attractive in many ways, but I was nervous about giving myself over. This, after all, had not been my plan when I left London on the fourth of August.

We approached London. The built environment subsumed the view. I closed my eyes and pictured my university room. I was glad I didn't have to return there. Then Sis. My memory did its job — she was still perfect. She was retained in aspic. Then Fernanda. The tears welled again. How would I ever get over her? For some moments I pulled up her face before me. But it was too much. I took a deep breath, slid shut the window and made my way back down the passageway. The past existed nowhere except in memory, the present was a nanosecond, and the future was nowhere extant. I just needed to come to terms with these facts. I still had a life to live. I needed to live it. All the death had to be put to one side, however difficult that might be.

As I approached the compartment, I thought the buzzing was coming back. I shook my head and it disappeared… I thought it disappeared.

The train continued: *clickety-clack, clackety-click.*

Terminus et Exordium

4 August 2024

I got out of the taxi and my head swam. But I trudged on with my stick, leaning on it every few moments to regain my breath. My phone had been bleeping during the journey from the station. I only now squinted at the messages: *Where are you? Are you ok? Please let me know you're all right.* I slipped it back into my shoulder-bag and made my way up the slope to the hospital.

It was not a hospital anymore. The neo-Gothic façades remained, but it had been turned into something else. The people living there were no longer insane — or at least they didn't consider themselves insane — and there was an air of enforced suburbia. I'd known the hospital had been converted to a residential complex decades ago, but to be confronted by it after so long, and with so many memories, affected me more than I'd expected.

I moved slow past the main building. When I reached what used to be the chapel, I had the unrealistic expectation of finding a bench where I could sit down. There wasn't one, but I found a low wall and eased on to it. My illness made itself known, exacerbated by the heat of the day. I took some moments to calm my swaying vision and tried to breathe deep to constrain the angina coursing down my left side and into my arm. My forehead was clammy with cold sweat. I shouldn't have come, but some deep resonance persuaded me I had to.

I spent ten minutes recovering and then pulled myself up to head on to the site of the TRU. The vegetable gardens were, of course, not there, and I became disorientated as I hobbled through some car parks and new outbuildings. But I knew if I kept heading up the slope with the sun to my left I'd get there. And I did. Although transformed into a domestic space, it was still recognisable. I approached the entrance and rested on my stick. The last time I'd stood on this spot, I was enveloped in grief. I was sure my world had ended. It hadn't. Maybe it would now. I closed my eyes and pictured her eyes.

'Are you ok?'

I came round with a start. My blurred vision made out a grey form, but then I was able to focus on a young man, his long hair drifting over his face.

'Moore?'

'Sorry?'

'Ah, no, I'm sorry. Yes, I think I'm ok.'

'Well, you look a little unsteady, ma'am. There's a bench over here. With your permission, I'll take your arm and we can sit there for a while. I'm in need of a break myself. Do you live here?'

'That's very kind. Yes, I could do with a sit-down and some company. I did live here once. It was a very long time ago though.'

We made the bench and he proceeded to open his camera bag. He moved aside some big lenses and slid out a small, old-fashioned silver flask.

'Never do fieldwork without the necessary sustenance,' he said, dipping me a charming wink. 'Would you like a tipple?'

'Why not?'

I gulped the whiskey and reeled a little. He took a big draught and sank back into the bench with his arms stretched out.

'Always does the job.'

'You're Irish?'

'For my sins. In exile over here for the last four years doing my degrees. Photography. This is my first job. I'm photographing all the old psychiatric hospitals for a book. Others do the writing, I do the pictures. Not much money in it to be honest, but I need to start somewhere. I'm nearly halfway through.

I have a day at each site. Trouble is, most have been converted like this place, so I can't get internal shots. I love it when I can—there was one up north especially, still derelict… very atmospheric. But I do like this place. There's something… haunted about it.'

'Yes… haunted.'

He creased his eyes in a smile. 'And you say you lived here? Were you a… err, a patient?'

I laughed. 'No. I was just staying here for a few months. I was like you—on my first assignment. It was quite a wild time. It made a big impression on me. Nothing in my life ever quite matched what I lived through here. A lot happened in this building behind us. I learnt much about life here; about how people's minds work… mine included. It ended in something of a tragedy, but the experience set me up well for life; a quiet life. I've been rather a recluse for the last five decades. The people I met here stayed with me afterwards, they became my family, I guess, but they're all gone now and so I thought it was time to return one more time. In fact, this is the first time I've been back since my stay here.'

'When was that?'

'I came here on this very day in 1970.'

'Whooh, that is a long time ago… oh, I'm sorry. I hope that's not rude.'

I laughed again. 'No, it is a long time ago. But sometimes, especially when I'm drifting off to sleep, the times come back to me very vividly, as though they were yesterday.'

The tears began to choke my voice, so I shut up. My new companion took another glug from the flask. I declined the offer of more.

'My mother was born in 1970,' he said after a few moments of consideration.

'And how old are you?'

'Twenty-four.'

'Yes, I thought you might be.'

He gave me a quizzical look, laced with the charm of his smile.

'The music though… 1970, that period. I love it. It's so much more authentic than the computer-generated pap we have these days. Hendrix, Pink Floyd, Led Zep. Hey, have you heard of a band called Van der Graaf Generator?'

My heart thumped. I closed my eyes and for an instant I was back in the E-Type with Moore over five decades ago, rattling through dark country lanes as a young woman about to embrace the pivotal equinox of my existence. I spoke the words: 'And in the end there beckons, more and more clearly, total –'

'ANNIHILATION!'

He parodied the exclamation and sat back with a grin of satisfaction. I laughed and I cried. He took hold of my shoulders gently as if recognising something had been enfolded. He let go quickly. I appreciated his tenderness and respect.

I breathed deep and met his eyes again. 'Yes, the music was better. You'd have liked to have been alive then.'

'Yes, I think I would. But we're stuck in 2024 and all the horrendousness. I just hope the situation isn't really as bad as they say. But things do seem to have become unstuck, haven't they?'

'Indeed they have.'

He sat back and we retreated from the charged moment to talk about more banal matters. Ten minutes later, I suggested I needed to get on, and he helped me up from the bench. I made an effort to stand straight up as if I didn't need my stick, but realised he probably wasn't fooled.

'Now are you sure you're gonna be ok? I can stay with you if you like.'

'I'll be fine. You have your photography to do. I may be an old woman, but I can still get around. And I have one other place I need to visit on my own. But I thank you for your kindness. I appreciate it, my young friend.'

'*Ceart go leor.*'

'Ah, now you do sound like Moore. What is your name? I'm sorry, I never asked.'

'Shelley… no relation, at least not that I know of. I actually prefer Byron. Do you know Byron?'

'Yes, I know Byron. I know Byron very well.'

'And you?'

'I've usually been called Blondie.'

'Blondie?'

'I know it may seem strange to you looking at my greyness. But that became my name. It's just the way of things.'

'Well, Blondie,' he said, taking my hands in his, 'it's been an honour to meet you. I hope you get to your special place. I will remember our coming together. Now, are you sure you'll be ok?'

'I'll be ok.'

I tottered off. I looked back once and he was watching me. I waved. He waved back. I knew he was the last person I'd ever talk to.

I made my way along a path away from the buildings and over a field. The landscape became familiar somehow, and I knew I would need to pass some barrier to get out of the grounds. When I reached the hedgerow, I was relieved to find a kissing-gate instead of the stile from my memory. It led out onto the lane I'd last trodden fifty-four years before.

The lane took its slight uphill incline and after about twenty minutes of ever-slowing, breathless progress, I reached the spot. The grove matched my remembrance. I stepped into it off the lane, relying on my stick for support. There was a large log lining the space. It couldn't possibly have been the same one from all those years ago, but for my current purpose, it may as well have been. Two ravens were beaking at each other on the log. They saw me, lingered for a moment, and then took off into the branches of the nearest tree. Were they the descendants of those telepathic nut-munchers Fernanda and I had engaged with long ago? I liked to think so.

I hovered for a while and then started the awkward and painful process of sitting down on the grass with my back to the log. Once settled, I realised how much pain I was in. My heart was careering and the whole of my left side spasmed, drawing up sharp burns to my neck. I was dizzy, dissociated and short of breath. I closed my eyes and attempted the deep-breathing Augusta had taught me. I pictured her face. She had been the last to die—blasted by cancer the previous winter. All the others were long gone: Albé, Moore, Scrope, Fletcher, Professor Hobhouse, even Epsilon. All dead… all dead.

As I relaxed, the hypnagogic state began to set in, and I was for brief moments back with Fernanda and Augusta in the darkness with our backs to the log, exchanging caresses and kisses. Their words came in broken delirium, saying nothing but meaning everything. I couldn't tell if my eyes were open or closed. There was a flickering. It coincided with a massive shot of pain through my chest and I reeled and collapsed to one side. My head hit the ground. I gasped for breath but the flickering ceased. I saw the grove move like a kaleidoscope around the clump of moss on which my head rested. A gloom came over me but then, for an instant, there was a clarity of vision, awash with brightness. A female blackbird landed right in front of me. She cocked her head.

'Tick-tock,' she said. 'Time to go.'

'Yes, I suppose it is.'

I didn't speak the words but I knew she'd understood them. There was a last brutal pulse through my chest and then darkness. But the darkness wasn't really darkness. It was something else. It evaporated. Annihilation turned out to be light.

The brook is in front of me. There is a buzz in the air. The light seems unreal; alive. The brook becomes a river and I walk into it. My head is immersed and the water fills my lungs, but I don't fight it. I begin to drift with the current. My life is reviewed in seconds, in eviscerating, impossible detail: all the mistakes, the sweetness, the dullness, the people, the seclusion, the depression, the joyfulness, the tears, the generosity and the grief... all there in an instant. But it shatters apart, almost before it begins. Someone grabs me and pulls me to the opposite bank. It is Albé. He draws me to his body. His warmth envelops me. He is filled with light.

'Hello, Blondie... you're dead. But don't worry, the dream continues. You're about to find out if you are God or not. We'll all help you with that.'

Sis, Fernanda and Augusta join us. They are joyful and full of past and present love. We all kiss and cry. We come together. I now know them without separation—like many minds within one. Orchid-shaped faeries dance and sing at our feet.

And voices from the deep abyss reveal a marvel and a secret. Be it so.

Author Profile

Neil Rushton attained a PhD from the University of Cambridge (Archaeology/History) in 2003. He is now a freelance writer, who has published on a wide range of subjects from castle fortification to folklore. His first novel, *Set the Controls for the Heart of the Sun*, was published in 2016. *Dead but Dreaming* is his second novel and brings together his research into folklore, social history and the philosophy of consciousness.

Twitter: @neilrushton13
Blogsite: https://deadbutdreaming.wordpress.com
Facebook: https://www.facebook.com/thefaeriecode/

What Did You Think of *Dead but Dreaming?*

A big thank you for purchasing this book. It means a lot that you chose this book specifically from such a wide range on offer. I do hope you enjoyed it.

Book reviews are incredibly important for an author. All feedback helps them improve their writing for future projects and for developing this edition. If you are able to spare a few minutes to post a review on Amazon, then thank you very much.

Publisher Information

Rowanvale Books provides publishing services to independent authors, writers and poets all over the globe. We deliver a personal, honest and efficient service that allows authors to see their work published, while remaining in control of the process and retaining their creativity. By making publishing services available to authors in a cost-effective and ethical way, we at Rowanvale Books hope to ensure that the local, national and international community benefits from a steady stream of good quality literature.

For more information about us, our authors or our publications, please get in touch.

www.rowanvalebooks.com
info@rowanvalebooks.com

Printed in Great Britain
by Amazon